THE

SPARKLE

IN HER

EYES

plus

Six More Short Stories

BY

Aileen Friedman

ISBN – 13   978-0-620-64434-1

Website
http://aileenfriedman.co.za

Facebook
https://www.facebook.com/groups/353447231333743/

Twitter
@aileenlf

Email
aileen2462@gmail.com

Editor
Franziska Denton
denton.fran@gmail.com

Front Cover Design
Simon Hattingh
seamonkey_studios@outlook.com
(The eyes on the cover were created from
a photo of my mother)

Book Cover Design
Andrew Van Sitter
Exact Copy - Somerset West
andrew@exactcopy.co.za

Thank you, Lord Jesus,
for your love and mercy
and for blessing me
with my family whom I love so much.
I am truly blessed.

Phil 4:13 'I can do all things through Christ who strengthens
me.'

A very special
THANK YOU
to
ANGIE EYBERS
For her support and for taking the time
to read these little stories before editing.
For your love and friendship, that is so
dear to me.
Love you forever
xxx

To
FRAN DENTON
A better editor one cannot find.
Thank you for your work and
above all your friendship.
Love you always
xxxxxx

Table of Contents

BEAUTIFUL SCARS

Beautiful Scars

Chapter One

There were few women, or men for that matter, more beautiful than I. I had luscious blonde hair and a silky olive complexion emphasized by dark blue eyes and a perfectly shaped nose and a rosebud mouth. My legs went on for miles, and I had a body most women would die to have. I was irresistible to anyone I considered encapsulating into my web. I got taught from a young age that my beauty was all I required to obtain fame and fortune. From the age of four, I was entered into local beauty pageants by my mother. It took only two entries until I won the first of my large collection of crowns. From then on it became an obsession for me to win at any cost. At six, I began modeling, and within a month, I had an agent and was being sought after for fashion shoots and TV commercials. By ten I had achieved great fame; my exquisitely beautiful face graced the cover of a young society magazine, and naturally, I was noticed by the influential socialites. By the age of just twenty, I was being flown across oceans for photo shoots and fashion shows.

My parents, both average looking and from poor backgrounds, relished my popularity and the new world I gave them entry into as the parents of the most beautiful girl in the fashion industry. I was an only child, spoilt beyond any form of control and I knew how to throw a tantrum anywhere and at any time to get my way.

At one stage in my life, I wanted nothing more than to win the title of Miss World. However, once I started modeling it was no longer necessary for my career, and I felt it beneath me since I knew I would win the title at any rate. While taking a break on a shoot, a less important model challenged me that perhaps I did not have the guts to accept losing the crown and that was why I did not want to enter the Miss World competition. How dare she test my beauty! Or my power to win! And so I entered. I put my modeling career on hold for a year to concentrate on the Miss World title. I was fully aware of what being Miss World meant and how it might benefit my modeling career. Not that it was necessary, as my beauty alone was sufficient.

The end of the year at the Miss World finalist competition I stood on stage among the last five finalists. The other contestants stood nervously smiling wondering if they had done enough to win the crown. Not me. I knew I had won it; I had done enough eye flirting and trapping of anyone important in my web to be assured of that crown. They announced the fifth runner-up, the fourth, the second princess and then they exclaimed in a fake hype that I was indeed the new Miss World. How had anyone doubted that I would win? The rehearsed tears rolled down my cheeks, and I exclaimed in false astonishment that I had won. The other contestants surrounded me with hugs, kisses, false adoration and congratulations. No one dared me and then didn't expect me to achieve the highest accolade, especially if it involved my perfect body.

The year of being Miss World went by so quickly that it hardly affected my modeling career. If anything, I was as I thought I would be, even more, sought after than ever before. I was the perfect Miss World – a patriotic South African who fought the plight of whatever the international politicians thought was important. After I had handed the crown over to the new Miss World, I knew nothing would stand in my way of one day being the most sought-after model spread across the covers of every high society magazine regardless of its genre.

Besides using my incredibly perfect body to advance my career, I used it to gain the adoration of any male I desired. It often happened that after a day of working from the early hours of the morning until late into the night all I wanted was to be comforted and told by a poor adoring man that I was the most beautiful woman he had ever seen. I knew this to be the truth at any rate, but it was good to hear it. There was, of course, a lot of envy from the other models. Shame, they could not be blamed for it. I was difficult to beat. I had been trained from an early age to detect any competition and eliminate it. Every model was competition to me, and so every model received the same treatment – don't mess with me!

I frequented nightclubs and as I was almost always in a different city the men did not know me. They thought I was simply too good to be true and that they were the luckiest men on earth to have even the pleasure of speaking to me. Unbeknown to my colleagues I would watch every man's eyes and take note of to whom he was taking a fancy. Once I figured it out, I would make every attempt to win him over simply so that I won and the other model would go home empty-handed or with a second prize. At times, the poor girl was almost in the man's arms when I joined the conversation, and within fifteen minutes he was mine. He had won the trophy woman for the night, and he counted himself lucky.

If I did go on a proper date, the privileged man was in his element; the poor sucker was actually under the misconception that it might lead to a second date. Usually, I ordered a salad at dinner, as maintaining zero percent body fat was a priority, but there were those dinners where the man had so much to say about my meal choice I agreed to have an actual meal. I picked at the food on the plate in front of me feigning a lack of appetite or making up any feeble excuse. By the time we left the restaurant, I had been to the bathroom and vomited the few bites of food into the toilet. The unsuspecting date thought he had, in fact, had a meal with me.

I never went back to my hotel room or apartment with a date; it was always back to his place. I left before he woke up and that was the last time he would ever see me or hear from me. It was all just so easy. The lack of female friends did not have any impact on me at the time. I was sadly under the misconception that everyone loved me.

Being a model meant that someone was always touching you. From hours before the shoot began someone was messing with your hair or your face and depending on the type of shoot, it was possible that even your body got painted. And then there were the people that clothed you, fiddling with the garments on your body until they fitted perfectly. I employed my own personal stylist and makeup artist to eliminate strange hands always touching my perfect body. I demanded my space in the always crowded dressing rooms. That this meant others had to be inconvenienced did not bother me. That was their problem, not mine, I was the one in demand and the main attraction, and therefore, I demanded what I wanted, and got it. I insisted on my changing area to be sterilized before I entered the building. The only brand of water I drank and whatever else my mood demanded was to be readily available at the snap of my perfect fingers.

Chapter Two

Along with the celebrity status that I adored, came the endless media, always around to take a photo of whoever I was with or wherever I was going. Whether it be a gala event, a party or even the shop around the corner from my apartment – there was always someone close by with a camera. I fed off it; it gave me such a high that I wanted it more and more. It came to the point that if I were attending a function, any function, I would tell whoever was outside my apartment where I was going and being sure to spread the word. Sometimes I phoned the newspapers under a false name and gave them the details of where Miss Jade Burnstein was going to be. It never failed, the media went crazy, and usually, I stole the limelight for the evening. I was beyond ecstatic facing the flashing cameras with all the attention focused on me.

During the filming of a TV commercial in Mauritius, I had a brief break from the cameras and sat alone away from everyone. It was most unusual, but this place touched a nerve I had not experienced before. I wanted nothing but peace, no flashing cameras, no media, no journalists asking the same boring questions – which I had never minded before – no staff standing by my side waiting for my next demand. I just wanted to sit alone under the enormous umbrella, lie on the sunbed and figure out what this odd sensation was that had suddenly come over me.

Alongside me in the commercial was a mini-me. A young girl, eight years old, and beautiful. Almost as beautiful as I was, but don't forget there was no one more beautiful than me in the world! But she was very similar in looks and physique. I imagined if I'd had a sister she would have looked just like her. But she had a gentle nature and the kindest smile. She never demanded but asked and never failed to say thank you. The only time I ever said thanks was if I was faking it to the press or someone of importance.

She had an endless flow of questions about my career and, in particular, my reign as Miss World.

I asked her if she would enter one day and she simply replied, 'No, never.'

'Why not?' I asked in surprise.

Who would not want to be Miss World?

'Mommy always says you don't have to wear a crown to be beautiful and to be Miss World. If you are loved, and in return, you can love others, you are the world to those around you.'

That this came from an eight-year-old little girl who possibly was the next me floored me.

'Well, I suppose there is some truth in that but if it means that you can have a wonderful career from being Miss World, then why not?'

'Different strokes for different folks,' she said and before I could ask if that was also what her mommy said she was whisked away by the costume department.

What she said meddled with my head for some time but once I was in front of the camera again her words dissipated into the confines of my memory. Whether I would ever have them resurface was not important right now. I was important, and the cameras were on me.

In the evening, I sat on the porch of my five-star chalet a stone's throw from the edge of the ocean. The peace and calm of this place were strangely overwhelming. I wanted to soak it in and remember every second I was alone in it. It was such an odd feeling, and sitting alone on this paradise island I began to wonder if I would ever have any children one day. I was still young enough at twenty-two to have this fabulous lifestyle for a few more years before contemplating marriage, let alone children. But I couldn't help but wonder if my child would be as beautiful as me. Of course, she would, what was I thinking? But maybe not quite as beautiful as there had to be male genes involved, but she would be beautiful nonetheless. I also naturally assumed my child would be a girl. What was I to do with a boy?

My hands fell limply onto my firm flat belly, and on impulse, I imagined a round belly that could one day encase a baby. I shuddered and felt like vomiting. What had come over me, what could possess me to delve into that part of my mind? If that ever happened, it would destroy my goddess-like body. I got up from the chair, feeling gingerly for my sandals and then made my way back inside and to bed. It was a restless night with babies popping in and out of my dreams, all of them grossly ugly and reaching out to me, their mother, for dear life. I held them for a short while then threw them into the arms of the first person that walked passed me; grateful those people did not have faces.

When I arrived on set the next morning, my makeup artist dared comment on the dark shadows under my eyes.

'I don't need your comments this morning, just do your job and get rid of them.'

She adhered to my demand and the next hour or so was spent in silence. I was insulted at the slightest suggestion that I was less than perfect. Still, that previous evening's strange emotions and dreams bugged me right up until I was in front of the camera, and then the memories were thankfully gone and forgotten. I was where I belonged, and I was the most adored and most important person that existed.

That evening I found an adoring fan that satisfied my desire to be worshipped and denied any repeat of the previous evening's oddities. Not sleeping in my bed also helped. Still, I made sure to leave his house before he woke up.

A day of filming in the small harbor was the assignment, the fishermen had left very early in the morning, but one trawler's crew was paid handsomely to skip the day's fishing. The captain was a rugged man with messy grey hair and an even messier beard. His voice was as rough as his appearance, and I think he last had a bath in the seventeenth century. The captain's son too was a fisherman by heart, there was no doubt about that, but he was neatly shaven, and his hair was cut short, so it had no chance of becoming windswept. He smelt pleasant and fresh; even his hands were clean and void of fish scales. He had a nice smile that cracked the skin around his eyes into suntanned wrinkles. He had long eyelashes that protected his warm brown eyes from the sun. I noticed these things because when we were introduced, he shook my hand for the longest time and stared straight into my eyes.

'Mercia, get me the hand sanitizer,' I demanded when he finally released my hand.

The man walked away after grunting something about the fact that he did not carry any germs. Unperturbed I wiped my hands and waited to begin shooting in my dressing area.

We were on the sea just within the entry points of the harbor walls. The wind was warm and the air humid. It was difficult to stand still on the trawler as it rocked from side to side over the lapping waves, made worse every time another boat passed our boat. We had to do take after take, and with each new take, I became more and more irritated and frustrated. The young man, I forgot his name, was kind and tried very hard to appease me and limit my complaining by controlling his boat as much as was humanly possible. It was not good enough for me.

'Can't you keep this stupid thing from rocking? It's ruining my performance.'

He simply smiled back, 'Cannot control nature, ma'am.'

'Well you can damn well try a little harder to control this stupid ugly boat,' I grunted for the hundredth time.

'It's a trawler ma'am.'

I was infuriated.

'Serge, get me off this thing now. You use what we have or do something else. I won't do this out here, and this man is not helping at all. He is probably rocking the boat on purpose.'

Serge and all the crew tried to convince me that I was unreasonable, and we should try the scene once more. I refused, put my gown on and went and sat inside the boat. The man and his father just smiled at each other and returned the boat to the dock. I stormed off in a huff refusing any more shoots for the day.

Without having to do another shoot on the sea, we finally finished filming three days later, and I returned to my apartment in Cape Town exhausted. It had been a strange few weeks, and the worst in me had surfaced, not that this bothered me much, though, as I was the star and the important one and could, therefore, behave however I liked.

When I viewed the commercial for the first time, I was surprised and jealous at how good the fisherman looked in front of the camera. People not knowing any different would think he was a model or an actor.

'Well he will never become a model or an actor, he is a common fisherman,' I replied when asked my opinion of the man, 'I was incredible considering the conditions I had to work under.'

My life in the city resumed again. I forgot my horrid ordeal with the fisherman and even forgot his face. If the ad came on the TV, I changed the channel and it hurt me for that meant I would not see myself and my performance. My agent phoned me one morning with news of a photo shoot in Argentina. The timing was perfect; I needed to be surrounded by new fans to adore me. We were on the plane and back home within the month.

<u>Chapter Three</u>

Long days and even longer nights of partying left me surviving on as little as two to three hours sleep; this meant that I had very little patience and was extremely irritable. It was also the reason I had on this particular day overslept by an hour. I flew out of bed, jumped into my jeans and grabbed the first shirt in my closet. I brushed my teeth on the way to my car. My hair had not seen the hairbrush. The makeup artist and stylist certainly had their work cut out for them this morning.

It was an hour's journey to the set in a small farm town in the middle of nowhere. Regardless of how close to a larger town it was situated, it was in my opinion in the middle of nowhere. I swerved between cars like a Formula 1 racing driver fighting to get to the front of the pack and only slightly yielding at stop streets. My Porsche had the chance to show off and in a 120km/hour speed zone, I was whizzing by at nearly 240km/hour. I knew how to handle my baby, and she knew how to obey my command.

I glanced at my phone for a second when I heard it ring; my left hand immediately let go of the steering wheel to pick up the phone, a reaction that took possibly less than a second. Still within that second my eyes glanced back at the road ahead of me, and I observed a cow crossing the road about hundred meters in front of me, traveling at the speed I was, a hundred meters were as useful as one meter. With my right hand still on the steering wheel I pressed hard on it pulling the wheel to the right, the car swerved and at the same time both my feet slammed the brake pedal. I missed the cow by an inch.

But my car propelled skyward; it whirred as the tyres spun without any traction and after another second it started to roll. It flipped over and over several times before landing with a thunderous smash, at least, a hundred meters away from where the cow was now merrily walking to greener pastures, oblivious to my predicament. Once the car met with the ground, it bounced tossing itself over repeatedly, banging every inch of the body on the road surface, over and over again. The sound of metal crashing against the asphalt was so intense it echoed through my head, the shattering glass sprayed out everywhere attacking my body that was imprisoned in the wreck.

The final landing point was softer, more like a thud, and I felt as though I was sliding down a hill on skis. The hood of the car scraped across the surface of the earth, over small rocks and grass. And as suddenly as it had all began the car came to a standstill. Another second went by before I gathered my swirling thoughts and could comprehend what had happened. I tried to loosen the seatbelt with my left hand, but it would not move. I tried to get the belt loose with my right hand, but my hand moved slowly and with every inch it sent a searing pain through my body. I had to use it, though, I had no choice and with a deafening scream, I moved my hand to the belt. But my fingers could not press the release button; they were too weak. I screamed in agony at every effort. What was I going to do? Where had I landed? I was unable to see anything from this upside-down position. The blood on my face and eyes didn't help either. As the seconds ticked by I tried to get my legs out from under the dashboard, they inched away slightly, and then pain so excruciating tore from my feet right up and throughout my body. I screamed and lost consciousness from the intensity, but only for a few moments.

As I opened my eyes dazedly, my head pounded against my skull, and I realized I was stuck, and my only way out of the mangled metal was help from outside. But who would hear me from wherever it was that I had now parked? With every move I made to scream for help or to see out of the bit of window that did not get crushed, my body yelled back in pain. It was impossible for me to move. As I sat trapped, a strange smell began capturing my senses. I looked through a haze at the crumpled dashboard in front of me and instantly knew it was smoke. Smoke! The car was on fire, and I was undoubtedly stuck in it, this could not be the end of my life. Not like this. I was not ready to go. I screamed for help, ignoring the pain. I shouted as loudly as I possibly could. What else was I to do? As the smoke in the car grew thicker, and I heard the sound of something cracking next to me; panic overcame me. I wriggled in my entrapped position, but the pain shot through my body forcing me to remain where I was. The smoke got thicker and scratched at my throat the louder, and more frantically I screamed. I desperately cried out to the quiet world that was unaware of my existence, of my predicament, of my desperation.

Through my faint peripheral vision, I saw lapping flames stretching past the edges and reaching towards the front of the car. The tips of the flames licked at my arm as they crept forward at a rapid pace, sizzling and seething at my demise. The heat in the car had increased rapidly; it was so hot – oh my goodness it was inexplicably hot – my blood was boiling over. The flames, burning rubber, and paint choked my failing lungs. I panted and gasped trying with all my might to scream for help, but all that I could voice now was a pitiful grasping sobbing squeak. The flames, not just the tips anymore were right on me, burning the left side of my body. I groaned at the pain, helpless, not able to move away from the heat, knowing I was about to get engulfed in the fire and to experience a pain few humans have ever had the misfortune of experiencing while still alive. It burnt so incredibly hot; I smelt my soft flesh and my luscious hair burning. I groaned in pain and agony as the flames ravaged the car and my body. My insides were about to combust. I prayed to a God that I did not know, that this would end soon. Though my mind was so drowsy and thick with smoke, I heard a sizzle and felt dollops of something heavy falling on my body.

'Ma'am! Ma'am, can you hear me?'

I heard a voice. Was I dreaming? There was a loud droning noise coming from a distance away. I also heard thudding noises and squelching sounds coming from what seemed to be the ground by my head. Something touched my body. I was sure of it.

'She's alive, only barely. Hurry, we only have seconds here.'

The world was a dark blur, and something moved in the darkness. Was I still of this world or was I already dead?

Chapter Four

I faintly heard sounds, the sounds of people speaking in hushed tones but with urgency in their voices. Then there was nothing but darkness and silence.

Sometimes I felt my body being touched with care, softly and gently, and then other times it was jolted and thrown around. The pain was a constant and with every touch whether gentle or not, it never left. A sensation of floating overcame me, and I heard a whup-whup-whup noise above me. Was I flying? I was sure I was as I felt my body tilt from one side to the other and then descend until it was motionless again. Then there was nothing but darkness and silence.

Bright lights were flickering through my closed eyelids. The voices were around me again, muffled and varied between orders and questions, high-pitched and low-pitched. My body was a blazing inferno yet something around me was cool. The fire inside me forced me to try and speak and tell someone, anyone, about the intense and excruciating pain I was enduring, and that my blood was boiling from the heat within me. Instead, I only groaned, unable to form a word.

Fluid flowed through my heated veins and with it a sense of slight relief from the agony. My jaw was pulled down, forcing my mouth to open to its full extent. Something was sliding down my throat, adding to my discomfort but my brain failed to tell my body to react to the procedure. I flinched as a cool liquid was rubbed over my skin, and at the same time, gadgets were attached to me. Then the cool feeling on my skin was being stifled by a wrapping movement. Over and over. Around my arms, my torso, my legs and then my head. Was I dead and someone with a cynical sense of humor had decided it would be funny to mummify me?

Then there was nothing but darkness and silence again.

How many days, weeks, maybe months did I lie there in that hospital bed, motionless like a corpse, wrapped like a mummy? At some point I became aware of people working on me, a woman's gentle voice was asking me how I was feeling today.

How was I feeling? How was I to know how I was feeling? Did I even have feelings right now? No, I did not. Where was I anyhow, was I even alive or was this all a very bad dream, or was I in hell or wherever people went when they died?

I tried to tell her what I thought of her stupid question, but instead, all that came from my lips was nothing. Not a sound. How did this silly woman think I could answer her when I had a thick pipe stuck down my throat? She did something with the gadgets connected to me and that familiar fluid flowed through my weak veins killing any feelings I might have felt before I rested in darkness again. I was beginning to enjoy this fluid stuff.

***

'Ms. Burnstein, can you hear me?'

I groaned while someone fiddled with a file loaded with papers. He conversed with a few other staff members and then walked toward the nurses' station. My eyes gradually brought the room into focus for the first time. The light was so bright, but wait; all was not in place. There was no vision in my left eye. I felt a surge of panic as I tried to lift my arm to touch my eye and it did not react. More adrenaline rushed through me and I groaned looking wildly out of my right eye, searching for someone to help me.

'Hello dear,' a nurse with a big smile said to me.

I flung a desperate questioning look at her.

Please help me! I begged her without actually saying the words.

I hoped telepathy worked right now. The doctor returned and instructed the nurse to remove the thick pipe from my throat. They fiddled with tape stuck on my face making sure not to mess with the bandages they had me enclosed.

'This is going to be very uncomfortable dear, but it will be very quick.'

The pipe reversed up my throat and out of my mouth. It was disgusting and while I tried to cough and vomit, my lungs stung in pain.

'Slowly dear, it's all right, that nasty little pipe is all gone now.'

21

She gently wiped the spit from my mouth, chatting all the time. My right eye never left her face looking beseechingly at her hoping she would tell me what was going on. Finally, the doctor spoke to me.

'Ms. Burnstein, hello dear. I'm Dr. Ronanski. I have a lot to tell you, but first, can you tell me your name?'

My name? My brain questioned the doctor. How did they not know my name, no wait, earlier he called me by my name I was sure of it! Were they just playing a nasty trick on me?

My right eye was obviously reflecting the panic I felt as he spoke in a soothing voice, 'I want to make sure I am treating the right person. Don't want to be giving you the wrong meds now do I?'

He smiled through a chuckle when he was finished speaking. I opened my mouth to speak, but again nothing happened. I coughed, and it hurt my chest so badly. I tried again after first clearing the phlegm that was sitting in my mouth. The nursed wiped my mouth again.

'Take your time dear, try slowly.'

'J...Uhm...Ja...' I coughed, clearing my throat once more, 'Ja...Jade,' I said very softly and slowly.

'Well done Jade,' the kind nurse said with so much elation that anyone would think I had won a prize.

'Can I call you Jade and not Ms. Burnstein?' the doctor spoke touching the bandages on my head at the same time.

I attempted to nod.

'Well Jade, do you know where you are and why you are here?'

I let my brain search my memory banks and dissect the room.

'Hospital.'

It was more a mumbled reply than a convincing one.

'Yes Jade, now do you know why you are here?'

Why? Why am I here? What happened to me? I shook my head, and it hurt. I frowned to ease the pain.

'Don't worry dear, try not to move too much,' the nurse said patting my hand.

'You were in a car accident. Try to remember Jade,' Dr. Ronanski coaxed me once more.

I clawed through my brain for memories of the accident. Flames flashed at me; smoke was choking me, I was crying for help. I remembered. Oh no! Did I want to remember this catastrophe? I would rather not! I nodded my head slowly and felt tears dribble down my face.

'Okay dear, it's okay, we are here to help you.'

This nurse was simply too kind.

'Jade, yes you were in a very bad accident, in fact, you are incredibly lucky to be alive. But saying that,' he paused, and I had to wonder if the "but" was worth staying alive for, 'you sustained second and third-degree burns on your back and the left side of your body. You also have a broken arm and leg.'

He stopped talking to; I presume, allow me time to absorb what I did not want to hear. I just stared back at him, not wanting to believe a word he was saying. It was hard not to believe him positioned in this room attached to pipes and wrapped in bandages.

The doctor continued, 'That you did not do any damage to your left eye is somewhat of a miracle Jade. We have it closed as a precaution against infection.'

He looked at me for confirmation that I understood what he was telling me. I didn't want to hear any more. If I was not beautiful, if I was not perfect then life was not worth living, this was not happening to me; it had to be a bad dream. My chest ached as I sobbed and the more I cried out that I wished I was dead, the more the pain seared throughout my body until I was not sure whether I was crying for my imperfect body or from the pain.

'I think that is enough excitement for one day. We will discuss treatment and perhaps take the bandages off tomorrow. But for now, Nurse Mary, you give our Jade here a nice dose of morphine that she may get some much-needed rest.'

He patted my arm as he stood up to leave.

'Jade, do you have any relatives? The only person that we were able to contact was your agent.'

I shook my head; the morphine was delightful.

'No,' I replied pathetically.

'Okay Jade, have a good rest,' he said, turned around and left the ICU, the nurses all walking away with him.

My agent was the only person who was concerned about me. Or rather she was the only person in the entire world that was in contact with me. Was there no one else? Did anyone even care that I had nearly died and that I was lying here alone and would look hideous for the rest of my life? If my parents were alive would they have bothered to visit? Why me, why did this happen to me?

I threw the questions out into the realms of space until I was in the oblivion of sleep.

Chapter Five

A few days went by, and I was increasingly more awake and aware of the people and my surroundings. What I noticed most was the number of visitors my fellow patients had during visiting hours. Some patients, especially on their first day in the ICU had a loved one sitting vigilantly by their bedside all the time. I had no one; I had not seen or heard from anyone since the accident; I felt so alone. I had probably always been this alone but had been so wrapped up in myself that I had not noticed.

'So Jade, today's the day we take these horrible bandages off for the last time. Aren't you pleased dear?'

My friendly nurse, Mary, was on duty again after having had a few days off. I was so pleased she was to be with me when they revealed what I looked like now. I needed her so desperately. While she was away, I had felt even more alone and lost. The other staff was just as kind and good at their job as she was but I needed her.

'I don't want to see!' I closed my eyes and allowed the salty water to cascade down my cheeks.

The bandage had been removed from my left eye two days prior, and everyone seemed overly impressed with its healing. I was just grateful I still had the eye, but now I wished I was rather blind and spared the visions of my burnt skin. Dr. Ronanski arrived and lifted my right hand holding it firmly in his strong but gentle grip.

He smiled and nodded, 'So after many skin grafts and good healing are you ready to see what the results are? Remember there is still a lot of healing that needs to happen, so this is not the final result.'

I shook my head again, 'I don't want to see.'

The words choked me.

'It's understandable Jade, and I won't lie to you and tell you that you won't get a shock when you see yourself. You will. But there are a lot of trained people right here to get you through all of this. Okay, let's start. We will begin with the bandages on your head and work our way down. All right?'

The unwrapping was terrible; the bandages seemed endless as they unwrapped and unwrapped and unwrapped me like a Christmas present. I felt like a rubber doll each time they lifted my torso to get the next round removed. The air felt cool on my body when I was finally free from the wrapping. My arm and leg that got broken were held together with steel rods protruding on the outside; I was an unfinished robot, but the steel rods were not as disturbing as the tight new pink flesh on my arm. I shivered and wanted to throw up. One of the nurses quickly stuck a kidney-shaped silver bowl under my chin.

'I have a large mirror that I am going to hold up so you can see yourself,' Mary said with a smile that was not very convincing.

'I don't want to see!' I cried as I spoke.

They nevertheless held up a large mirror in front of me. I took a while to lift my eyes up to it. When I did, I saw a horrible, distorted person with no hair looking back at me. I was shocked to my core and frightened and terrified and repulsed all at the same time. It was not me; it could not be! I was beautiful; I was perfect. This person was, was, what was this person? This person was a piece of regurgitated flesh, a freak.

'No, no, no!' I burst into loud sobs causing my chest to ache as I clutched at it with my good right hand. I looked at my right hand holding my chest and looked at my left hand lying still beside my body, big silver pins protruding through the replaced skin. I looked back in the mirror at the ghost of a beautiful person looking back at me.

'No, please no,' I sobbed without end.

A few minutes passed, the mirror removed, and Mary consoled me. Her words meant nothing, and as kind, as they were, they were meaningless to me. Then Dr. Ronanski tried.

'Jade, I know it looks and feels like a disaster at the moment, but after good care and physiotherapy, you will be wonderful again. You have been extremely lucky that your eyes and front facial features got spared any disfigurement. The cosmetic surgery to your left ear is not even noticeable. Once the skin has completely healed and you are a lot stronger, you can have hair implants done. It will be a long journey, but it will be an easy one if you let us help you, Jade.'

The doctor wanted so much for me to believe him as he held my hand and kept his eyes focused on mine. I sank back allowing the pillow to swallow my ridiculous looking head. I detected tears in everyone's eyes; this was not the world I wanted to live in; I would prefer to be dead.

I sank into days of depression, into days of limbo, of feeling utterly numb and worthless, constantly crying at the reminder of what I saw in the mirror. I kept seeing this abhorrent person looking back at me. The eyes, nose, and mouth, were the same, but the left side of my head was bare, with burns, scars and an ear that only sort of resembled the other one. The hair was thin, wispy and lifeless on the one side of my head, and there was absolutely no hair on the other side. The imperfect scarring on the left arm extended round to my back. The skin grafts had done what they possibly could to repair my arm and torso however burnt skin never repairs one hundred percent. I was to look this way for the rest of my life. Oh, how I wished I was dead!

'Come along dear; we are going for a ride.'

Mary arrived at my bed with a wheelchair and a porter. After a lot of protesting I did not get my way, and after a lot of effort, I was sitting in the wheelchair. Covered with a light blanket, we made our way down the corridor to a lift and the second floor. When the lift doors opened, we exited and turned right down another corridor and through a set of double doors.

The ward was full of children of all ages, they were smiling and laughing but there was one major difference in these children – they were all burnt just like me. How could they be laughing and how or why were they so happy? We were barely in the ward when the children spotted us and came bouncing up to me all speaking at the same time. They touched my arm and my hair, or lack thereof, and it made me shiver with disgust. I could only just bring myself to touch my body, and that was also only when it was necessary.

Mary cheerfully greeted and hugged every child introducing them to me one by one explaining that I had been in a car accident and got burnt. One or two of them exclaimed that they too had burnt in a car. They seemed to find it amusing, but I just sat there. I did not like children, so why would I feel touched by these burnt ones? And yet I was. Some of them were by far more burnt than what I was, some almost completely disfigured and yet through their thin, taut skin they smiled. One little boy only had one eye and the use of only one side of his face and no ears, and yet he smiled at me, happy to see me. I started to vomit, and a cute little black-haired girl shoved a plastic bowl under my mouth. She took a wet wipe and wiped my mouth for me when I finished. Her face glowed when I said thank you, and she didn't walk away but stayed by my side smiling every time our eyes made contact. She swayed her body from side to side, and I wondered where she had got burnt; it was clearly not her face. I plucked up the courage to speak to her, her name evading me for the moment.

'Why are you here?' I asked perhaps a little too bluntly.

She lifted her shirt, and I wanted to vomit again. Her entire body horribly burnt and yet she was happily smiling when she showed me her scars.

'Mary, Mary!' I called desperate to get out of this place.

Back in my bed, the inevitable tears and sobs made their way to the exterior of my being. How was it possible that those children were happy and smiled when they looked as hideous and grotesque as I did?

When Mary arrived on duty the next day, she arrived with a porter and a wheelchair again.

'Oh no Mary, please no, just leave me here.'

'Nope, those little children have been asking all about you and want you to visit them again.'

I found myself in that ward again surrounded by burnt happy faces, all except one.

'Where is…Uhm, what's her name, the one with the black hair?' I asked Mary.

'She is at the hospital chapel. She goes there every day.'

'Why?' I asked very confusedly.

'You can ask her yourself when you see her again.'

Chapter Six

It became a daily routine to go down to the children's burn unit. Every day saw a change in the number of children, some days there were fewer as they went home and other days an increase as children were added to the ward. Without knowing, I was being drawn into their little cushion of happiness and found myself smiling a few times. The little girl with black hair, Leah, was still there and always remained at my side as soon as I arrived. We talked a lot, and I even read her stories from her favorite books. All the children would gather around me when I began to read, and eventually, I was given the books to read the minute I entered the ward.

Physiotherapy was painful, and I hated it since it bore the reminder that I was less than perfect. The steel pins were finally removed from my broken leg and arm and replaced with specially fitted casts made of hard plastic. I was grateful not to have the old white plaster stuff that they normally used.

One morning I hobbled into the children's ward on crutches and, as usual, was greeted by happy little faces. Leah said hello briefly then turned around and headed towards the door.

'Where are you going Leah?'

'To the chapel,' she replied so matter-of-factly that I was rather curious about this chapel.

'May I join you today?'

She simply waved her hand to indicate that I could. I didn't hesitate just in case she changed her mind. She walked with a brisk limp, and I hobbled along next to her with my crutches, still getting used to them, and before long we were at the entrance to the hospital chapel. It was quiet, peaceful and lit dimly but had an atmosphere of serenity, not gloom. I had no idea what to do there, so I followed Leah. She made her way to a seat two rows from the front and sat down. I sat down too. She bent her head and closed her eyes, but I had no idea what she was doing so just sat next to her and stared around at the room. My heart beat slower and steadily, and I sat back and leaned against the backrest of the pew, it hurt the scars on my back, so I sat forward again. As I did, I felt a sense of calm wash over me; it was the first time I had felt so relaxed since all the madness of the accident began. The stillness, the calm, the peace filtered through my body, and I simply sat there staring ahead at nothing. Leah lifted her head and looked at the cross hanging in front of the chapel with love in her eyes.

'What am I supposed to do?' I finally whispered to her.

'Nothing, just pray to Jesus.'

'How do I do that?'

'Close your eyes and talk to him. Ask Him to heal you, but first, ask Him to help you to come into His life.'

This little girl, no more than twelve years old was so confident in her Jesus, she seemed so mature for her age, and she knew her faith was all she needed to survive. I closed my eyes and spoke to Jesus, not knowing at all whether what I was saying was wrong or right. I just told Him how unhappy I was and asked Him why I had to live like this. Strangely when I was finished talking to Him, I felt warm and refreshed, as if I had unloaded a burden I had been carrying around for eternity. The calm feeling I had remained and I felt at ease. When we returned to the ward, Mary looked at me curiously, and I smiled back at her. She came up to me and gently hugged me. I had no words to explain the peace I was feeling.

Every day until Leah was finally able to leave the hospital we went to the chapel together, and on Sundays Leah's parents joined us and it was such a pleasure to have the simple hospital chapel service with them. Leah's father was a minister, which explained a lot about her dedication. The last Sunday we spent together Leah's father handed me a book. I looked at it bewildered. Was I meant to read it? I could not remember the last time I had read a book.

'Don't look so scared of it,' he laughed and Leah giggled, 'it is a Bible, God's Word spoken through his apostles. It is the guide to life and eternity.'

I looked at the black leather-bound Bible in my hands. I flipped through the pages and noticed highlighted passages marked in pink.

'What are the highlighted parts for?'

'Those are scriptures of importance, which will help you hopefully, find Jesus.'

'Thank you,' I said.

Then Leah handed me a small booklet, 'It will help you read the Bible.'

She was too special and I bent down and hugged her so hard it hurt us both. The hospital seemed empty without Leah, but every day I went to the children's ward and read to them and played games with them. I also went to the chapel every day and found myself longing to know Jesus more and more. My prayers slowly became less about me and more about the children who were as burnt and scarred as I was. The hair implants took as well as the doctors had expected and my broken limbs healed well too.

***

Eventually, the time came for me to leave the hospital. I was hesitant to go, I was safe here, cared for and had a support system in place around me. I was not prepared to care for myself yet or ever! What if I bumped into someone that knew me from the modeling world? That world seemed an eternity ago, and clearly, it was not the world that missed me. In the entire time since my accident, my agent had visited me once, and it was obvious she had only done so to clear up business matters. I had no idea what I was going to do with my life now; I only knew how to be a spoilt, selfish, self-absorbed career-obsessed perfectly beautiful model.

My apartment smelt musty, and I felt lost in my home. I was so incredibly alone. I shuffled up and down the apartment, wandering around trying to find a comfortable spot to relax. I lifted up magazines and newspapers, went through all my mail and threw most of it away. I tried to watch TV, but even that finally got switched off. There was just nothing in the apartment that convinced me that it was mine, or made me feel that I belonged. I stood by the kettle for yet another cup of herbal tea waiting as the water came to a boil. On the counter in the kitchen was a flyer from the hotel I had stayed in when I had done the disastrous shoot in Mauritius. I flipped it over and read its offers and was startled when my phone suddenly rang. When was the last time I had received a phone call? I could not remember.

'Hello, this is Jade speaking,' I answered in what I remembered my professional tone to be.

'Hello Jade, this is Leah's father.'

I was so relieved to hear his voice on the other end of the line and not anyone related to my past.

'We want to invite you to come to church with us tomorrow. We can fetch you and drop you off, and Leah will be so happy if you say yes.'

He was gently persuasive but I resisted, and that evening I did as I had always done and wallowed in my self-pity, wondering why the only friend I had in the world was a twelve-year-old girl when before I'd never given children the time of day. What was I going to do with my life? Modeling certainly was not an option anymore, and unfortunately, it was the only thing I knew how to do. I was unable to do anything too physical as my lungs had weakened considerably from the smoke inhalation and just going down to the local store was a huge effort. In the past, I had always been hounded for an autograph or photo, and I had thrived knowing I was being noticed – now if someone so much as looked at me for a second too long, I wanted to slap them. I was also growing very weary of the false sympathy shown by some.

A knock on my door early one evening was an unusual sound; it startled me and I contemplated not answering so I waited, hoping whoever it was would go away. But the knock came again – and hesitantly I plodded to the door opening it just enough to see who it was.

'Hello, Jade. We made you a cake.'

It was Leah holding up a cute pink cake with silver balls sprinkled all over the icing. I stepped back and opened the door to allow Leah, the cake, and her parents to enter.

'Please excuse the mess I look, and that goes for the apartment too. Coffee or tea?' I offered and I had to admit to myself that I was very happy to see them.

We settled down in the living room to eat Leah's yummy pink cake. She told me how she had made it herself with only a little help from her mother. Her parents, Merwyn and Molly, were contagiously happy people, they reminded me of the Gummi Bears; Leah was their only child.

'So what do you plan on doing in the future Jade?' Merwyn asked before slaying the last slice of cake.

'I have no idea. I only know the modeling world and, well, I can't go back to that now can I?'

Instinctively I rubbed my left arm and the back of my neck.

'Well, would you mind if we came, say, once a week and had a little study with you? It might help you. We hope it will help you.'

I knew Molly was referring to a Bible study, and I remembered how easy and calm the hospital chapel had made me feel.

'That might be nice. Yes, I think so but as long as you bring cake like this with you.'

I was surprised at my willingness to accept. We arranged to meet every Thursday evening at six-thirty, and after a couple of sessions, I looked forward to it eagerly. I made sure my home was spotless for their arrival, and when their knock sounded on the door, I opened it almost instantly with a smile.

'Have you ever been in a place where you have felt relaxed and at peace?' Merwyn asked before, as always, eating the last slice of cake.

I had to think about it. Thinking about it took me to the many places and the many countries I had visited. It took me back to my previous world of fast and furious chaos, but suddenly in all that rush an image of a beach and a silent mesmerizing sunset brought my memories to a standstill.

'Yes, in Mauritius, once,' I replied, still holding that image in my head, clinging to it for a few more seconds.

'Is there any reason you can't go back there for a while? A few weeks in a place like that will be just the medicine you need, and you won't be recognized there.'

'That is not a bad idea. I'll look into it. Thanks.'

After several weeks of studying with this wonderful family, I gave my life to Jesus. I was baptized in my bath by Merwyn and welcomed to my new life by a very over-excited Molly and Leah. The following Sunday I ventured out of my apartment and to church. I was overwhelmed by the friendliness and love

I received from everyone. Why did it have to take such a major catastrophe in my life for me to find the Truth? But I had found it, and it was exhilarating.

The Mauritius idea was growing on me more and more. I lay in bed staring at the ceiling and wondered what kept me in this town; nothing! I had no job and had no job lined up in the near future either. I had no friends except Leah and her parents and, yes, I was going to church now and had met some lovely people, but were they a reason for me to stay here? No! Molly suggested a lady from church who could sell my apartment, and so I phoned her and gave her the mandate the very next day.

Chapter Seven

It took another two weeks to settle any other loose ends, and when I next took stock of what I was doing I was on the plane, Mauritius bound. Hopefully, the apartment would not take too long to sell, but I had enough money to get by for a few months if it didn't. The plane landed, and I took a shuttle to the same hotel I had stayed at previously and checked in. A new environment, and the start of a new life.

After two days of doing nothing but lying on the beach or at the poolside – always under an umbrella and clothed with a light long-sleeved cotton shirt as my injuries and hair still required a lot of healing – I went to town and bought a scooter, my new mode of transport. I laughed at myself when I pulled off for the first time, but before I did, I got the salesman to take a photo of me on it so I could send it to Leah. She would find it very amusing.

The next thing was to find an apartment to rent. There were plenty but none that were in really good condition and with my weakened lungs, dust was an issue in most of them. I wanted to find a place that could accommodate Leah, Merwyn, and Molly as well. As soon as I sold my place, I was flying them over for a holiday. I owed them so much. Without them, I did not want to think of what type of person I would've become.

Luckily Merwyn had found the details of a church nearby, and so I attended it. It was a small church that looked more like a cottage than a church, but it was cool inside – a blessing to escape the humidity outside. The people were mostly fishermen and their families, and they welcomed me warmly.

It was a stroke of luck that I walked into a block of flats situated right on the beach one day. I asked the landlord, an elderly man if he knew of any apartments available to rent. God was guiding me as there were two available. They were identical, but naturally, I took the one with the sea view, and I moved in a week later.

After a month in Mauritius, I was recovering far better and faster according to my new specialist than he had ever previously recorded. But it was time for me to find something to do. Although my chest was still weak and probably always would be, I had a good amount of energy each day.

On a bright but humid morning, I took a stroll along the beach and landed up at the harbor. The quaint harbor had not changed since I had been there last. The trawlers were all out at sea busy with their daily catch, and it left the harbor looking like a forgotten and deserted port. I remembered the fishermen and the disgusting smell of the fish and shivered when I remembered the person I had been then and how I had treated them. They had been so kind and accommodating, and I had been nothing but a selfish, spoilt brat.

I sat on a dilapidated bench soaking up the sea air for a few minutes, watching seagulls fight for food before I took a slow walk back along the same route to my home. Along the way I saw, hidden among the palm trees, an old but very neat house. There was a "For Sale" sign plugged into the ground, and so I stored the number on my phone and continued my slow pace home, all the while my mind calculating and contemplating the possibility of buying it. What would I do with it if I did buy it? Turn it into a bed and breakfast? Rent it out and stay in the apartment? But first I would have to find out the selling price.

It was such a lovely day, so instead of going inside, I plonked myself on the beach just in front of my apartment block. There were so many tourists about at this time of year, and by ten o'clock in the morning the beaches were packed, and the bay was buzzing with jet skis and glass-bottom boats taking enthralled tourists to the various spots of interest. I watched with fascination and a bit of envy. With my damaged body, I was not able to suntan or go on these wonderful adrenaline adventures. But on second thoughts I realized I had never really been the adrenaline type anyhow, I had always been too concerned with looking anything but perfect in my self-centered life before the accident.

'Jade?'

A male voice interrupted my thoughts and before looking up at where the voice was coming from I immediately panicked.

Who would know me here?

A man with neat blonde hair and a shade of ruggedness that creased his wrinkles depicting the many hours exposed to the sun stood before me; looking at me expectantly.

'You that fisherman, sorry I don't remember your name...' I was flabbergasted he had remembered my name let alone recognize me.

'Yep, that's me, the fisherman Markl. How you doing?'

I chose not to answer his question.

'How did you recognize me?'

'Very seldom forget a face.'

Even a face that has changed as much as mine has, with hardly any hair and hidden under a huge hat?

'So! What you doing here? Another modeling shoot? Do you need a boat again?' he chuckled.

I was very sure he had vivid images in his mind of how it had ended the last time.

'Are you in a hurry since you're trying to get your questions asked in one breath?'

Markl put his head back and laughed, then plonked himself on the sand next to me. For a few seconds, there was silence, only the sound of waves disturbed it.

Markl fidgeted with the sand before he said, 'I know about your accident. I guess I am just surprised to see you here.'

'Shoo my tale of woe spread all the way here,' I said, sarcasm sliding off my tongue.

'Sorry,' his reply was one word, and yet it touched me like a million with its sincerity.

We sat in silence until he changed the tempo back to upbeat as it was when he first spoke.

'So why you here?' he asked again, determined to get an answer this time.

'I live here.'

I had to smile at his expression of disbelief.

'Really? Where?'

I pointed to the building behind me and specifically to the window of my apartment.

'You're kidding me! Since when?'

I sighed. He was not going to cease with his detective questioning until he had all the nitty-gritty details, I was sure of it.

'This is how the story goes...'

And I retold my whole sorry tale. Usually, when I had to share my experience, I was left feeling depressed and distraught, but with Markl the more I spoke and even gave very graphic details, the more it felt like a release from the burden. It was so easy to talk to him. When I got to the part of my baptism and told him about attending the little church on the island, he interrupted me for the first time.

'No ways,' he exclaimed, 'that's where I go! I haven't been for a while – been at sea during the time they have service. Wow, what a story! Who would've thought the diva Jade I met so long ago would find her way to Jesus.'

He shook his head in pure wonderment.

'Okay yes rub it in! I was a horrible person.'

'Yes, you were.'

He had a glint in his eyes and a smile as wide as the ocean, and I detected a genuine joy in his voice.

'So what are you going to do now, or are you working already?'

More questions to appease his curious mind. It was then that I told him about the house I had noticed for sale.

'Oh, I know that house. The owners are old and want to return to live with their children in France. If you want to put in an offer you had better hurry as that is prime property.'

I realized he was probably telling the truth since I remembered him knowing everyone and everything the last time we had met. I guess he'd been here all his life.

'Do you want to meet the owners now and have a look at the house?'

'Now?'

Why was I surprised at his eagerness, I should have expected it.

'Yes, come!'

He stood up and jiggled the sand off his bum, then offered me his hand to help me up. As I stood up, my hat blew off which had never happened before. It threw me completely off guard, and I was so embarrassed I scampered after it and put it back on to hide the awfulness as quickly as possible.

'What's the fuss? You look good with short hair.'

I ignored him, too embarrassed to form a rebuttal.

The owners gave me a tour of the property and that I immediately fell in love with it was not difficult at all. Over a delicious cup of vanilla tea, I made them an offer, with the condition that my property in South Africa sells first. All I had to do was give it to the Lord in prayer, and if it were His will, then it would be mine. My heart wanted it I could not deny that.

Markl walked me home along the beach and decided it was time for a little revenge as he goaded me non-stop over my previously despicable behavior. He found great pleasure in mimicking me – and he did it very well too I might add, but mostly he was astounded at my changed life. He kept emphasizing how the Lord works in people's lives in ways we will never understand. By the time we reached my building I was out of breath and very tired. Markl, sensing my fatigue and with a promise of meeting at church the next day, reached out his arms and held my shoulders with his hands, rubbing them affectionately. I shuddered at his touch – not that it was unpleasant, it was very pleasant – but he touched my ugly scars without hesitation, without concern that I was imperfect. He was indifferent to my ugliness and smiled as he said goodbye. As I showered, I felt the touch of his hands still resting on my shoulders. How did I not repulse him?

Chapter Eight

My property in Cape Town was not selling, and I ran out of time on the offer of the house, and that left me bitterly despondent. I still had no idea what I was going to do here on this paradise island. Weeks went by, and still, my apartment was not sold. I was getting worried that my money was going to run out, and besides, the boredom was beginning to kick in.

Markl and his father Estaban invited me to lunch after church one Sunday. While sitting on their porch sipping tea and admiring the beautiful view over the harbor, Estaban told me fascinating stories of his many years at sea. He spoke of his late wife with such passion I felt like I knew her, and he talked admiringly of his son who had clearly inherited his mother's looks. Estaban was a rough diamond but a placid man with a gruff voice, who chewed his pipe that was never lit. I liked him. He enquired about the offer for the house and listened as I gave him the disappointing news.

He cleared his throat with a cough, 'I have a possible solution for you.'

'I'm listening.'

'The house next door is available to rent. I know the owners well, they live in the south of the island, and I can ask them to lease it to you like a B&B.'

'You'd do that for me?'

'Well yes, but all I can do is ask; the rest you will have to do.'

I jumped from my seat and hugged him surprising myself with my reaction. Estaban blushed and stuck his pipe back into his mouth. Suddenly I remembered, almost having forgotten how I looked.

'Do you think I can do it? I mean with, you know, my scars?'

Markl and Estaban replied in unison, 'Of course!'

Estaban went inside the house and picked up his mobile phone, dialed a number on his way out and was greeting the person at the end of the line by the time he was back in his rocking chair. He ended the call after giving an up-to-date news flash on the local fishing industry, then put his phone down on the table and rested back in his chair, rocking forwards and backward in a calming motion.

'He wants to meet you this weekend, Saturday.'

Since Estaban had a spare set of keys for the house – in the case of emergencies – we spontaneously took a tour of the house. The men were full of ideas of what needed to be done to turn it into a comfortable and pleasant B&B. Listening to them the excitement rubbed off, and although I had no idea how to run a guesthouse, it was a challenge I was keen to take on. The house had the same beautiful view of the harbor that Estaban and Markl's had; it had so much potential.

***

The following Saturday I met with the owner. It was simply a formality as Estaban had pretty much sealed the deal with his first phone call. The lease was signed with a few addendums, and there it was – my future in Mauritius. Financially it was not a solid plan as I still had to renovate and get paying guests. I needed my property in South Africa to sell soon.

The men were working long hours at sea as it was peak fishing season, but Markl had organized one of his friends that had a construction company to do the main renovating and painting. I spent every day doing whatever I was capable of, my weak lungs prevented me from doing as much as I wanted to and by the end of each day, I was completely exhausted. However, it was satisfied exhaustion. I stood back and inspected the wall I had just finished painting and decided a break was in order. I took a doughnut from the plate in the kitchen, and with a glass of orange juice, I sauntered off to the porch. Once I had placed the juice on the table, I sat on the little balcony railing and leaned against the pillar slowly eating the delicious doughnut. Where were the days when anything with bread or starch did not cross my lips at all? I grinned as I savored every bite. The sun shone gently on my face, and I relaxed completely, my mind clear of any thoughts of the past. Nothing filled my mind for several minutes until Markl's lovely face appeared in my thoughts.

If you would be my kiss, I would be your hug.

I opened my eyes in shock. Did I just think that? Why would I think that and why was Markl occupying my mind in that way? Flustered, I got off the balcony railing and sat down in an old worn-out chair I had found in the house and moved to the porch. I gulped down my juice hoping to wash away the image of Markl and those crazy ideas of him. But he kept creeping back, smiling at me with his sparkling eyes and sun-stained wrinkles. Could it be that I was in love with him? No, I never fell in love, well not before the accident in any case! I contemplated this for a very long time and simply had to conclude that yes I was. I was in love with Markl. I had never felt this way before. I had never felt my heart flutter when my eyes met another man's the way they did when I looked at Markl.

I was finally in love.

But what was the point of being in love now when I was so much less than perfect? And in any case, why would Markl want to fall in love with me when he could do so much better than a woman with scars and wispy hair?

Back in the house, varnishing the window frames of a guest room, I managed to get Markl out of mind, but not for long. Every time I stopped to check my work I envisaged Markl standing next to me pointing out the spots I had missed. In my mind, I, in fact, had a conversation with him about my handiwork. I envisioned his smile, and I smiled back at him. What was I going to do when he was around, now that I was aware of my new revelation?

<u>Chapter Nine</u>

The renovations were finally complete except for a few little jobs that I was easily able to do myself. I had been shopping to my heart's content and was very impressed with the décor items and linen that I had purchased. The little three bedroom guesthouse looked cozy and homely. The pastel color shades in the rooms gave them a cool, breezy feel that kept the humidity and heat of the Mauritian weather outside. I had finally received an offer on my property, a lot less than the original selling price but at this point, I just wanted to get rid of it. The buyer's mortgage was approved a few days later, and then I had to wait for the legal work to be finalized and then finally I would be able to relax over money issues.

Markl and all the other fishermen had a few days off when fishing was impossible due to high-speed winds, torrential rains, and massive swells. I invited Markl and Estaban over for dinner, a simple meal to say a huge thank you for everything they had done for me. We enjoyed one another's company immensely and the evening flew by with our laughter and chatter. I told them tales of the renovation, and in return, they told tales of their fishing trips. We ate every morsel I had made and finished both bottles of red wine. During all of this, I tried desperately to avoid too much eye contact with Markl, afraid my nerves and silly discovery might cause me to say something stupid and ruin the evening by chasing him off.

Estaban decided it was time for him to retreat to bed and I presumed Markl was going to leave as well. I stood up to start locking the back doors and to gather the dishes for the dishwasher. But Markl was not leaving. He put the kettle on and prepared the cups for chamomile tea. My nerves were wrestling with me. I had not been alone with him since my little discovery. When the tea was ready, he made his way to the porch and beckoned for me to follow, which I duly did. I sat on the balcony railing as I always did and rested my back against the pillar. He sat down on the balcony railing next to me. My nerves were fluttering madly through my body, and I could feel my skin flush. We sat in silence for a while looking out over the harbor. The wind and rain had subsided to a breeze and a drizzle and the lights from the buildings danced over the water. I couldn't take the silence any longer.

'Why have you and Estaban been so kind to me?'

Markl sighed, and then he looked towards the sky and sighed again, I was instantly worried and so afraid that I had said the wrong thing. I looked at him through the shadows of the night and wanted to tell him not to answer since it seemed to have unsettled him. He looked down at the strip of timber we were sitting on and sighed again, still not answering me. I was about to say something when I felt a strange sensation caressing my mind, soul, and body. A sensation I had never experienced before. A sensation that invited me to want more. I felt the gentle touch of his lips against mine, softly checking whether I would accept or reject him. When I leaned into him, he slid his hand behind my neck and pulled me into his embrace. The passion and craving for each other parted our lips, and we succumbed to the yearning of our needs that turned the kiss from soft and sweet to powerful and strongly overwhelming. I felt my body lift into another dimension, to a universe where if he were not holding me I knew I would have flown away.

Managing only for a brief moment to tear ourselves apart from each other, both out of breath, Markl whispered, 'I've always been in love with you, even when you never gave me the time of day. When I saw you on the beach, that day I knew God had sent you to me.'

He stroked my face and gently kissed the tip of my nose, my lips and my lips, and my lips again. I gave into the wonderment of love. His fingers caressed my back and arms and my scars, and for the first time, I felt nothing but elation, even my scars tingled with glee. He kissed my neck and ran his fingers through my hair, and there were no shivers of shame only that of pure ecstasy.

'I am going to ask you to marry me one day,' he said in a low almost seductive voice while resting his forehead on mine.

I lifted my eyes to him, 'And I am going to say yes.'

He lifted his head and looked at me very seriously.

'Marry me please?' he said almost pleadingly.

A glow lit up my face and joy filled my heart and I laughed, 'That day came by very quickly!'

He giggled, and if I wasn't mistaken even in the light of the night, I noticed he blushed a little.

'Yes.'

With my hands holding his face I said again, 'Yes.'

He flung his arms around me forgetting we were still sitting on the railing of the balcony, nearly tipping us over the edge. Finding our balance again just in time we laughed, kissed, hugged, kissed and laughed again in jubilation. We rejoiced in our love for each other.

Reluctantly Markl dragged himself home. Sleep eluded both of us, and we lay in our beds just meters away from each other. We messaged each other until the sun let us know it was a new day, the first day of the rest of my life. Was it possible to be so happy?

Before the sun was above the horizon, Markl was knocking on my door. That we had not slept did not show, the adrenaline of happiness ensured that we were still wide awake and bright-eyed.

'Let's make my dad breakfast and tell him,' he said as soon as I had opened the door but after he had kissed me hello of course.

We skipped over to their house like two excited children running after candy. I detected a tear in Estaban's eye when Markl burst into the kitchen holding my hand and giving him the news. He was too excited and too happy to wait until after breakfast was served to get it off his chest.

'I am so happy my child, my son has been in love with you for so long,' He said hugging me lovingly.

I looked at these two wonderful men that had come into my life with direction from God and had to pinch myself to believe I was so lucky to get blessed with a second chance. Over breakfast, we discussed the wedding.

'Why wait?' Estaban said, 'I met Markl's mother, and we got married two weeks later. It worked out for us.'

Markl's eyes were bright as spotlights with the idea while he reached over to take my hand in his.

'What do you think or do you want to wait for a while?'

It was impossible to misinterpret the pleading in his eyes, he wanted me to be his wife sooner rather than later, and I only had to say the word.

'As soon as possible,' I replied.

He jumped up from his chair, did a little celebratory dance and ran to get his phone from his room. He phoned the minister of our church and his close friends, and before I was able to count to three, it was all arranged for the following Saturday on the beach at ten o'clock.

***

I took one last look at myself in the mirror, hardly recognizing the woman that was gazing back at me. This woman had on a light cotton summer dress, with lace sleeves and a wide straw hat. This woman was glowing radiantly in the ambiance of love. This woman was gentle, considerate and kind. This woman was able to be loved and to love in return. This woman filled herself with God's love. I was in love with the woman that was staring back at me in the mirror, who was smiling excitedly at the prospect of getting married within the next half an hour. I remained standing in front of the mirror, closed my eyes and thanked God for my accident, for my scars and for returning me to the paradise island to find my true soulmate and to find my true family.

Suddenly there was a sturdy knock on the door, and my heart jumped ten beats. The time had finally come and I dashed to open the door, greet and hug Estaban and get to the beach. It seemed to me that Estaban was just as eager as I was and we almost ran to the car and from the car to the beach. On the beach, a foot away from the edge of the ocean, everyone was waiting for me. There were Markl's friends who were now ours, the minister and then to my extreme surprise, and I squealed when I saw them – Leah, Merwyn, and Molly.

'A little surprise from me my dear,' Estaban said happily to have surprised me so.

I embraced him with so much love I was unable to hold back my tears of joy. We linked our arms and began our short walk to Markl. My eyes linked with those of my very-soon-to-be husband, and as though there was a string between us, we were drawn towards each other. Markl and Estaban shook hands and Estaban gave me a gentle kiss on the cheek before Markl took my arm, and we stood before God and our witnesses.

'You may kiss…'

We enraptured our hearts in our kiss of sheer love before the minister was able to finish his sentence. Everyone laughed and clapped and threw petals over us, but we were oblivious to their existence. The first to congratulate us was Estaban, and then I made a beeline for Leah and threw my arms around her, unable to control my happiness at them joining me for this momentous occasion. I wanted eagerly to introduce them to Markl and Estaban, but they had already met the previous night. My surprise was entertaining to them, and we all burst out laughing.

Chapter Ten

We moved into the private section of the guesthouse immediately but always had our meals with Estaban. At first, he was resistant, us being the newlyweds, but we won the debate in the end. Married life was truly blissful even when Markl was away for the long hours required of fishermen. My love for Markl grew daily if that were at all possible, so much so that there were times I felt my heart and lungs would explode. I even got blessed with the occasional guests and as the peak tourist season arrived my bookings increased until the B&B was fully booked for an entire month. I had made good friends with the other girlfriends and wives of the fishermen as well as with the people in our congregation.

One morning I awoke to feel awfully sick and after a week or so it got increasingly worse. Markl was concerned and went to tell his father about it. Before I knew it, they both burst into the room.

'You're pregnant!' Markl yelled and laughed at the same time.

My eyes grew enormously round.

'What?'

'You have morning sickness. It must be,' Estaban said sending Markl to the store to buy a pregnancy test.

He must've run all the way there and back because he returned panting and wheezing.

He handed the little box to me, and Estaban told me, 'Pee on the stick.'

I blushed and disappeared into the bathroom. I heard the footsteps of the two men pacing up and down in the bedroom. Then I heard them stop as I flushed the toilet and I had to giggle to myself. I sat on the seat of the toilet and waited as per the instructions on the package. If I saw two little blue stripes, I was pregnant. The minute I had to wait seemed like hours.

'Jade honey, everything okay?'

I sensed Markl's anticipation. I opened the bathroom door, and the two men stood dead still curiously looking at the plastic stick in my hand. I wish I could have filmed them both at that moment so that I would never forget the looks on their faces. I shook the plastic stick and tried as hard as possible to keep a straight face.

'Pregnant,' I said.

Markl screamed and danced his little jiggle, and by the time he was holding me, he was so happy his eyes were overflowing with tears. Estaban sat down on the armchair in the corner of the room and bowed his head. I was dizzy from the idea, trying to comprehend that another human being was developing inside of me. After a visit to the doctor, it was officially confirmed that we were indeed going to have a baby. The close community in which we lived rejoiced at the news that Markl spread like wildfire. I became petrified at the prospect of being a mother and the responsibility that went with it, but Estaban always eased my mind with his wisdom and knowledge. Knowing he would be close by was certainly a reassuring thought. Leah, Merwyn, and Molly were as thrilled as we were and promised to visit once the baby was born. I had reserved their accommodation at the guesthouse before they changed their minds.

The morning sickness was just too terrible. It went on for months, forcing me to employ someone at the guesthouse because I was simply too ill most of the day to attend to the guests. Markl and I moved back into Estaban's house and renovated the spare room into the nursery. Nine months was way too long but, at least, the last three months I was free from nausea and gratefully not too large, especially in the Mauritian summer heat. I was extremely tired, though. The doctor did mention that the extra weight I was carrying it did put a lot more strain on my weak lungs, but he assured us that it was not anything to concern ourselves over.

For the last two weeks of the pregnancy, Markl and Estaban stayed home. Estaban had arranged with a friend to take their trawler out to sea so that they would be at home when I went into labor. Every evening we sat on the porch discussing names and things we would do with our child. Estaban related many stories of when Markl's mother was expecting him, and the sadness in his voice echoed his heart's longing for his late wife, especially at this time in our lives. I promised to name the child after her if it was a girl. The boy's name was still not agreed on; there were just too many names we both liked.

A Saturday like any other Markl moved to get out of bed but suddenly jumped up and yelled my name. I opened my eyes and felt the sheets soaking wet beneath me, then felt the most excruciating pain in my abdomen and cried aloud.

'The baby is coming!' Markl yelped and ran calling out to Estaban to get the car in a hurry.

We arrived at the hospital within half an hour later with the contractions ten minutes apart. After hours of intense pain, the doctor finally informed us that it was time to push as the baby was ready to make its appearance. At this stage, I was ready for a cesarean, an epidural, anything to take this pain away. Markl held my hand while I wrenched the life from it as I squeezed it so hard, pushing until it felt as if every blood vessel in my body would burst. There was a brief moment of silence, and then a tiny wail echoed throughout the room.

'Welcome to your baby boy,' the doctor said as he handed me the tiniest little thing I had ever seen.

Markl burst into tears with me, and we gazed upon this perfect treasure that was our own.

'I love you,' he repeated over and over choking on his emotions.

When they took our baby to get cleaned, Markl went to give Estaban the great news that he was now a grandfather. I had an image of the two men embracing each other, too emotional to speak and too overjoyed to care who saw their tears. The nursing staff wheeled me into the ward, and my greatest blessing was handed to me. I kissed his forehead and thanked God once more for giving me a second chance in this life. And what a second chance it was! Markl sat in the chair next to me with our child (after his ordeal called birth) lying content and peaceful between us. We were unable to tear our eyes and hearts away from him as we were in complete awe of our miracle. We finally agreed on a name that suited him – Kylar.

Chapter Eleven

Time went by quickly, and I didn't fall pregnant again even though we tried when Kylar turned two. There was no medical reason for my not falling pregnant, but we never dwelled on it. If it were meant to be it would be, we told ourselves. Kylar, a walking clone of his father in looks and mannerisms, was the joy of our world. I shuddered whenever I thought of my past where I had been so immune to the idea of having a child.

The guesthouse was running smoothly, and the woman I had employed to help me stayed on as she was doing such an excellent job, and I wanted to spend as much time with Kylar as was possible. But even without working and Kylar not being a difficult child I was still often so tired.

The year he turned four I got my energy back and began to be involved with as many community projects as I could. It helped me get through the times in peak fishing season when Markl and Estaban were rarely home. Slowly though, and much to my disappointment, I felt my energy levels sagging again, and one day I decided to visit our doctor. He seemed oddly concerned over my lungs – these seemed to be more concerning to him than the original fire damage. Eventually, he did some tests that were sent away, and it would be a few weeks' wait until the results became available.

The men were always up early every morning regardless of the fishing schedule, and I had adopted the same habit. We ate breakfast and prayed together every morning. One morning when they had just left to go to the harbor the phone rang.

'Hello Mrs. Jaxson, this is Dr. Bacchus.'

Three hours later I returned home from the hospital, drained and exhausted. Kylar was, fortunately, asleep when I got home, and I knelt beside his bed and prayed.

'Oh Father, thank you for Your love, for Your salvation and Your Son Jesus. I pray, oh Lord, please hold my family strong in Your loving arms when they have to hear what I must tell them. Please, oh Lord, guide them and protect them. I pray, oh Lord, that they will not mourn my going to join You but will rejoice in the life we had together. Please, Lord, help them to raise Kylar in Your favor. Thank you most precious Father for the second chance. You gave me, there are no words to describe how grateful I am, but You know that Lord. I come to You soon, but until then, please give me the strength and knowledge to help my family through what will surely be a very difficult time. Thank you for loving me, Lord. In Jesus' name, I pray. Amen.'

I put my head on the bed and cried till my weak failing lungs hurt so much I had to stop. I looked at my beautiful son sleeping peacefully like an angel and thought of all the plans and little things I would have to put into place so that he and Markl never forget how much I loved them.

Chapter Twelve

The old man, his son and his grandson sat on the porch of their home, sipping hot chocolate and watching the sunset among the thick balls of clouds in the sky. It was a chilly evening as the autumn winds blew directly off the ocean bringing with them the colder taste of winter. They all had their warm sweaters on to protect them from the air and the gusts of the wind that swirled around the porch.

'Looks like the typhoon season is coming early,' Markl said to his father as they both rocked in their weathered rockers that had seen centuries of change from their prime positions overlooking the harbor and the glorious vast expanse of ocean.

'Hmmm, the weather station is already starting to send out the warnings,' Estaban replied clacking his teeth on his unlit pipe.

They both sighed and returned their gazes to the ocean, their hearts still heavy, and the events of the funeral that morning fresh in their minds. Kylar vroomed his toy monster truck up and down the wooden slats of the porch, the wheels making a diggy-dig noise as they rumbled over the grooves. He stopped, took a deep breath, picked up his truck, walked over to Markl placing the truck next to the rocker and climbed onto his father's lap. He too stared out over the ocean, at the small sailboats, fishing trawlers and other enormously expensive catamarans and large yachts. The sky grew darker as the sun slid below the horizon, becoming a bright orange ball forming a jigsaw puzzle with the clouds.

The chairs squeaked as the men rocked forward and backward in a soothing motion, the creaking noises playing a tune of their own as the three generations of males in the Jaxson family sat glued to the movie of the world they knew so well playing out before their eyes. Kylar leaned back into Markl's chest and sniffed as he snuggled closer wrapping his arms around his father's neck. Markl cuddled his son with love and compassion and rubbed his back comfortingly.

'It will be okay son. It will be okay.'

He was trying hard to reassure his son that living the rest of their lives without the woman they called wife and mother would be okay. He fought down the chunk of painful sorrow flooding his chest, trying to keep it from bursting into a river of despair through the tears that brimmed at the edges of his eyelids. Estaban grunted and stuck the pipe back in his mouth ensuring his emotions did not spill over.

'Your mommy was sick son; it was better that God took her to be an angel so she can watch over you and your daddy without having all that pain. Now she can smile all the time watching you just like a guardian angel.'

Markl bent his head forward into Kylar's neck hiding the tears dribbling down his cheeks. Kylar took a staggered breath as the pain his heart was encasing broke at the seams and at that moment the desire to rather be in his precious most adored mother's arms was overwhelming. He longed for her; he longed for her touch, her voice, and he longed to be loved by her. He wanted to feel her arms around his tiny body and have her fingers run down his cheeks and then her forefinger tap his nose as she smiled at him and whispered, 'I love you.'

His heart broke open, and he cried aloud with longing for the mother he had just seen buried in the family graveyard, and while he knew how much his father loved him, he knew that he had just buried the most important person his world had ever known.

Markl held him tightly, his chest heaving as he sobbed his sorrow. Together they cried for a person who had been loved so dearly and for a moment, time stood still allowing the passion of love to comfort their hurting souls.

Estaban stood up from his rocking chair with a grunt and walked to the edge of the porch wiping his face with his sleeve. Markl rocked the chair soothing their heavy hearts, and slowly they calmed their tears until they stayed at bay for the time being. Estaban moved from his spot on the porch and walked to the front door hesitating by his son and grandson and affectionately placing his hand on Markl's shoulder. Markl placed his hand on his father's and leaned his head on their hands appreciating Estaban's compassion without any words. They did not need words; their actions spoke volumes.

Markl stood up from the rocking chair with Kylar in his arms and followed his father into the house. He laid Kylar on the couch and put the TV on hoping something decent was on for his son to watch. After flipping through almost every channel, SpongeBob was selected, and Kylar curled up hugging a cushion bringing his knees into his chest. Markl covered him with the crocheted blanket that his mother had made for him when he had been a baby. When he was sure Kylar was comfortable, he went to the kitchen and joined Estaban at the kitchen table. He sat down with a thump, totally exhausted.

'It will take time son. The best remedy will be for you to get back on the sea and Kylar must get back to school and be around his friends. Kids get through these things much quicker than we do.'

'Yeah, I know you're right. I can still remember when mom died. I just never imagined in my wildest dreams I would ever be in the shoes you wore.'

'It's what they call life son. Fortunately, for you, I am still around and ever more so, God is around.'

He smiled and patted Markl on the shoulder. It had been a long day starting off at four in the morning, not for any other reason than it was a habit. When a member of the community passed on in this laidback little Mauritian town, it was felt in the hearts of everyone, and they all felt it was their duty to help carry the burden. Thus, a little after six that morning the first of the community had shown up with a plate of food or snacks for after the funeral service. And so it went on until the memorial service at noon, then to the graveyard for the burial service and then everyone remained to show their respects to the Jaxson family and to have tea and snacks after the service. The community, closely knitted together despite the continuous influx of tourists, was held together most strongly when someone was hurting. Everyone felt that if they left the bereaved family, they would be letting them down, and the family would not be able to cope, and so they hung around until someone else made the first move. It meant for a long day.

Markl put his arms on the kitchen table and rested his head on them. He closed his eyes just for a few minutes and not any longer or else he might find himself falling asleep right there. Sleep was not a bad option even if it was only seven in the evening.

'Think I might go sleep,' Markl said forcing himself up from the table.

He lifted the fast asleep Kylar off the couch, and carried him to his bed, tucking him in before climbing in on the other side. Kylar did not stir once even when his shoes were removed. Markl's head had barely hit the pillow, and he was asleep.

Estaban went back outside to the porch biting on his pipe and sat in his faithful rocking chair. He rocked himself a few times before he stopped, put his head in his hands and burst into the tears that had been long in waiting. When he eventually got his breath back, he sniffed and wiped his eyes and looked to the sky.

'Well Rue, you finally get to meet her now, I know you will both watch over us down here.'

He stopped talking as his gruff voice crackled and his heart broke at the longing for his beloved wife who had left this earth fifteen years ago. The passing of his dearest daughter-in-law had brought back the agony he had felt long ago.

As always, at four in the morning, the three men sat on the porch drinking coffee. Although not preparing for a day at sea, they found solace in their usual routine. As always, Estaban read from the Bible, and they prayed together. Kylar sat at the top of the stairs leading from the porch to the front garden. He stared towards the harbor watching the birds fluttering around the trawlers encouraging them to get a move on and get their haul in as they were hungry too.

'Aunty Mea says Mommy was beautiful on the inside, it did not matter what she looked like on the outside,' Kylar said casually, still watching the seagulls.

Markl flew from his rocking chair in a rage and stomped to the edge of the porch almost breaking the timber railing with his grip of steel as he fought down his anger.

'Your mother was beautiful inside and out. Aunty Mea needs to learn to keep her opinion to herself,' he snarled.

56

'No need upsetting yourself son. You know that woman is as silly and harmless as women come. She meant no harm,' Estaban said waving his hand at Markl and shaking his head.

Markl's grip on the railing loosened, he took a deep breath of early morning air, closed his eyes and let go of the railing.

'Let's go down to the harbor, and watch the fellows go out,' he said reaching for Kylar's hand and patting Estaban on the shoulder as he walked past his father.

Estaban bit his pipe and followed them. Down at the harbor they felt at peace, they felt eased from the anguish that filled their hearts, and even though they weren't going out to sea themselves, they felt better for being there. They felt God's presence holding them together should they fear to break apart. They drew on God's strength in guiding them through the passage of grief.

FULL
CIRCLE

Full Circle

I am very proud to say that a condensed version
of
Full Circle

won a Top Five Award
in the
Kwarts Short Story Competition
2013

www.kwarts.co.za

&

It is also published among a few other
short stories from authors
all over the world in

"i" An Anthology of Short Stories

by
First Step Publishing

www.firststepcorp.com

Chapter One

The plane bumped down softly and no sooner had it come to a standstill, when most of the passengers stood up, impatient to disembark. As if their eagerness would help the process go any faster – not at all – and so there they stood.

'Nana, you ready to go?' Gorgie asked as he held out his free hand to help me out of my seat. The plane was now empty of passengers, bar one or two elderly persons like me.

'Thank you, dear, I am.'

Gorgie was the most darling grandson any grandparent could ask for; from the moment he was born a unique bond had developed between the two of us. Now, at thirty-five, he still spent a lot of time with me and had passed down his loving nature to his son Lance, with whom I too enjoyed a very special relationship. At times, the closeness the three of us shared was much to the annoyance of the rest of the family.

Gorgie, Lance and I found our way through the King Shaka Airport in Durban to the car rentals and made our way swiftly to Amanzimtoti, my childhood hometown. A place I had not been back to in sixty years! Yes, I was extremely nervous as I stared out of the window, finding specific landmarks and trying to remember what everything had looked like so many years ago.

'You remember any of it?' Gorgie asked, sensing my anxiety.

'It's changed so much, but yes, some of it does still look familiar, to a degree...'

'You're going to be just fine. I'm sure no one will even remember what happened sixty years ago, Nana.'

As we approached Amanzimtoti, I could feel my body tensing up, my heart pumping a little faster and my hands beginning to shake more than they usually did. Such a feeling of anxiety was not good for my heart even if I was an extremely fit and healthy eighty-one-year-old lady. I lived in a granny flat in Gorgie's backyard and could still get myself around by taxi or bus without any help from anyone.

'Stop at that pharmacy on the left, please.'

'Are you okay Nana? Do you need a doctor?'

Gorgie's face paled as he glanced at me and I knew he thought I'd have a heart attack from nervousness.

'I'm fine dear; I just want to find out if an old friend is still around. One of the few that never judged me…' I trailed off.

As we slowly drove down the road, Gorgie was looking for a parking space; I couldn't help but see things the way they had looked sixty years ago. Yes, the town was completely different, but I could still see the bakery, the hardware store and the pharmacy next to one another. I could still see Mr. Petersen standing in the doorway of the hardware store, watching everything that went on in the streets like a guard dog on duty. I could almost smell the aroma from the bakery, inviting me in to buy a few cakes that I could not resist…

Gorgie parked the car and switched off the engine. The silence woke me from my daydream. He got out and made his way around to my door, opened it and held out his hand to assist me out of the car.

'Should I come in with you Nana?'

'No, you wait here. I won't be long.'

Hesitantly I walked towards the pharmacy, feeling a tiny hand slip into mine. Lance was not going to sit in the car; the curiosity of a six-year-old child was far too strong to hold at bay. The pharmacy, although redesigned with modern furnishings and fittings still had the feel of my era. My nerves stirred in the familiar surroundings.

'Did you work here Nana?'

'No dear, but my friend did. I want to find out if she's still living nearby.'

'Will you be sad if she's dead like your other friends?'

The truth of a child's words.

'I'll be disappointed,' I said as I felt my heart drop.

There was no time to dwell on the subject as a young lady came up to me and asked if she could be of assistance.

'I'm looking for an old friend. She used to work here, a very long time ago, and I was wondering if anyone might know of her. Her name is Daphney McNally.'

'Let me ask the owner. If I'm not mistaken, he's related to her.'

She scurried off to the dispensary area and a couple of minutes later returned with a very tall gentleman in her footsteps.

'Good day madam, how may I help you?'

His voice meant nothing but business. I told him I was enquiring after Daphney and that we'd known each other many years ago. To my surprise and delight, he disappeared and came back with a piece of paper. On it was the address of an old age home where she was living.

'I hope she recognizes you; she's my wife's grandmother.'

'Julia? Are you talking about Julia?'

'Yes, Julia is my wife.'

I thanked him, at least, a hundred times and hurried as fast as my little old legs could carry me, back to the car.

'She's alive, we going to visit her!' Lance yelled as we approached the car.

'Who is alive?' Gorgie asked curiously.

'My friend Daphney, and she lives at the retirement home a few blocks from here. Can we go there now before we go to the hotel?'

Gorgie just bowed.

'Your wish is my command, madam,' he mischievously offered as he opened the car door and presented his hand once more.

Very happy that I would get to see an old friend again, I relaxed in the car seat and closed my eyes.

Chapter Two

'Maybe I should freshen up a bit first before we go to Daphney,' I said as the car began to make its way around the corner creeping toward the retirement home.

'I wanted to suggest that,' Gorgie said, patting my hand and then pulling over to wait for the opportunity to do a U-turn.

'Where are we going?' Lance quizzed from the back seat, clearly confused as the car now continued back in the direction we'd come.

'To the hotel to check in and freshen up, and then we will visit Nana's friend,' Gorgie told him before I could.

'Her name is Daphney,' Lance answered smugly, and both Gorgie and I chuckled at the straightforwardness of a six-year-old.

Lance was so excited at the prospect of living in a hotel that he ran straight into the room to what he presumed was his bed. He stood next to it, and his face dropped. He looked at us with such a sullen expression that my heart wanted to melt.

'What's the matter, honey?'

'It's not like in the movies. It's supposed to be a really big bed, and I'm supposed to have my own room.'

Gorgie sat on the bed and looked at him gently.

'Now where did you get that idea in your head, mister?'

'It's always like that in the movies.'

Lance sat next to his dad on the bed and bounced a little, his head bent towards the ground, clearly not very impressed with this three-star hotel.

'I bet the food here is just as good as any fancy hotel in the movies.'

'Really, do you think so?'

He brightened at the thought of food.

'I surely do.'

Gorgie picked him up, and they went to inspect the view over the town from the balcony. I joined them trying to remember what had existed where.

'Back then it was just a little holiday village, with a few apartment buildings and hotels. The lagoon seemed to be a lot bigger then…'

I gazed out toward the sea; it was high tide, and I could hear the waves crashing on the beach. The air was as humid as I could recall Natal weather to be. The lagoon to the right of our balcony glistened in the sun, looking peacefully undisturbed.

'I remember there was a hotel next to the lagoon; we would go there on Saturday evenings and listen to a band play. That's where I met him. He was the guitarist in a band…'

I had to smile as I flooded my mind with the memories of those wonderful carefree childhood days. They did not last long, as those days had been short-lived.

'Did that man die?' Lance innocently asked.

'He did,' I replied as I turned around and walked back into the hotel room, nervous at the realization that so many wounds were about to be exposed.

'It's going to be okay Nana,' Gorgie said as he followed me into the room and put his arm around my shoulders, hugging me lightly.

He truly was an adorable grandson.

It was just past lunchtime when we were finally on our way to visit Daphney. The closer we got to the retirement home, the more the butterflies in my stomach increased their fluttering. Around every corner, Lance would ask, 'Are we there yet?' Or, 'Is this the place?' with typical childlike curiosity. Gorgie had to hold Lance's hand tightly to keep him reigned in. The last thing we needed was for a six-year-old boy with energy at around the 2000% level, running loose in an old age home. Just the thought of it sent me into a frenzied state of concern.

I walked into the lobby, and an elderly lady with a kind face greeted me. After telling her who I was there to visit, I signed the register, and she ushered the three of us into a living room, furnished with light green cushioned chairs and pale pink floral curtains. I sat down nervously, not sure what to expect. Gorgie just kept patting my hand comfortingly. After a few agonizing minutes, the lady from the reception returned – a hunched and wizened grey-haired woman at her side. I scrambled to my feet as I recognized my dear friend immediately. Her hair and aged skin could not hide the striking features that were Daphney. She stared at me, not hearing a word of what the lady at her side was saying, and the broadest smile graced her face. She knew who I was.

'Oh, oh, oh, oh can it be true? Meri? Meredith Chase, is that really you? Oh, oh, oh...'

She left the lady's support and spread her arms towards me, hurrying to wrap them around me.

'Daphney,' I spluttered her name through my tears, and the emotions swelled in my throat, 'oh my dear...'

We embraced each other for the longest time, clutching at each other so tightly our fragile bones could easily have snapped but scared that if we let go, it would all be just a dream. Eventually, standing back, I held Daphney at arm's length and took a good look at her, as she did me. It was incredible that I'd found my friend after sixty years, one of the very few I'd trusted and one that had never judged me for what I'd done.

'When did you get here? Why are you here? I never thought I'd see the day when you returned. I thought I would never see you again! Oh, my friend, I am so happy.'

Daphney began to cry and embraced me once more. I did not want to let her go. When we remembered that there were other people with us, I finally made the introductions. The lady who had brought Daphney to me had red eyes, and her face was wet with tears, and when I looked at Gorgie, I noticed that his face was in a similar state. Lance just had a look of pure amazement on his face.

'Gosh, your grandson is handsome,' Daphney said as Gorgie blushed, his brazen skin glowing with a hint of red.

He was exactly that – dark hair, slightly grey on the temples, tall, a bronze tan and hazel eyes. What was not to like? Lance looked more like his mother, with his blonde hair and blue eyes but blessed with the bronze skin tone of his father.

'I look like my mother,' he said matter-of-factly, to which we all giggled.

The kind lady who introduced herself as Sheila excused herself and promised to return in a few minutes with tea and cake. Daphney and I sat as close to each other on the sofa as possible while Gorgie took Lance out to the beautiful gardens to explore.

'So now, how did you find me? Oh gosh Meri, I still can't believe it's you, sitting here right next to me!'

It was with difficulty that we kept the next flow of tears at bay, but our smiles stuck to our faces like masks.

'On the way into town, I asked Gorgie to stop at the pharmacy you used to work. It was a shot in the dark, but it worked!'

'Oh yes of course. My son-in-law owns it now.'

We gave detailed accounts of our children and grandchildren. I told her all the places where I had lived, and about my second marriage, how wonderful my husband had been to our children and me – he had adopted Damian, Gorgie's father, as soon as we were married.

'So Meri dear, what on earth has brought you back here?'

Sheila returned with the tea and cake as I was about to answer. I felt it best to postpone my reply until we were alone again. Lance came bolting through the door at the prospect of food, with Gorgie in tow – those boys and their appetites.

When the boys went back to the garden, and Sheila had removed the empty dishes – not a crumb in sight – Daphney and I took a slow walk out to the gardens and wandered down pretty pathways lined with colorful flowers and little garden gnomes. We found a bench under a large willow tree that stood on the bank of a small stream, which I remembered meandered through the entire town and eventually flowed into the lagoon.

'Have you heard about our old school's Christian initiative?' I asked, not sure that even though Daphney lived here, she would've heard about it.

'Yes, I have heard a little about it. But how does it involve you?'

'Well, somehow they knew what had happened all those years ago and that I am now a servant of God. Somehow they found me – this internet technology is amazing,' I smiled, 'at any rate, they found me through Gorgie and invited me to give a little talk to the school children. To encourage them, you know, that no matter what life deals you, God is the answer.'

I sighed and looked down, straightening my floral skirt. Daphney took my hand and linked her fingers through mine, our old joints flowing with love as they intertwined.

'They could not have found a more perfect candidate, Meri. You have so much to offer, so much advice and wisdom for those kids.'

'Will you come too, please? We can pick you up on the way there. I would appreciate it.'

'Wouldn't miss it for the world!'

She squeezed my hand reassuringly, and I sighed with relief. I knew that although time had passed and our lives had changed so dramatically, love for a true friend would never change.

'Thanks, my friend. I knew that God would spare you till we could see each other again. I am so grateful for this day.'

We hugged each other, and this time, we did not bother to restrain our emotions.

Chapter Three

As I walked into the foyer of the school, I could not help the feelings of nostalgia that ran through my veins. We looked at all the photos proudly displayed along the walls, bragging of past pupils and their achievements. Lance, however, was only interested in finding one that had my face on it and when he did he squealed with delight.

'Look Nana! That's you; I'm sure, you look so funny.'

We all had to laugh and true enough, there I was, in our class photo, sitting next to my dear friend Daphney. The headmaster Mr. Lancaster introduced himself and escorted the four of us to the staff room where all the staff members were waiting for my arrival; and a buffet of tea and biscuits. It was somewhat daunting walking into the staff room. So much had changed and my memories were so different from what I encountered at that moment.

After tea and cake, the assembly bell rang, and all the teachers made their way to the stage in the school hall. A hum of voices and pounding feet could be heard down the passages, as the children made their way to the hall and ushered to their assigned seats. As the honored guest, I had to walk into the hall alongside Mr. Lancaster – down the middle aisle and up to my seat on the stage. Fortunately, he offered me his arm, steadying me and making sure he kept to my slow pace. The assembly procedures had not changed, and while sitting in my seat to the left of the stage, I giggled as I found the seat where I had sat in the gallery in my final year. The nonsense we would get up to in that gallery during assembly made me want to burst out laughing just at the thought of it!

Then the nerves set in and my hands started to shake as Mr. Lancaster began to introduce me to the entire school. The headmaster strode over to my seat and presented his hand to help me up and walk me to the podium in the center of the stage. My legs wobbled as I grasped his arm tightly, and I felt sure that the pale blue dress I had on was not the right one to wear – who knows why I thought of that then. The applause finally ceased, and the children sat down in their chairs once again, intent eyes boring into me, and utter silence, waiting for me to start. The front rows on either side of the aisle were always reserved for guests, and I sought out Gorgie, Daphney, and Lance, who smiled and waved at me. I gave dear Lance a little wave back, took a deep breath and moved closer to the microphone.

'Hello. It is so special for me to be invited to speak to you all today. It has been sixty years since I was last in Amanzimtoti.'

A murmur filled the hall, but I continued, my voice still shaky.

'I went to school here. It was very different then, but in a strange way, it was the same. The assembly procedures were exactly the same.'

I put a huge emphasis on the word "exactly," which caused a giggle to ripple through the hall. I explained where I'd sat, and I waved at the young lady who now occupied the seat, she blushed as she waved back, much to the amusement of her peers. I cleared my throat, my voice grew stronger, and I continued, 'Life in my final year at this school was fantastic. We were so excited to be seniors, to finally be heading out into the big wide world to fulfill our dreams. I met the man of my dreams that year. He did not go to this school and was three years older than I was. At the time, he was working for the old AECI plant. We fell madly in love and the year after I finished school we got married. You must all remember that getting married so young was normal and almost expected in those days.'

I could hear mumbles from young girls disapproving of such a notion. I smiled and went on speaking.

'We were so in love, and within our first year of marriage I was pregnant – again this was a normal way of life in those days.'

I couldn't help grinning at the looks on some of the young girls' faces. They looked horrified at the thought of being married and pregnant by the age of eighteen.

'We were blessed with a son. I was completely and utterly in awe of the miracle of birth and our gorgeous baby boy, whom we named Damian.'

I looked at Gorgie who handed Lance a gadget on which he liked to play games. His father gently put the earphones in his

69

ears, and I was grateful for the common sense Gorgie had, not to allow Lance to listen to my story of woe and pain.

'With each day that passed, the bond between Damian and me blossomed, and with each passing day, my husband grew more and more jealous of the time that I spent with Damian and not with him. He withdrew from our little family unit and developed a temper I had never known he could possess. Damian was utterly dependent on me, and as a mother, there was no thought in those days of going back to work a month after giving birth. You stayed at home and raised your children; it was your duty. Our son was equally dependent on his father, and yet my husband only increasingly saw him as a threat.'

I took a deep breath. It had been a long time since I had reached into the memories of those horror years and even more so to speak to strangers about them.

'The first time his jealously became too much to bear was on a quiet evening at home. We were watching television when Damian started crying in his crib. I got up to attend to him, and my husband flew into a fit of rage. I was so shocked I just stared at him. I did not know what to do or say. I just stood in the middle of the living room floor frozen, while Damian's crying increased rapidly. Realising I had to comfort my son, I took a step toward the crib, and the next thing I knew, I was on the floor, with blood dripping from my mouth.'

I swallowed nothing, my throat was suddenly dry from talking, but I had to continue.

'My husband stared at me with a look of confusion, anger, and disbelief on his hard face. He could not believe what he had done and immediately regretted it, swooping down to help me up and apologizing profusely, begging for my forgiveness. He even took charge of Damian while I cleaned my face in the bathroom. As he held Damian in his arms, I returned to see a picture of love between a father and his son. I thought that would be the first and last time such an incident would happen. But I was wrong.'

Daphney held my gaze and winked at me even though her eyes were welled up with tears.

'The tantrums and violent behavior increased as he found it easier and easier to explode over the smallest things. I became a nervous wreck, and Damian could sense that, which in turn affected him as he cried more and more just to be held. Any simple little thing could set my husband off – such as the food not being quite ready when he was hungry. The acts of violence grew with each episode until eventually he used his fist and would not stop hitting me even when I was cowering on the floor.'

The hall was silent; no one wanted to breathe even for fear of disturbing the chilling story they were listening to. Gorgie and Daphney both looked at the floor; I think looking at me was just too hard for them to bear. I swallowed the tears and the cry that wanted to escape from my throat. My hands shook almost uncontrollably, and for a moment, I wondered if I would be able to get through my testimony.

God, please give me strength, I silently prayed as I paused to compose myself for the audience of children and teachers alike waiting in anticipation.

'Toward the beginning of the violent outbursts, my husband would apologize profusely afterward, and I would always forgive him, thinking he would not do it again. After a while, he stopped bothering to apologize, and instead threatened that if I ever did whatever it was that I'd done wrong again, the beating would be even worse. And every time it was. I was too afraid to go outside for fear that someone would see the mess I was in.'

I looked at Daphney, her face stained with tears.

'My friend here,' I pointed to her, 'came to visit me one day, concerned that she had not seen me for some time, and she was horrified at what she found. She put Damian and me into her car and drove us straight to the police station. I protested, but she finally convinced me to lay a charge of assault against my husband. And the police immediately arrested him. He got released on bail that his friend posted, and arrived at the house in the early hours of that morning. He dragged me out of bed, threw me against the wall and threatened to kill both Damian and me. I pleaded. I begged. I cried. He just kept hitting me. Somehow I managed to get out of the room and run to the kitchen – the room furthest away from Damian's.'

Shaking, I took a tissue from the pocket of my dress and wiped away the tears that ran down my face. I tried desperately to compose myself so that I could get the rest of this awful story told.

'He came toward me like a bull on a rampage. He had a belt in his hands, and I knew he would not stop until I was dead. As he approached me with his arm out to deliver the next strike, I grabbed the frying pan that was drying on the dish rack and swung it at him with all my strength. It hit him on the side of the head, and he staggered backward and fell, hitting his head on the kitchen table on his way down. He was dead before he reached the floor.'

You could cut the silence in the hall with a knife. I stopped talking and tried to compose myself, wiping away my tears and swallowing the lump jamming my throat closed. Then I took another deep breath, my lips quivering, and I went on.

'I didn't know what to do. I screamed I cried, I fell to the floor next to him, shaking his limp body wishing it to come alive. Then slowly reality dawned on me, and I went to the phone and dialed the police, and then Daphney and then I went to get my child that was still crying. The police and Daphney arrived together, and I was in a total state of shock, horrified that I could have done such a terrible thing. I was even unaware of the blood that ran down the side of my face, dripping onto Damian as I held him.'

Everyone was frozen to their seats, mesmerized.

'After a lengthy police investigation, I was freed from all charges of manslaughter, culpable homicide and others. But, how did I get over such a tragic and horrific crime that I'd committed? Well, the truth is that the images of that day, and all the pain and guilt I felt, never left me. In desperate need of counseling, and trying to find peace within my soul, I went to church with my friend.'

Again I looked at dear Daphney, who smiled back at me, blowing me a kiss.

'I was told that day that forgiveness comes from God. We are all sinners. That God died for all our sins. And if we give our lives to God, we can start our life anew. Our past is exactly that – the past. God gives us a clean slate. That from that moment on, if we walk the path of righteousness for the rest of our lives, with God we will have peace, we will have an understanding. We will have love and live in abundance. We will live forever. And if we do not live for God, His love and protection cannot work for us. That day I chose to live for God. That day I chose to live in peace and in love with God. That day I chose life forever. From my story I do, with all my love, hope that you young ladies will realize that it is so important to find a man that will not abuse you and most importantly, one who loves God. And to you, young men, I hope that you will serve God and be kind and gentle to your girlfriends, and one day to your wives. Life without God is no life at all.'

There was a moment's hesitation, and then Mr. Lancaster stood up and began to clap his hands. Not even a second later the hall erupted, and for what seemed like forever I stood there – having bared my soul to strangers, in a town that I had left, in a place I'd thought I would never see again.

I had come full circle. I could live with what little time God had left for me, in complete peace and happiness. Through a horrific tragedy, that I thought I would never get over, I'd found peace and love and happiness, but only by the mercy and grace of God.

RENOVATED HEART

Renovated Heart

Chapter One

The constructor's van pulled into the driveway while I took a deep breath, exhaled slowly then repeated the same action several times. At the last exhale I was still not prepared for the next few weeks' chaos that was to ensue in my home. The van switched off, the back canopy door flipped open, and several workers peeled out talking loudly in their native tongue that I did not understand. They then proceeded to pull out pieces of equipment and tools from the back of the van where they had been sitting and placing them on the driveway. I wondered if the back of the van was a bottomless pit since there was a seemingly endless stream of tools.

Finally, the driver, whom I presumed was the foreman, ended his phone call and got out of the van. He strode directly over to the workers and started talking or rather it looked more like lecturing as they responded half-heartedly. He then took off his cap, held it with both hands and walked towards the front door. I left the window and got to the door as he knocked and was greeted with a pleasant smile.

'Good morning Ms. Conley. I believe we are to start with the renovations on your house today.'

I was about to reply when he continued, 'My name is Kai Naihe. I will be the site foreman for your project.'

His right hand left his cap and presented itself to shake my hand as a formal introduction. I offered my right hand and shook his. It was a firm handshake; his hands were slightly rough in line with his form of work but gentle at the same time. He had a manner about him that immediately made me feel at ease and that it would be okay to trust him.

'Please call me Darla. I guess you had better come in and get started then. Your office did phone to confirm that you were on your way. They even gave the registration number of the van, the number of staff and a description of what you looked like, very efficient I must say.'

'We want our clients to feel they can trust us and that hopefully we will get recommended at the end of the contract,' he hinted impishly.

I opened the door to its full extent and indicated that he should follow me to the back of the house. He followed, carrying a bunch of plans and his cap. We exited the back of the house, and I waited for him to take in the design of the house and the surroundings. I showed him the building on the side of the house which originally was a shed, and that was now to be extended to join the main house as a fully equipped cottage. But that was not all that was to get done; I wished it was.

The house was old and in dire need of some serious restoration. By the end of the project, the house might have none of its old features still visible. That was not what I wanted, and I hoped the designers and builders had got it into their heads that they had to preserve as much of the history of the house as possible. They had promised to do just that, but there were always issues that prevented this as so many of my friends had told me. My friends with their delightful stories from their experiences of renovations had made me extremely nervous, and at one point I almost canceled the whole project. The only reason I went ahead with it was the need to have my mother live with me. She had been living in a wonderful retirement home, but she was not exactly happy. Her desire for her freedom and routine drove us to look for a home that would accommodate both of us and still allow our individual lifestyles. We definitely would have made life a lot easier for ourselves buying property that had all that we wanted in place from day one, but for whatever reason, we had both fallen in love with this old rundown house.

Kai placed the plans and several other objects on the ground and took a look around the shed and the outside of the house. Then he opened one of the plans and with it spread out open in his hands he re-examined the shed and the house. As I watched what he was doing, I suddenly remembered the table and gazebo I wanted to give them to work from in the garden.

'Uhm...Kai,' I hoped I had pronounced it correctly as I did not remember his surname, 'in the shed is a table and a fold-up gazebo. I thought you might want to make use of it. If not, that's also fine.'

He turned around slowly still glancing between the plans and the house and with a quick look at me thanked me very politely. I went inside to the only room that was barely liveable – the spare bedroom. I heard feet traipsing through the house a dozen times; voices echoed between the walls and every action such as putting down a bucket or laying down plastic was loudly audible. I realized from that first afternoon that my intention of living in the house during the renovations was not going to be at all possible. I had foolishly given notice in the apartment I was living in and had moved out at the end of the previous month. Had I known what the living conditions would turn out to be like I would have stayed in my apartment until the house was completely renovated, cleaned and polished?

I had to make up my mind in a hurry – did I move in with my friend for the next six weeks or should I go to a hotel? My best friend, Rylee, lived in a small townhouse on the other side of town. She had, at least, five cats that I knew of, and there was the distinct possibility she had found a few more lost and lonely felines to rescue since my last visit. I had no objection to owning a cat or two nor to her desire to own so many, but personally, I preferred dogs. Large ones for that matter. So I had to ask myself repeatedly if I would be able to withstand the onslaught of feline affection for six weeks or more. One other worrisome issue that would come with living with Rylee would be her immense need for partying and consuming more alcohol in one evening than I was able to manage in a month. She was a woman of many contradictions. The other alternative – hotel or B&B – would obviously cost me a rather large sum of money which I needed for the renovations. If I went to the hotel and after a few weeks had discovered that I was unable to afford it, and only then went to ask Rylee, it was possible I might offend her. A tap on the door interrupted my thoughts.

'Sorry to disturb you, Ms. Con…Darla, I only wanted to let you know that the delivery trucks will start arriving within the next half an hour.'

Kai stood in the bedroom doorway waiting for my response.

'Okay. Thank you.'

He turned to make his way back to the backyard, but I quickly continued, 'I think I will make other living arrangements. This noise, dust and I will not get along very well.'

'It will probably be the best option.'

He nodded and left, placing his cap back on his head once his back turned on me. He fascinated me. He was so well-mannered it was almost unnerving. I knew he was not a local man and definitely from another country. He was probably in his late twenties or early thirties. He had olive skin, brown eyes, and wavy black hair, and he was tall and from what I observed, decently built too. My mind left Kai and swung back to my decision making, pondering on my two options but not for very long.

'Hi Rylee,' I said when she answered her phone in her professional tone.

First, we made idle chatter catching up on the day's events then I asked, 'So can I still take you up on your offer to stay with you?'

'Silly, of course, you can. When I get home we will fix up the spare room; it's minute as you know, but I'm sure you will be comfortable. It's going to be awesome to have a human conversation every night instead of only feline chatter.'

I was not sure how to respond to that but thanked her and confirmed that I would be at her place by seven that evening. Rylee's townhouse was on the cheaper side of town, not that I minded or had any issues with that, it just meant that I had to drive at least fifteen minutes longer to the hospital where I was doing my final year internship in the pediatric ward.

My usual route to run every morning also had to be altered now that I was living on the other side of town. After a few mornings, I found a decent route and got back into the rhythm of jogging, but I still missed my normal route along the beachfront, and so I changed my mind and drove to my usual starting point and ran my old route along the beachfront. I was far happier and content with this arrangement.

Every day after my shift at the hospital ended I stopped in at the house to check on the progress and to discuss any issues with Kai. He was always the same gentleman that I had met on the first day. Sometimes when I stopped by at lunchtime I'd find him sitting alone in the sun reading; he was an intriguing fellow. Kai would go over the details of the progress always giving me a guided tour as well. It was on the very odd occasion that he phoned during the day for any matter, and by the end of the first week I trusted his every decision even if it was a major change that had to be made.

One evening the air was nippy and fresh after an earlier rainfall of an hour or so. I'd had my morning jog as always but felt the need for another run in the crisp air. As I ran along the beachfront passing the masses of people taking an afternoon stroll or also jogging, I noticed a few men kneeling at the edge of the ocean with their surfboards lying on the sand next to them. I stopped, why I do not know, and watched them wondering what they were doing. When they stood up, I recognized Kai. I took a short breath and remained to stare at them as they picked up their boards and made for the ocean to surf.

That's odd, I thought to myself and continued with my run constantly looking back at the surfers and in particular at Kai.

Chapter Two

The weekend brought with it an abundance of parties and nightclubs for Rylee. I went along to the first one on a Friday night but left after a few hours. We were complete opposites, and it was a wonder that we were such good friends. Funny enough I preferred the company of her many cats to her parties. With my car safely parked in the driveway, leaving room for Rylee to park in the garage whenever she decided to stumble home, I reached to open the front door. It pushed open when I touched the lock with my key. Puzzled I swung the door open and stepped into the small entrance hall wondering if I had not locked it properly when I'd left earlier. The lights were on too, but I was sure I had switched everything off. The cats were lazing around which was, at least, normal. Cautiously I made my way to the bedroom. The light was also on, and I smelled a strange odor the closer I got to the room.

When I entered the room – by now walking on my toes just in case – my heart stopped for a second before I let out a horrified yelp. Standing at the bedside table scratching in the drawer was a man less than gracious and determined to get whatever he could to sell for drugs, alcohol or both. He turned and ran towards me, and I froze for a split second, stifling a scream, and then I came to my senses and turned to bolt out of the room. A string of vulgar obscenities flew from his disgusting mouth leaving his bitter breath lingering on the back of my neck. Panic overrode any rational thinking, and I screamed trying to escape the hand that had a hold of my jacket. His other hand held onto my forearm so tightly it hurt, and the touch made me want to throw up. I had to fight back or…I did not want to even think of what he was going to do me…I had to fight back. I swung around and with my fist threw a punch at him. I had no idea if the punch would even land on him, but it did. Better than I could have anticipated. It landed in his throat, and he released my arm, instinctively grabbing his throat, this gave me just a few seconds for an escape. Or so I hoped.

As I got to the bedroom door, he was grabbing my jacket again. I wriggled my arms out of the sleeves and kept running, holding my car keys for dear life. My cell phone was still in the pocket of my pants. He threw my jacket to the side and grabbed my arm again, pinning me to the wall. I kept screaming; he slapped me in the face that the sting was so intense tears sprang from my eyes, but I still had to fight even if all I wanted to do was hold my throbbing face. My foot shot into his leg; my pointed cowboy boots made an impact as he bent forward from the pain and I slipped out from his grasp again. Had I made it out of the house? My mind was spinning with instructions, questions, and panic. His hand gripped my leg, and I fell to the floor just inches from the door. He pulled me towards him and pull himself towards me, all the time threatening to do awful things to me. I had to resist. I kicked and shouted for help, but who would hear me? I was almost underneath him. He stank so badly, his breath was nauseating, and he was so dirty, but I ignored all that and desperately tried to free myself.

I screamed out loud, 'Oh Lord, please Lord help me! Help me!'

A few more minutes of desperate struggling, kicking and begging and then I felt a surge of confidence filter through me knowing that I was not going to get harmed any further. I flung my free arm at him making no impact whatsoever. Then I realized I was still holding the car keys in my hand, and amid all my irrational thinking I had enough savvy to release the pointed part of the key and use it as a weapon. With a loud grunt, I plunged forward and wildly stabbed at him, not caring where I stabbed him. I took the adrenaline induced energy and dug the point of the key into him, not once but three times until he collapsed on the floor beside me holding his pulsating bloodied face and crying in agonizing pain. I got up and finally made it out of the house to my car. Somewhere in the mixed up chaos flooding my thoughts, I managed to start it. I reversed out of the driveway so fast the rear bumper hit the asphalt, sounding like a head-on collision. I shoved the gears into first and put my shaking foot on the accelerator, speeding off like a maniac.

I don't remember changing any gears at any stage from the house to the service station two blocks away. I raced into the driveway, and while the car was still idling, I sat choking on my hysterical sobs, my body uncontrollably shaking from the shock. An attendant approached the window to ask if he could assist me. At the glimpse of a person in my peripheral vision, my hysteria up-scaled into manic hysteria. The attendant sensing that something was not right, and probably also noticing the blood on my hands, face and matted in my blonde hair, ran to the convenience store and told the manager to phone the police.

I fought with my unsteady hands enough to get my phone from my pocket and pressed any number on the call log. I did not care who it was as long as it reached someone. The blaring sound of music and people shouting to hear each other speak greeted me above Rylee's voice.

'Hello hello!' Rylee shouted through her slurs.

I tried to answer her, but she did not hear me. I hit the end call button and hit another number on the call log.

'Hello,' a male voice answered.

My mouth opened, but my throat so choked up I was unable to get any words out.

'Hello Darla, you there?'

His voice went up a notch.

Forcing the words out, I brokenly begged, 'K…Kai…help.'

The tears ran into my mouth as I swallowed the stutters of anguish and fear.

'At the BP in Strand.'

Unable to say anymore I let the phone fall from my shaking hands and cried and cried so loudly I'm sure I was heard from the other end of the street. And by now there was an audience around the car and so many people mulling around. A stream of blue and red lights was swirling around the area. A police officer knelt down at the window of my car. He tapped gently on the window to get my attention.

'Ma'am, can you wind your window down, please?'

He showed me his badge and smiled. I shook my head still sobbing, my hands holding onto the steering wheel were still shaking so wildly it was obvious to everyone.

'Can you unlock your door then ma'am? Please, we want to help you.'

It took a few minutes to get my brain to register that I should do what the policeman asked me as he was going to help me. With an immense amount of effort, I managed to relay a message to my hands to let go of the steering wheel and unlock the door. The second the policeman heard the click of the door he opened it. He reached in to help me get out the car, but at the sight of his arms coming towards me, I screamed, throwing my arms at him envisioning the man that attacked me.

'Darla, Darla!'

I knew that voice and fought through my inner panic to find where it was.

'Do you know this lady?' the policeman asked the man with the voice.

'Yes, she called me a little earlier. Said she needed help and mentioned this place.'

He bypassed the policeman in a flash and stood next to me reaching for my hand.

'Darla, hey, it's me, Kai. I'm here.'

My eyes were heavy, and I was exhausted but hearing his gentle, well-mannered voice sent a wave of relief through me, knowing that he was here with me. He was soothingly persuasive and finally coaxed me to trust him and allow him to take me to the ambulance that was nearby. As I stood up, my knees buckled but before I collapsed, he caught me in his arms and carried me to the ambulance. The paramedic instructed him to lay me down on the gurney carefully. When the paramedics lifted me into the ambulance, I would not let go of Kai's hand, and so they permitted him to travel with me. He held my hand all the way, but he looked down and had his eyes closed the entire journey. I wondered if maybe he was very tired.

At the hospital, I was given medication to make me relax and sleep, and they cleaned me up. The staff of the hospital and police tried to get information from me as to what had happened. I was eventually more forthcoming and in bits and pieces explained what had happened, the fear still so viciously fresh. Kai stayed with me until I was fast asleep.

Chapter Three

In the early hours of the morning, the hospital was buzzing with activity. At first, I had no recollection of where I was or why I was there. When a nurse who brought me a fine cup of coffee hinted at what had happened, I remembered it all too well. The tears came and lingered on my face, but after the coffee, I felt somewhat better.

'The gentleman who was with me last night…'

The nurse butted in before I was able to finish my sentence,

'Oh, what a lovely fellow, sat here till the wee hours of the morning never taking his eyes off you and never stopped praying all the while he sat there in that chair. Such a lovely man. He be a keeper that one.'

She took her gadgets with a smile and left.

What is she on about? I asked myself bewildered.

The doctor was next to visit me, and when he was satisfied that I was stable albeit traumatized, he said I was able to go home. I looked at the brightly colored curtains and wondered to which home I would go. A phone was ringing for a few minutes or so before I realized it was my cell phone in the drawer.

'Hello?' I answered.

'Hello Darla, it's Kai. How are you feeling?'

'Kai! Oh, Kai…Hi. Thank you for last night! I am so sorry if I caused any trouble for you and put you in such an awkward position.'

A wave of distress took residence in me, and tears flooded my eyes again.

'No, no really I am pleased you phoned me, and I was able to be with you. Are you okay?'

'I can go home,' I said fighting the desire to hang up and cry.

'Where is home? Rylee's house or the one being renovated?'

'No, not Rylee's house. I can't go back there, not now. I would never be able to sleep there.'

I wondered as I said that if Rylee even knew about what had happened.

'Do you need a ride?'

'Can I call you back if I do? I need to make a few phone calls.'
'Of course. Please Darla, if there is anything I can do, please call me.'

His kindness was so welcoming it warmed my heart. I called Mother first, and she naturally felt shattered when I told her where I was and what had happened. I tried to make it sound as if it was nothing too traumatic but Mother knew me better than I knew myself. I also left out the part of stabbing the attacker in the eye with my key, but I was sure she would find that out from someone. She would not rest until she had all the details.

The word spread around the hospital that I was a patient, and so it was that I had a constant flow of phone calls and visits from all the staff. I had to promise my superior that I would visit the children before I left as they were so worried about me. I phoned Rylee between all the phone calls and visits. She sounded really tired when she answered, and I remembered that she had probably only arrived home a few hours ago.

'Hi Rylee, it's me, Darla.'
'Darla hi, what's up? Where are you? What happened here last night? You have a party or something?'

She was dead silent and probably waking up more and more as I relayed the horror of the previous evening. I had waited for a few seconds before she responded when I was finished speaking.

'No Darla, no, I am so sorry, I should have phoned you back. I am so sorry.'

She cried and cried. I cried too, again. Kai sounded disappointed that he did not have to fetch me but was satisfied when I promised to phone him later in the day. When Rylee arrived in the hospital room an hour later, she was distraught, flinging her arms around me apologizing over and over that she'd remained at the party and then had not returned my call. I, in turn, tried to convince her it was not her fault, I was okay, and it was all over. But the nurse, overhearing us, kindly reminded me that it would take time for me to come to terms with all that had happened.

We left among loads of good wishes, hugs, and kisses. Mother had arranged a room at the retirement home, and when we arrived, I was inundated with wishes from the sweet elderly residents. Living here for the next few weeks were going to be very interesting, and I was sure, entertaining.

After a few days of being pampered by Mother and the residents, I went back to work. I loved being around the little children; they brought so much joy into my life even if they were ill. They were such a contrast to the elderly, and yet in many ways so similar. They kept my mind free from the reminder of what could have happened and the horror of the whole experience. It was when I was alone in my bed that I struggled to keep myself free from the nightmare. I found myself asking God for help.

Chapter Four

After work one day when my shift ended at about lunchtime, I took a drive to the house to catch up on the renovations. Kai had kept me updated by phone on a regular basis, but I wanted to see it for myself. The driveway was crowded with building materials forcing me to weave my way around the objects to get to the front door. Upon entering, I felt the change in my bones. That old musty smell was gone, and a new smell of clean, fresh paint and varnish had taken its place. I hoped they had kept the old style of the design and features and looking around; I realized it had been a while since I had last been there; so much had been done and completed.

Where is everyone? I thought to myself as I exited the house and went to the back garden where I finally found the workers sitting in a corner eating their lunch. One of the workers realized I was looking for Kai pointed his finger at the far end of the garden. Kai was reading, sitting on the grass leaning against the fence that got good shade from the midday sun. I contemplated leaving and returning later rather than disturb him as he seemed so engrossed in what he was reading. He glanced up from his book and called my name just as I was about to turn around and leave.

'Sorry, I did not want to disturb your lunch time. You seem to be very interested in your book too.'

He smiled and simply replied, 'No worries, how are you doing?'

He asked not just out of decency but from real concern. I could tell this by the tone of his voice and the expression on his face, and I felt pleasingly moved. I told him all about the retirement home and the residents. The love affairs I had stumbled upon and the jealousy among some of the ladies. It was like being in high school again. His face lit up pleasantly as he laughed at my stories, conversing with him was just so easy.

'So I want to thank you for the other night and so does my mother. Will you be willing to brave a dinner at the retirement home? Please don't feel obliged; you don't have to if you don't want to. I will understand.'

'I would love to. It will be very interesting I'm sure.'

'You are very brave I must say. The ladies are going to pounce on you.'

I laughed as I imagined the little old ladies hanging all over Kai.

'You want a tour?'

'I don't want to interrupt your lunch really.'

'Come,' he said insistently, placing his book carefully in his backpack.

'Thank you,' I replied as we slowly paced toward the house.

First, he showed me the new cottage for Mother. It was practically finished and almost exactly as I'd envisioned it. I knew she was going to be comfortable living here. Then we gradually moved on to the house, and he paid special attention when showing me the old features I'd wanted to keep and apologized profusely about the one doorway that they'd been unable to save. I was disappointed, but he had informed me earlier that they were having problems with it, so I'd expected it, and the replica they'd made did not look too obvious. He went through every room in detail, and anything I was not happy with or sure about was written down in his notebook with the promise to make the necessary changes. The old restored features and the new ones all fitted together well. After I had taken up his entire lunch period, he walked with me back through the maze of equipment and materials to my car.

'Have you heard anything from the police?' he asked hesitantly, unsure if I was ready to speak about the incident at all.

'Yes, a man was rushed to the state hospital that same night with his eye half hanging out, and they naturally called the police, and so they have him in custody now. They will let me know when the court hearing will take place.'

He nodded slowly.

'Thank you for the tour, I appreciate it. Will Saturday be fine for dinner? Sorry, it is short notice.'

'Saturday is fine, should I wear a bulletproof vest or something like that?' he chuckled.

I giggled too. 'Probably something like that.'

When I got back to the retirement home and told Mother dinner was set for Saturday, it was practically seconds before every old lady knew Kai – the hero – was coming for dinner. They scrambled to find their very best outfits, many even made appointments with the resident hairdresser, and when in a matter of minutes she was fully booked for the day, they made appointments with outside hairdressers. They fussed about as if royalty was making an appearance. The kitchen staff and head chef went into operation mode and headed up the best five-course meal they were capable of making.

'Please, you honestly don't have to make such a fuss.'

'This man made a special effort for you and besides we don't often get a chance to go all out in the kitchen,' Billy the head chef said with exuberance.

There was no way to deter him now.

I sent Kai a message when I finally got to my room: *'Oh boy! Are you very sure you want to come here? I should have rather taken you out somewhere. These people have gone overboard.'*

He replied: *'Lol shld be fun.'*

Rylee joined me for an evening jog along my favorite route passed the beach. It was not her favorite form of exercise, but she was still riding a wave of guilt and making a very big effort to change her partying ways. She had also moved to a townhouse two blocks down from my house. Off we went, keeping pace with each other. For a woman that rarely, if ever, did any form of exercise she was relatively fit and kept up with me without breaking too much of a sweat. The sun, still warm, was suspended in the universe as a massive, round, perfectly shaped ball illuminating the sky with a bright red color. It looked larger and closer to the earth than it should have. I stopped mid-stride and gazed at the red ball. I stretched out my hand. I could almost touch it – well in a perfect world, yes. Rylee came walking back, realizing she had been running on her own for at least ten meters and confused as to why I had stopped and why on earth I was trying to touch the sun.

'Isn't it perfect and stunning?' I said in complete awe of the spectacular theatrical display the universe was performing that evening.

'Never mind the hot sun, look at the hot men,' Rylee drooled pointing toward the ocean.

'Oh, that looks like Kai again. They did the same thing the other night.'

We watched as the men knelt at the edge of the ocean before picking up their boards. This time, they did not go into the ocean but made their way up the beach. What to do? Continue running or stay? While I pondered, Rylee rambled on about how hot these men were. If she hadn't broken out in a sweat from running, she was certainly breaking out in one now.

'Hey, Darla!' Kai called a few feet away from where I was still standing contemplating – too late.

'Hi, Kai, this is Rylee,' I pointed toward Rylee, who was by now oozing lust at the men that had approached us.

Kai introduced us to his five friends, and we all exchange pleasantries. Rylee zoomed in on Kai, explaining how sorry she was for not having taken my call and how grateful she was to him for having been there for me.

'I will have to thank you properly one day soon.'

Wow, she certainly does not waste any time, I thought, annoyed at once.

'Well I need to get going again otherwise it will be dark before I finish my run. Speak to you soon Kai. Bye guys, nice meeting you all.'

I tugged on Rylee's arm, and she huffed and batted her eyelids flirtatiously as she said goodbye.

'Oh, my word you never said your construction dude was so fine - I want him.'

She babbled on about, in her opinion, an instant attraction between them. I was irritated beyond measure and just wanted to get home. She was entitled to date whoever she pleased, and that included Kai, so I don't know why it bothered me so much. I kept quiet about the dinner on Saturday night just in case she invited herself along.

Chapter Five

Kai arrived at the retirement home about fifteen minutes early. He pressed the buzzer and Benson the security officer let him in and ushered him into the green living room. Benson picked up the phone at the reception to inform me my visitor had arrived.

Gosh, he looks so dashing! My brain reacted delightfully to what my eyes saw. He stood up and smiled at me; I detected that it was a nervous smile. He was dressed casually in a grey shirt that complemented his bronze complexion and dark hair, jeans with a black belt and shoes that gave him the looks of a movie star. I felt sure the ladies would swoon so badly they might pass out. Rylee would completely freak out, and I giggled inwardly. Maybe I would get a photo taken, put it on Facebook and then wait for her reaction, this time, I did laugh out loud.

'What's funny? Am I overdressed?' He questioned very concernedly!

'No, I will explain later. You look very nice, certainly better than your daily clothes I've seen you in.'

I was sure he blushed.

'Well let's meet the masses. I hope you are ready for the onslaught!'

I led the way first to the blue room where I had asked Mother to wait for us. I wanted to introduce her to Kai first for fear of not getting a chance once the other ladies got hold of him.

'Thank you, son, for rushing to Darla when she called you.'

Mother hugged Kai with sincere affection and when she released him the tears streaming down her face confirmed her gratitude.

She wiped her face with a tissue and amid the sniffs said, 'Enough of this, come let's eat.'

Her smile would forever melt my heart. She linked her arm in his and started toward the dining hall entrance. Kai grinned and held out his other arm to me, requesting that I link my arm in his. I did so. Gosh, it felt good!

'You need protection?' I smirked at him trying to forget the fuzzy feeling I had just felt.

The big doors swung open as we entered through them. Everyone stood up, be it a little slower than normal considering the average age of the residents.

'Be prepared to be treated like a superhero,' I said as I eyed Betty swarming in on Kai.

Poor Kai. Everyone literally attacked him. He probably had more kisses in a matter of half an hour than he'd had in his entire life. His hand was shaken by the men so many times that by now it was likely swollen. I felt sorry for him, but he took it all in courteously. When Mother had finally freed him and managed to get him to his seat between her and me, Chef Billy was finally able to stop sulking and complaining that his food was getting cold. Before we ate as was the norm in the retirement home, Uncle Larry said a prayer.

'Amen,' Kai said when Uncle Larry had finished.

A delicious avocado stuffed with seafood was the starter for the five-course meal. We ate it in silence; it was so yummy, and then we wiped our mouths with the serviettes and sat back feeling very well satisfied.

Then Kai cleared his throat.

'So your friend Rylee, she is very forward...' He looked at me waiting for my response. Well!

I did not want to have this conversation right now.

'Yes, she is. She does not mean any harm, but she is, as you say, very forward. What prompted you to mention that?'

'She phoned me last night and invited me to a party.'

'She did? Goodness!' I was stunned. 'I'm sorry if you had wanted to go, you could've canceled with me.'

Kai took a sip of his juice and paused before replying, 'Are you crazy and miss getting treated like a superhero celebrity?'

I snickered, 'But honestly Kai...Ooh wait, did you tell her you were coming here tonight?'

'No, should I have?'

'So when are you going out with her?'

Curiosity was killing me.

'I took a rain check.'

'Oh.'

Then the next course was brought in, and our taste buds were sent into a frenzy of tantalizing tickles as we sipped our soup. I had no idea what soup it was; it had bits of veggies and chicken in and other spices that simply set off a blaze of flavors in our mouths. No one spoke until every drop of the soup was devoured. I wanted to continue my conversation with Kai, but Betty was once again all over him, and when the other ladies noticed they vied for his attention too. I couldn't help but notice some of the men getting very jealous of their ladies perving over Kai.

'Sorry ladies can I just tell Kai something please? You can have him back in a second.'

'The men look like they're getting a bit jealous. I'm so sorry, but you have to treat these lovely elderly people like kiddies sometimes, so can you talk to them a bit.' I whispered in his ear.

Kai glanced at the men and nodded.

'Excuse me, ladies, please,' he said standing up and moving toward the men, and if I am not mistaken, he looked relieved.

The ladies, however, looked very disappointed. We had very little time to talk in between the courses that truly were beyond anything I had ever tasted. After the soup, we had lamb shanks, roasted beef, mutton curry and an array of roasted veggies flavored with different herbs. The dessert was out of this world – tiramisu; need I say more? Chef Billy was terribly wasted in the retirement home kitchen; he should have been cooking meals like this for the whole world to savor.

I did manage to steal a photo of Kai and me on my phone – a very cozy one at that – and I uploaded it to my Facebook page. I couldn't wait for Rylee's reaction. Then I walked Kai to his car, well, the van he used for work, it was just cleaner.

'I am sorry you had such a hard time with all the ladies; I really should have taken you to a restaurant instead.'

He turned to face me before opening the door, 'Oh no! It was a great evening. Thank you again.'

He seemed to hover by the car door.

'Though I might take you up on that restaurant offer sometime.' He had the most adorable smile.

'Thank you. I'd like that.'

I knew I was blushing. He leaned forward and kissed my cheek. His lips were soft and smooth, and the kiss glued itself to my face. I mentally stuck it there forever.

'I'll see you at the house,' I said as he climbed into the van.

I realized as I was walking back indoors and to my room that I had no idea where he lived and that I didn't know anything about him. The retirement home was silent in contrast to the last few hours. Shame, they were all so exhausted from the excitement, and I'm sure the ladies were dreaming of Kai by now. I lay down on my bed after a warm shower and checked my phone. Rylee had seen the photo and 'liked' it on Facebook. I knew she was going to phone me in the morning, but fortunately, I had the day off, and so I switched off my phone.

Chapter Six

I surfaced from the wonderful world of Dreamland at almost ten o'clock. It was not often I had the chance to sleep in and so the days it was on offer I took gladly. Mother and her friends were outside in the garden, and so I snuck out for a run along my favorite route before I was told a thousand times over how much they had enjoyed the previous evening. I made a mental note to buy something special for Chef Billy to say a huge thank you. My taste buds were still relishing the flavors of his dishes. Rylee had phoned, and I quickly called her back when I parked at the beach.

'Good morning,' I greeted her when she answered.

'Hey, finally you're up. So are you and Kai an item?'

I knew it must have bugged her the whole night.

'No, I had a thank you dinner for him at the home last night. He was treated as if he were royalty, it was unbelievable; those ladies are something else.'

'Oh okay. I asked him out for dinner, but he said he had something else on. So I am glad he did, and he wasn't blowing me off.'

That was an angle I had not considered!

'Come and visit this afternoon,' she insisted as we said goodbye.

As I jogged, I couldn't stop thinking about the idea of Rylee and Kai together. I was not at all happy and even knowing I had no claim on Kai it bothered me. I told myself over and over to stop being ridiculous! Rylee was my best friend, and if they should hook up, I had to be happy for them. I stopped at the beach, sat on the little wall and watched the surfers. Not thinking for a while was peaceful.

'Hello,' Kai said sitting down on the wall next to me.

A lady and a little boy were with him.

'Hello,' I replied looking at the woman and her child.

Is he married? Crikey! Why didn't he say anything?

'This is my sister Kaia and her son Selby.'

They both smiled at me and said hello. I stifled a sigh of relief.

'Your names are almost the same!' I had to state the obvious.

'Yes, our parents went for simplicity,' Kaia chuckled.

Selby ran to the sand with his buckets and spade and immediately started digging. We spent a few minutes chatting. Selby was five, and they were from Hawaii and were visiting Kai while on holiday in South Africa. Now, at least, I finally knew where he was from originally. Kaia politely asked how I was coping with my dreadful experience and also offered to help in any way she could. Kai and Kaia were so much alike I guessed they were twins.

'Are you twins?' I had to ask.

They both laughed, and Kai told me that it was a common occurrence to get asked that question, but no they were born fifteen months apart. They might as well have been twins with so little time between them. Kaia went to Selby, and while I had Kai to myself for once, I needed to satisfy my questions with answers.

'The other day, well twice now, I have seen you and your friends kneeling at the edge of the ocean. What is that about?'

'We pray before we surf and when we come back out.'

'Oh,' I said unsure of what to say next.

'You know the night you phoned me, well at the same time as the phone rang I was praying for you.'

'Why?'

'I don't know. I just landed up praying for you – for health, safety, that kind of thing.'

'This might sound weird, but during the struggle, I called out to God to help me. I have no idea why because I have never known God or church things in my life. Seconds afterward a calm came over me. I never understood it, but I was able to react more clearly, and that's when I managed to get free, granted it was with violence, but it definitely would have turned out worse.'

'God works in the most amazing ways. I only found salvation in Him when I moved here and met my friends, the ones you met on the beach the other day.'

I remained silent for a while contemplating what he had just said; this was probably the reason he was such a kind and pleasant person.

'Is your family Christian?'

'No. Kaia has been studying with me and is thinking about committing to God, but I think she is concerned about what her husband's reaction will be when she returns home and that is holding her back. My parents have no issues with my faith, and I am hoping that when I go back at the end of the year, I will be able to teach them the Gospel.'

'You're going back?'

My heart sank into the concrete wall.

'Yes, I must.'

'Oh,' I said, and the sadness spilled over in my voice.

'If I invite you to a study will you consider coming?'

'I don't know; you will have to ask and find out.'

My lips creased into a smile. Kai looked at the ocean, his mouth in a lovely smile, and slowly it faded as he turned to look at me seriously.

'Will you come to a study on Wednesday evening?'

'Yes, it sounds interesting, but I will first have to check my schedule at work, I am not sure what shift I will be on.'

'Good.'

'What made you move here?'

'After I got my degree in structural engineering I took a gap year and came out here. I fell in love with this place and stayed. But now I have to go back to my family for a while; it's been three years since I last saw them and I need to sort out my interests in the family business.'

Our conversation was cut short by the gleeful Selby calling Kai to inspect the mansion he had built in the sand. I said goodbye to them all and proceeded with my run that had taken a very different turn, one that I hadn't anticipated when starting out. As I jogged along, I thought about all we had said to each other. So he was a Christian, I still wasn't entirely sure what that meant, but I was looking forward to finding out more. The fact that he had been praying for me when I had phoned him pricked my conscience. But what had upset a beautiful day was the fact that he was leaving. When he had said that I instantly realized that I could easily have been more to him than his client or friend. There were feelings stirring within me for him that excited my heart.

When I relayed all this news (except the tickles of affection I was harboring for Kai) to Rylee later that afternoon the only fact she was interested in was when Kai was leaving, and she would have to act fast to "nab him." She infuriated me, and I left her house earlier than planned.

***

Work in the pediatric ward had upgraded from the usual busy to the hectically insane. It seemed that every virus was doing its rounds attacking the precious little children. There were days when double shifts were a necessity as there were simply not enough staff members to cope with the onslaught of sick kiddies. It resulted in a no-show at the Bible study. I was disappointed as I was interested in learning more. Also, it had been ages since I had been able to visit the house to view the progress, and if I wasn't mistaken, there was only about a week of work left before completion. Mother dearest was so excited, she had already packed up all her belongings and was practically out of the door of the retirement home and moving into her new cottage. Since I was so busy, she had offered to pack up my things for me, the stuff that was in storage I still had to sort out, though.

Finally, I had a Wednesday evening free, and instead of opting for the much-needed sleep my body desired I went to the Bible study. Rylee had been going (she had invited herself) every week but for reasons other than to study and I wondered if during this time she had, in fact, made an impression on Kai. Neither had ever mentioned anything to me, so I was left guessing. As the crow flies, Kai's apartment was not very far from my house, and it was easy to find. When I knocked on the door, Kai opened it and presented me with a fabulous warm smile. I was introduced again to his friends and to some faces I had not seen before. Rylee greeted me with an affectionate hug as always.

'So happy you made it finally, please take a seat,' Kai said offering me a comfortable armchair and then sitting next to me on the stool he had dragged from the kitchen. Rylee was completely focused on Kai and not impressed that he had selected to sit next to me. He handed me a black book, similar

to the one I had often seen him reading. I looked at the title –
"Bible."

Oh right, now I get it! I finally clicked. I was somewhat lost
during the study but certain things that were said and read
stung me. "He died for your sins," and, "In Him, you can have
eternal life," and, "He will carry all your burdens."

After the study, while I was enjoying a cup of coffee Kai got
out of Rylee's clutches and joined me with his coffee.

'You look like you're in the middle of a storm. What's up?'

There was no way I was going to tell him that Rylee was
irritating me beyond words the way she hung all over him, so I
confessed my confusion rather.

'I got a little confused in the study…'

He nodded. 'I did too. What if Mitch and I came to study with
you? They did this for me too, or would you prefer not to
continue at all?'

'No, I want to, it is very intriguing actually. It will be a bit
difficult at the retirement home, so perhaps we can wait until I
have moved into the house and Mother can perhaps study with
me.'

He nodded again and smiled. 'Okay, let's do that. It will be
amazing; you will see.'

His face fell when Rylee appeared at his side, demanding his
attention. I said goodbye to everyone and left.

Chapter Seven

I was extremely grateful that things at work had slowed down so that I was able to arrange a few days' leave to move finally into an old but new house. Mother dear was beside herself with excitement. The retirement home had a swinging (meant literally – those old people loved to dance) party for us on our last evening as residents there.

Kai had arranged to bring the furniture from the storage unit to the house with Mitch. On one of the wettest days of the year, with rain pouring down amid threatening hail I signed the final piece of paper. I was now the proud owner of a freshly renovated house. When the rain had subsided Kai, Mitch and I took a slow walk from the house to the cars, discussing when the Bible study was to start at my house.

'I have an idea,' I said excitedly, 'how about we start this Tuesday, and at the same time, we have a barbeque as a housewarming? We can invite the whole group if you like.'

They seemed to like the idea, and so we all had a date for Tuesday. Mitch left, and it was only Kai standing hesitantly by the door to his van.

'So besides the barbeque, we still have the matter of dinner at a restaurant remember?'

'Oh, I wasn't sure if you still interested, so I kept quiet.'

'You don't want to go?'

'No…Yes…I mean yes, I do still want to go.'

He looked away. It was one of those days when the sound of the ocean was excessively loud, and it looked like he was listening intently.

'Okay, I will speak to you soon. Congratulations on your house again and remember to phone me if anything is wrong or for anything…'

He did not finish and instead climbed into his van, waved at me and left. Dinner, alone with Kai, I liked the idea a lot.

When Rylee showed up after work, we shared a pizza, and she and Mother helped me unpack a few rather soggy boxes. Not much longer mother was exhausted, excused herself and eagerly went to sleep in her new home. Rylee and I gave up with the boxes and instead sat in the comfort of the living room each with a glass of red wine. I felt it was the right time to speak to her about Kai before I went to dinner with him.

'So what is happening between you and Kai?'

'Oh, he is the hunkiest man on earth.'

'That isn't what I asked. Are you guys going out, had a date? What?'

'Yep, we see a lot of each other; it's only a matter of time before we make it public.'

I felt my heart sink. Could this be true? Was Kai the smooth operating kind? I had a hard time believing it, but I also had no reason to doubt Rylee.

'Oh okay, wow I never knew.'

'Well you have been so busy lately I have hardly seen you to catch up on any news.'

That was also true. I invited her to the Tuesday evening barbeque and study and with a heavy heart decided to abandon the idea of Kai and me. I would never stand in the way of my best friend. But a niggle refused to budge, nagging at me that it was not true. My brain had an ongoing fight with itself over the pros and cons of Rylee's revelation. Even my daily jogs along the beach were preoccupied with it, so much so that I never even looked to see if Kai was on the beach or surfing.

Tuesday evening arrived, and while the fire was going, we all sat to begin the study in the living room (Mother was treated like a queen by the young men). I tried to keep my distance from Kai as much as possible, and Rylee made it easy by forever attaching herself to his hip. It fuelled my ideas that she was, in fact, telling the truth, but then he was at my side every chance he got which made me think otherwise. I did not know what to think, and it was beginning to infuriate me.

Mitch opened with a prayer and blessed our house. We started the study by examining who Jesus was, his birth, background, and childhood. These things I remembered from school but it was still good to have my memory refreshed. We ended the study when Jesus was teaching in the temples and had gathered his disciples. It was all relatively simple, and yet I still did not find the reason for the commitment these Christian people had. I was eager for the next study to seek this understanding.

As the men stood by the fire, and Rylee stood glued to Kai, Mother and I made salads in the kitchen.

'I thought you had a thing for Kai?' she asked softly so if anyone were entering the kitchen they would not hear her.

'Yeah well, apparently Rylee and Kai are something of an item.' My reply was so half-hearted it was barely audible.

'Well, I don't see it at all. Yes, she is all over him, but he is not interested in her in the least.'

'And you can tell that how?'

'Call it old age, intuition, experience or maybe it's just obvious.' I sighed not wanting to discuss this any further as I was already exhausted from over-thinking it.

'Well Rylee says it is so, so I have to respect her as my friend.' Mother shook her head. 'You are wrong.'

Then she left the subject there taking the salad bowls to the dinner table. I followed her with my hands full, and while we set them on the table, Kai walked into the house with Rylee right on his heels. I gave Mother a knowing look, confirming my side of the story.

She shook her head and very quickly muttered, 'We will continue the conversation later.'

By then we were no longer alone as Kai was asking for oven gloves and an oven tray for Mitch. Rylee just hung on him like a flea.

***

It was such a pleasure to be in my home with my things and to be able to do as I pleased and Mother felt the same. A few of her friends had come to visit her and had already planned a tea party every Thursday morning in her cottage, and after a week, she was so happy there was a pink glow to her complexion.

I had to skip the study for the next week due to the schedule of my shifts at work, and when the following Tuesday evening came along, I was ready and waiting to fill my mind with the fellow named Jesus. Other than the Rylee/Kai affair all I was able to concentrate on was this man they called Jesus. What did

He do that calls everyone to His name? I had to find out. Mitch arrived excusing Kai as he had to take his sister to the airport; she was on her way back to Hawaii. Rylee also did not pitch up for the study and automatically I presumed she was with Kai. Another notch for my argument with Mother.

As Mitch continued from where we had left off the last time, I was fascinated by what I was learning. It had to be so because the Bible was written by those that had walked and lived with Jesus. Even Mother was intrigued, and she delved into the facts and asked a lot of questions. Mitch went to the Bible and the scriptures for all his answers satisfying us both every time. Mitch ended the study when Jesus was arrested. I was sickened. Another week before I found out what the deal was. We had homework to do, and I already had a mountain of studying to do but this was too important, and I was too curious not to make time for it.

I phoned Rylee the next morning.

'Hi. You weren't at study last night. Everything okay?'

I had no intention of letting on that all I wanted to know was if she had been with Kai.

'Yeah, one of the kittens was vomiting so much, so I took her to the vet, shame poor little thing was so sick.'

'You have kittens now? When did you get kittens? How many do you have?'

'Only two. I could not resist their little faces in the window of the pet shop.'

She giggled and swooned. It was obvious that she was holding them in her arms as we spoke.

'Rylee, how many do you have now?'

She hesitated, perhaps quickly doing a head count.

'Nine,' she said.

'Nine cats in that tiny house?'

'So?' she replied indignantly.

Chapter Eight

Over a week had gone by without a word from Kai, and I slowly became convinced that Rylee was perhaps not spinning a yarn. During a slow day at work, while I was taking my time taking temperatures and other vitals, the phone at the nurses' station rang. Annette called me indicating the call was for me and upon answering a deep voice greeted me.

'Ms. Conley, this is Mr. DuPont. I want to inform you the court hearing for the case against the man that assaulted you is on the twentieth of November. You are required to attend. I will make sure you get the notification to appear in the next few days.'

I thanked him and put the phone down trembling.

'What is wrong?' Annette asked as she observed the grey pallor of my face.

'I have to appear in court in November. I don't know if I will be able to face that man...'

Without realizing it, my face was stained with tears within seconds.

'Someone must go with you dear and take lots of calming meds. Your lawyer will protect you, and he will guide you every step of the way, I'm sure of it.'

I turned and went to our private bathroom, took a few deep breaths, drank a lot of water and washed my face. I still had work to do which had to get done on schedule. However, I knew this news would limit my ability to function as I should.

When I arrived home, Mother calmly listened as she made me a hot cup of chamomile tea.

'I will go with you,' she said determined to support me.

'No, you won't. I am adamant about that; you will not enter that courtroom.'

'Why not?'

'Please Mother, it will be bad enough for me to muster up the courage and face that man without having to worry about you losing your temper and trying to attack him.'

'Oh, I won't do that! Don't be silly.'

'You won't? Can you promise me you won't?'

Mother didn't reply, and I knew that she knew I was right. I knew I had won this debate.

'Will you ask Rylee to go with you?'

My phone rang, and I answered without looking at the caller ID.

'Hello.'

'Hello, Darla.'

'Kai. Hi.'

After some brief small talk, he asked, 'Have you heard from your lawyer?'

'Yes, Mother and I were just discussing it.'

'I also have to appear in court?'

'You do? Why?'

'Well, they want as many witnesses as possible apparently.'

'Oh. I'm sorry to have you involved in all this.'

'Don't apologize; I've told you that.'

We both had hesitated before he continued, 'So how about we have that dinner at a restaurant, and we can talk about it some more?'

'Okay, yes that'll be nice.'

***

Kai insisted on fetching me on Saturday for our dinner date. I was to find out where we were going once I was in the car. Whether it was to be a date or not my heart fluttered about so much simply at the thought of being alone with him. Saturday was in three days, and my nerves would be fried by then with anticipation.

Rylee popped in at work the following day, and without realizing it, I told her about dinner with Kai. She was surprised, and I quickly recovered stating that it was to discuss the court case. Rylee, nonetheless, was not impressed, and as soon as she left I phoned Kai, hoping that I would catch him before she did. I reached him first.

'I told Rylee about our dinner date.'

There was no reaction from Kai for a few seconds then slowly he asked, 'And I should care why?'

I was baffled.

'Are you and Rylee not dating?'

'Why on earth would you think that?'

Now I was perplexed and rather than try to tell him all that Rylee had told me on the phone we agreed to discuss it at dinner. I was grateful dinner with Kai would happen before the next Bible study as things might be a little uncomfortable or strained until I found out what was or was not going on between Kai and Rylee.

Saturday morning I woke up, and the first thing that entered my thoughts was what I was going to wear for our dinner date. After much debating I was ready, and I double-checked myself in the mirror. I had decided on a black lace mid-length dress, suitable for formal or casual, with deep purple high heeled shoes. Kai was tall, so my usual problem of being taller than my date was for once irrelevant. My hair I left loose, and it curled around my face, and grey eyeliner enhanced my hazel eyes.

Kai arrived on time and was as dashing as I'd imagined he would be. He complimented me, and I was completely dazzled by his charm. He had made reservations at a cozy restaurant in the next suburb; it had been ages since I'd been in that area. Once our drinks were served and we had placed our meal order, I needed to get the Rylee/Kai issue out of my head once and for all.

'Okay so I have to get this off my chest, I hope it won't ruin our evening.'

'Rylee?' he replied nodding.

'Are you two dating or going to date or something?'

'Where did you get this idea from?'

Kai mumbled something and bent his head.

I was about to reply when from behind me I heard a cheerful, 'Hi guys!'

Rylee! She did not just gate-crash our dinner date, had she?

'Rylee! What on earth are you doing here?' I asked considerably exasperated.

'I was at the club across the road and remembered you said you were having dinner with Kai, and then I saw his car parked on the road, and so I thought I would pop in and convince you guys to join us,' she blurted out in one breath.

Before either Kai or I had a chance to answer, she sat herself down at our table, called the waitress and ordered a glass of wine and a salad.

'What are you doing?' Kai asked Rylee.

She was unfazed by his question.

'Well, I haven't eaten so while I'm here I might as well eat.'

'What about your friends at the club?' I stated.

'Oh you know those friends and me, we come and go as we please.'

I was not at all sure how to handle this situation, and I looked pleadingly at Kai to sort it out. However, he was too much of a gentleman to make a scene. Rylee, I was sure was aware of that as well. She turned all her attention to Kai, rambling on about her day at work and the vibe at the club, and constantly moaning about how long her food was taking as she wanted us to eat and then go party. Oh, how I wished I had come in my car! The food arrived, and Kai and I ate in silence. Rylee spoke nonstop; even when she had food in her mouth, she continued speaking. I am sure the meal on any other occasion would have been delicious but not on this night. It tasted as bitter as I felt about Rylee's constant jabbering.

Kai paid for the meals, and we left, Rylee shoving her arm through his as soon as he stood up. If ever I felt like a third wheel it was now. We walked into the club, blasted by the loud music until our ears adjusted to the sound. Since Kai and Rylee walked arm in arm, it looked like I was without a partner as I followed them through the crowds of people. As I walked, I was whistled at, smiled at, winked at, "skissed at," requested to dance and even asked to go home with a total stranger. By the time I reached a chair to sit on I was livid. No, this was the end of the evening for me. I got off the chair and made for the entrance door once more, this time exiting it. I walked back across the road to the restaurant, sat down in the waiting area and phoned a taxi. I could see the club from where I was sitting and noticed Kai hurriedly coming out of the door and looking up and down the street. He stood there for a while looking up at the sky with his hands on his hips, and then he looked down and stared at his feet. After a moment or two, he turned and went back inside, dragging my angry heart along with him.

The taxi pulled up to the curb, and I thanked the manager and left. I wanted to cry all the way home, but instead, I fumed over Rylee and her behavior. Now I had even fewer answers to my Rylee/Kai affair and, this time, I was going to forget the whole thing. Forget Kai, forget Rylee, and forget any feelings ever existed. My shift began at four in the afternoon the next day, so I went straight to bed and switched off my phone.

After a restless night's sleep I finally surfaced at eleven in the morning, and when I waddled to the kitchen for a good dose of coffee, Mother warming herself outside in the sun caught my eye. My coffee and I joined her.

'So what happened last night?'

'Good morning to you too and nothing happened.'

'Well Kai was here very early this morning, and let me tell you he looked frazzled. He said you disappeared last night, and he has been trying to phone you ever since. So what happened last night?'

'Can I please enjoy my coffee first?'

I sat back in the chair and allowed the sun to kiss my skin. It felt invigorating as the rays poured life into my pores. I knew that Mother was silently stewing as I took my time drinking my coffee. Eventually, I drank the last sip and rested my cup on the grass and sighed.

'So what happened last night?'

'Jeepers, give me a break. I will tell you.'

Mother sighed tapping her foot with impatience. I contemplated having a shower first before telling her, but that would simply be cruel, and so I let out another heavy sigh and replayed the whole previous night's episode for her. Her foot was now drumming.

'That little devil! Imagine throwing yourself at a man like that. It is disgraceful.'

'Well, she wants him so she can have him. I am finished with it all.'

'Phone Kai.'

'Mother, please just leave it now. I'm going to shower.'

When I reached my room, I switched on my phone. It beeped like crazy with notifications of text messages, WhatsApp messages, and voicemails. All from Kai. I read a few, and yes he was rather frantic, apologetic and pleading for me to contact him urgently. There were no messages from Rylee.

I dialed his number, and before the first ring finished he answered, 'Darla!'

'Hi. I got all your messages...'

He rattled off a million questions – Where had I gone? How had I gotten home? Why had I switched off my phone? I listened without interruption.

He finally finished, and I asked, 'Which question am I supposed to answer first?'

At first, he did not react then he gathered his composure and replied, 'Can I come over? I need to set the record straight here. Please.'

As much as I wanted to ignore this whole affair I had no hope of ignoring the plea in his voice.

'Okay, but only you, by yourself. I will speak to Rylee another time, if ever.'

I added the "if ever" and immediately regretted it.

'I need to shower and do a few things so you can be here in an hour.'

He thanked me, and we hung up. Now the anxious beating of my heart thumped awkwardly in expectation of what he was going to say.

Chapter Nine

I opened the door, and Kai's face was so distorted I wanted to hold him and assure him everything was going to be all right. But that depended on him.

'Let's go for a walk,' he suggested when I indicated he could come in.

I closed the door behind me shoving the key into my pocket. As we walked, I kept looking out for Rylee expecting her to show up at any minute. We walked together in time, at a slow, casual pace, the spring air and sounds of the birds in the tall trees along the sidewalk were relaxing. I sighed, releasing a lot of tension in my neck and shoulders.

'Darla,' he hesitated a little, 'I am so sorry about last night. I was worried sick when you left, and I couldn't find you.'

'I saw you come out of the restaurant, but you went back in again. I was waiting in the restaurant for a taxi.'

'You took a taxi home?' He looked mortified.

'I had nothing but indecent suggestions from almost every male skulking about from the time we walked into that club that when we reached the chairs to sit, I'd had enough. I don't enjoy clubs to start off with, and you obviously were attached to Rylee, and I was not going to spend the evening being the third wheel and being hit on by every drunken idiot and their mate.'

The anger in my voice surfaced making it very clear to Kai how I felt about the turn of events. We had reached the beach and sat on the little wall dipping our feet into the sand once our shoes were off.

'You have it all wrong. So very wrong.'

'Well correct me then.'

We both stared at the ocean for a few seconds; the sun was gleaming off the water as the waves (or lack thereof) trickled onto the shore.

'At first, I thought you had invited Rylee when I saw her walking into the restaurant. I was so disappointed, and then when she opened her mouth, I realized it was all her and her foolish notion that I am remotely interested in her. I noticed then too that you were very annoyed, and when we left I was hoping you would not go to the club, and I was not sure if you did not want to go. I also did not want to get between you two as friends.'

He took a gulp of air and continued, 'Of course thinking about it I realized how last night must have looked to you when she put her arm around me, and we walked into the club. But when we got to the chairs, I got hold of one to offer you and you were gone. I thought that maybe you had gone to the bathroom, so I waited for a while.'

He got off the wall and started walking on the sand toward the ocean. I presumed I had to follow, so I did.

'When you didn't return I started asking Rylee and her friends if they had seen you. One of them said they'd seen you leave, and that's when I went outside hoping to catch you. Well, I didn't so I went back inside and looked around again. When I still couldn't find you, I left and drove around the streets for some time before going home. And of course, leaving a thousand messages on your phone.'

He stopped walking when he finished speaking, and we sat down on the sand. Well, I was feeling very foolish right about now. I cleared my throat trying to formulate my reply.

'I had it completely wrong. I am very sorry Kai.'

'No need for you to apologize – well yes you do for not answering your phone,' he grinned, 'but for the rest of what happened, I am to blame. I should not have allowed Rylee to manipulate the evening. So I am very sorry. If anything had happened to you, I would never have forgiven myself.'

He looked at the sand with that same distraught expression on his face.

'Okay, so how about we were both wrong, and we forgive each other and move on past all of this? But first I need you to tell me why Rylee insists that you are dating.'

'I honestly have no idea. I have never asked her out, never even mentioned her in conversation to anyone. At first, when she was always talking to me and phoning me, I thought she was just forward, as I told you and I accepted that, but after a while, it became annoying. So I tried to ignore her as much as possible.'

'I just cannot understand her sometimes. I'm sorry if she made everything all messy like this…'

I too looked down at the sand and drew little circles with my fingers.

'Don't apologize for her. Come,' he said standing up and offering his hand to help me up.

He did not let go of my hand, and I was going to make sure I held his just tightly enough so he couldn't let go. His hand felt perfectly fine in mine. I noticed the sun had moved along the horizon indicating the approaching evening, and I checked my watch.

'I will have to start getting back home, I have to be at work by four,' I said reluctantly, wanting to remain in his company so much longer.

Strolling back home we were forced to let go of each other's hands to avoid a signpost, but as soon as we were alongside each other again, he put his arm around my shoulders and pulled me toward him in a half-hug.

'We all good then? Back to normal?' he asked.

I smiled and nodded swinging my arm around his waist and half hugging him too. We left our arms around each other all the way home. When we reached his van parked along the sidewalk in front of my house, he turned to face me, wrapping both arms around me in a delectable hug. I was so wrapped up in his arms, soaking up the awesome feeling of being wanted. I easily could've forgotten myself in them. Before completely relinquishing his hold of me, he kissed me ever so softly.

'No more Rylee nonsense. See you Tuesday night for study.'

He climbed into his van while I almost fainted from sheer delight. My delight turned into frustration when five minutes after Kai had left Rylee was on my doorstep.

'I have to be at work in an hour,' I curtly said as I let her into the house.

'I just have to tell you the news,' she exclaimed full of excitement, 'last night Kai and I…'

Before she could continue to embarrass herself with another lie, I cut her off.

'Stop it, Rylee.'

She stopped speaking although her mouth stayed wide open.

'Kai has been here the whole afternoon, and frankly, I believe his version of last night before I even begin to hear yours.'

Her eyes went as wide as saucers.

'I don't know what your issue is and why you have this need to lie about a relationship that does not exist. What is wrong with you?'

The irritation in my voice was audible, and my aggressive stance was intimidating. She stuttered something and then made a feeble attempt at recovering her composure after the embarrassment.

'Well, I was going to tell you that we agreed to be friends and that I met the most amazing man instead…'

'Yes Rylee, whatever. I have to go to work now,' I replied and walked away.

She quietly let herself out.

Chapter Ten

At work, I wondered if our friendship was ever going to recover from this episode. However, it was impossible to dwell on for long as the sweet kiss from Kai overruled any activity in my mind and body. Tuesday night arrived more slowly than I begged it would. Kai arrived, albeit a little late, settling my nerves and my thoughts that he wasn't going to pitch. A quick hug assured me everything was fine between us.

Mitch proceeded with this intriguing news about Jesus. We started at the part where Jesus was captured; an arrest made up with blatantly false accusations and how He took it all in as the scriptures declared he would. I learned how they barbarically beat Him and humiliated Him and made Him carry that heavy cross all that way until the other man helped Him. And when they nailed Him to the cross, I was utterly gutted. How could they do this? I had no control over the tears that escaped me when we read how He hung on that cross slowly suffocating, enduring such immense and excruciating pain without complaining. It was too much to bear, and I cried. What savages were these people that ordered this? But even more so I was in complete awe of His suffering. When Jesus died, I struggled to understand what the point of it all was. But Mitch went on explaining that He arose again after three days and defeated death. That because Jesus lives forever and if we obey Him we too can live forever. I desperately desired to know how I could live forever. Kai sat next to me smiling like a Cheshire cat.

'Through baptism,' said Mitch.

He showed Mother and me how when we are baptized when we get completely immersed in water, and we are then buried in Christ and are cleansed from all our sins. Everything wrong that we have ever said or done shall be forgiven, and when we come up out of the water, we are a new person living with the Holy Spirit of Jesus within us. And it is only by this grace given by God through baptism that we can have eternal life. It was a remarkable revelation when it all made sense. There were no questions as to why, if or how, it all made sense, and it was so simple it was ridiculous. I had one question left to ask.

'So when can I get baptized?'

Kai clapped his hands full of elation.

Mitch simply said, 'Praise the Lord.'

Everyone in the study group except Rylee – who had decided to visit her new boyfriend instead – gathered at the edge of the ocean early the following evening. We stood in a circle holding hands as Mitch prayed for mother and me, praising God in our acceptance of His salvation. Mother and I held hands as we entered the cold waters of the ocean. Mitch and Kai followed closely, and when we were knee-deep, we stopped. Mitch held Mother, and Kai held me.

They ask us simultaneously if we understood what we were about to undertake, and we both answered with "yes." They asked if we believed Jesus was the Son of our Creator and the living God, and we answered with another "yes." Then they asked if we believed Jesus had died for our sins, that we would get cleansed of all sins through baptism, and then finally if we accepted Jesus Christ as our savior.

I held Mother's hand as we replied together, 'Yes.'

And with that, we were both immersed into the water holding hands and came up new people – born again – in Jesus Christ.

'Amen!' everyone exclaimed and clapped hands before hugging us with congratulations. While Mother and I shivered wrapped in towels, Mitch prayed once more asking God to guide our lives in Him forever. As we walked back to the cars, Kai wrapped his arms around Mother.

'So Griselda, it took you a while to become a real person!'

The humor washed off Kai's tongue.

'Watch it, fella, be careful how old you make me out to be. But yes, it has taken me a little longer than usual I guess.'

'Better late than never,' he replied remaining at her side until she was in the car.

We all went back to my house and celebrated with tea and biscuits. Much to my delight, Kai was the last to leave. I said goodbye to him at the door with an affectionate hug that he return willingly.

'So happy you committed your life. It is so amazing you will see.'

'I tend to remember you saying that to me once before,' I laughed at the memory.

'See you soon.'

He gave me another longer lingering hug, kissed me tenderly and left. Every sensory organ in my body was reeling with delight over this momentous occasion and of course the kiss.

I floated on a cloud for the next few weeks flying the flag of the Gospel. Rylee was truly sorry for missing study and my baptism. After a long heart-to-heart, we healed our friendship; her attendance at study became regular as did her interest in God's Word. She was baptized at church one Sunday after service.

Kai visited me regularly, and we finally went on a proper dinner date that turned out to be a most splendid evening. As much as I wanted to, Kai was hesitant to commit to any form of a relationship since he was leaving in December. He said as much at dinner when he admitted to having more feelings for me that he knew were fair toward me.

I had to respect his decision even if my heart was screaming out, 'Who cares if you're leaving and we're together now?'

Chapter Eleven

My life was peaceful until a few days before the court case. Mother kept dosing me with calming medication at any chance she had. I had seen my lawyer a few days before, and he assured me that I had nothing to worry about, they had enough concrete evidence to convict the accused. I did not doubt his ability or the evidence; it was the fact that I had to be in the same room as that man once more that concerned me.

The morning I had to appear in court there was a tap on the front door and both Mother, and I startled – we were both on edge. Kai walked into the living room wearing a navy suit; he was so elegant and dashing and way too handsome for his own good. I forgot all about the case, even if it was only for an instant. At least, if I only gazed at him, it would be a good distraction in the courtroom.

'Hello Griselda, how you doing?'

He waited while Mother assured him she was fine, and her friends were coming over to keep her company.

'How are you holding up? Okay?'

He took my hands in his with care and compassion.

I nodded. 'Not too sure yet. I keep hoping they will phone and say it's all canceled.'

'It's going to be fine. I spoke to the lawyer again yesterday, and he is very confident.'

'Okay,' I uttered the word but had no conviction in its meaning.

Kai had prayed with Mother and me before he and I left in my car.

We walked down the aisle of the courtroom; people filled the rows on either side. No one looked at us but rather looked forlornly toward the front. We met our lawyer and found a seat behind what would be his desk once the case was called up. My hands were sweating and cold, and I felt my heart rate increase its pace by a few beats every time a door opened behind the judge's podium. Eventually, a tall man opened the door and stood to the side bellowing for everyone to rise until Judge – I cannot remember his name – was seated. Then we were told to sit. My heart was racing, and I was hoping that we were the first case on the roster so I could get this over with and get out of the suffocating room. It was not to be, we were the third on the list, and so we sat and watched the people and the proceedings. Kai had his arm around me, and his hand gently stroked my arm where it rested, it was very soothing.

Then the judge called the next case that was ours. I took a deep breath and tried to stifle the panic rising within me. Kai took both my hands with his free hand and kissed them tenderly.

'It is going to be fine. Trust God.'

I sat in the seat next to the lawyer trembling, and when the door opened to allow the accused entry, I gasped. My knees were rattling. He entered and looked directly at me through his one eye. The other eye had a black eye-patch over it.

'Did he lose his eye?' I whispered to my lawyer.

'Apparently yes.'

What have I done? I berated myself over the physical damage I had caused this man.

The judge cleared his throat, and I tried to concentrate amid the chaos in my head. He read out the case number and its matter.

'How do you plead?' he asked the accused.

The accused man was already standing, and his lawyer replied on his behalf.

'He pleads guilty, your Honour.'

Guilty! I sat up straight. Was that it? There would be no need to stand witness or argue any cause? Was it possible that it was all over so quickly? Oh, how I silently pleaded that it was.

'Well if he is pleading guilty then it is just a matter of sentencing. We will adjourn for lunch, and I will pass down sentencing at three o'clock.'

He banged his gavel hard on his desk that sent a vibration ricocheting through my bones, and I jumped from fright.

'That's it?' I exploded with relief.

'That's it,' replied my lawyer perhaps a little disappointed that he would not have the opportunity to strut his stuff.

I stood and hurried to Kai crashing into his chest wrapping my arms around him. He reciprocated and held me so tightly, reassuring me that it was all over. Everyone had exited the courtroom except for two women sitting on the opposite side of

118

the room to us. As we walked down the aisle, the one woman charged towards me, screaming and waving her finger at me as if it was guiding her to me. I back-pedaled into Kai, but she kept coming, screaming that it was my fault that her husband had lost his eye and that he had not done anything. I cowered into Kai's chest while our lawyer got himself between the enraged woman and me. The security guards, upon hearing the commotion charged in taking hold of the hysterical woman and removed her from the courtroom. I found a seat and sat down inhaling and exhaling deeply and trying very hard to steady the pounding of my heart. Kai sat next to me and engulfed me in his arms, and when I had my breathing more or less under control, he helped me to my feet, walking me out of the courtroom.

We found a little coffee shop a block away from the court building, ordered coffee and quietly breathed in and out until our heart rates were beating normally again.

Kai spoke first. 'You don't have to go to the sentencing, and with that woman there it probably is best that you don't go.'

I shook my head, nodded my head and then shook my head again and finally shrugged my shoulders. I was exhausted, and all I wanted or needed was a good uninterrupted night's sleep. Kai pulled his phone from his jacket pocket and dialed a number; I sipped at my hot beverage in a daze. He phoned the lawyer and told him that we would not be at the sentencing to which the lawyer amiably agreed.

Mother fretted over me like a true mother hen from the second I walked in the door. I was ordered to my bed, given some more of those calming meds and cuddled lovingly by a mother who utterly adored her daughter. It was not long before I was asleep and then Mother got the low down on what had happened from Kai in the living room.

Chapter Twelve

I woke up in the wee hours of the next morning, sat up in my bed and put on the bedside lamp. On the dresser was a massive colorful arrangement of flowers. Their fragrance kissed my senses pleasingly. Removing the bed covers, I went to inspect the flowers, looking for a card that I found stuck between two red roses.

It read: *'Darla, it's all over – 3 yrs without parole. You are an incredible woman and very special to me. Let us allow God to guide our lives in His direction. With lots of love always, Kai xxx.'*

I read it over, over and over again, held it against my heart and even kissed it as if I was a young teenager getting her first love letter. I sent him a message, presuming he would be asleep at this early hour, to thank him, but got, *'It's a pleasure'* seconds later. He was awake! I phoned him.

'Why you not sleeping?'

'I have no calming meds. You took them all,' he laughed.

'Thank you so, so much for the flowers! They are beautiful. When did you sneak them into the room?'

'No need to sneak you were snoring so loudly a gorilla could have delivered them and you would not have heard it.'

I laughed out loud. He did have a wonderful sense of humor.

After a few days of working through and dealing with the episode and outcome of the day in court, I was finally at peace again with the world and myself. I still had to teach myself to let God be in control, but I was working very hard at it. Even Rylee had quit her wild days and was in a very serious relationship with Nolan, one of the friends from the study. But with the sweet there is always sour; the day was drawing nearer to when Kai had to fly back to Hawaii, still uncertain as to his future.

The sauce I was stirring pulled my thoughts into its swirling motions; there was one thing I irrevocably knew – I was in love with Kai. Just my luck to fall in love with a man who had to leave the country! I was so deep in thought I did not hear the tap on the front door or that it had opened, neither did I hear Kai call out my name and walk along the wooden floors in his flip-flops until he was standing behind me.

'Hello,' he whispered in my ear.

A shrill cry left my lips and resounded against the walls. My hands flew up into the air taking the spoon with them which elevated the pot that simultaneously fell over spewing the sauce all over the kitchen floor. What a mess! Kai did not escape either; his shirt got speckled with red sauce that undoubtedly was going to stain.

'Kai, are you crazy? Sneaking up on me like that!' I scolded him above the rapid beating of my heart.

Immediately I grabbed a floor cloth and started mopping up the sauce. An apology came amid bouts of hysterical laughter.

'I thought you heard me come in. I did knock and call you.'

'Did I answer you? If I'd had a knife in my hand, I would not have been held responsible for my actions.'

I was still shaking; Kai was still laughing.

'I'm sorry I've ruined your shirt.'

'Let that be my punishment,' he grinned still highly amused.

'Well since we're not going to be eating this, let's say we order pizza.'

We snuggled on the couch like a romantic couple – only we weren't – our tummies full of delicious pizza, and became engrossed in a very funny movie that was on TV. The movie finished and I channel-hopped for a while but finding nothing further of interest to either of us, I left it on the channel I had started with and muted the sound. I reached forward, rested the remote on the table and leaned back into the couch and nestled in Kai's arms.

'So you're all packed and ready to go?'

I looked at him – he was staring at me intensely, looking into my soul with his eyes. He shook his head slowly, leaned forward and kissed me ever so softly. He paused, not moving his mouth more than a few millimeters away from mine, his free hand caressing my cheek, his eyes never leaving mine. There was no point resisting any further, we both knew we wanted each other; the chemistry that was passing between us was far too electrifying to stop. His lips touched mine again, sending excitable signals of delight down my spine. My arms reached around him, folding him closer into my embrace; he held me tighter, and our kissing increased in pleasure as did our urgency for each other. Somehow sanity prevailed, and we eased apart gasping for air. Kai placed tiny kisses on my forehead, my nose, and my cheeks which did not exactly help the cause instead only increased my desire never to release him from my embrace again.

'I'm sorry, I should not have done that,' Kai said leaning his head back into the couch.

'What? Why?' I asked still trying to get my breath back.

It was so unfair; it was like taking a child to a store full of candy and then telling the child it was not allowed to have any candy.

'It's not fair to either of us if I'm leaving and might not be able to come back.'

He lifted his head, and I saw the pain written all over his face, this was hurting him as much as it was hurting me. It was killing me. I nodded and rested back into the couch, and his arms, the unbelievable feeling of fitting perfectly together consumed me with sorrow, and as I sighed sadly, the tears rolled down my cheeks. Kai put both his arms around me, and while he held me close, I was sure I heard a sob escape from him too. We remained there on the couch in each other's arms, mostly silent, for the rest of the evening.

Chapter Thirteen

All day my heart thudded in my chest, even the cutest little kiddies could not crack a smile on my face. I felt so heart sore at the possibility that I might never see Kai again. Worst of all I tried hard to understand the purpose of falling in love with someone I was never going to be able to be with and who loved me back. Even if the actual words had not been uttered, it was clearly understood by both of us. The memory of his final goodbye last night and the sadness in his eyes left my heart in shreds.

At home, Mother left me alone to wallow in my self-pity, but she said firmly, 'Only for today.'

I watched the clock on the wall like a hawk, waiting for four fifteen to strike for then my heart would be taking off to the skies on its long journey across the seas. I sighed again and flopped onto my bed. Perhaps sleep would take away the despair that was overwhelming me. The air conditioner quietly whirred cooling the room to a bearable temperature as I lay on my bed repeatedly paging through the photos of Kai I had on my phone. I heard a disturbance in the living room and presuming it was Mother I ignored it and pulled the light throw over my head trying to forget my sorrows.

'Darla!'

I threw off the cover, sat straight up, and in one movement flew off the bed and bolted straight into Kai's arms. He crossed his arms over my back pressing me into his chest so hard we melted into each other. I drew back, put my hands on his face assuring myself this was true, and I was not dreaming.

'What happened?'

'I couldn't go,' he said as he put his head against mine for a few seconds, 'I love you. I couldn't leave without you.'

Before I replied, I hugged him and thanked God for answering my prayers.

'I love you too, so much.'

I kissed him, and he kissed me back with the same fervor as the previous evening. Eventually, we calmed our hormones down enough to talk.

'I got as far as the boarding gates but I...I...Couldn't go through them, not without you.'

He grabbed me and held onto me as if I were about to disappear into thin air.

'What are you going to do now? Your parents, aren't they mad at you?'

'No, they understand. So when does your internship finish at the hospital?'

'In a week, why?'

'Well this is what I am hoping for,' he smiled his perfectly handsome smile, kissed me and continued, 'when you're finished at the hospital, you get your visa, and you come with me to Hawaii while I sort out the family business issues there.'

He was well impressed with himself for working this out.

'Really, you want to take me with you to your country? Won't your parents mind?'

Kai held my hands up to his lips and kissed them; he was still smiling, and the glint in his eyes sparkled.

'When I told them my sad love story,' he pulled his face all sad, 'and told them I wanted to stay with you, they suggested if it were possible I remain here until you can come over with me to meet them. They do in any case want to meet their future daughter-in-law!'

Did I hear correctly?

'Kai, their what? What did you say?'

He threw his head back and laughed, 'Darla, my love. I love you; I want to marry you. My parents want to meet you, after all, you are all they have heard about from me since the day I started working here on this house. When you opened the door on that first day, I almost ran away because I knew I was in love with you from that very second.'

I burst into tears. I was so happy that this man, this beautiful man of God, loved me.

In God's infinite wisdom we are led by Him. If we take His hand and allow Him to lead us, a life of fulfillment and joyous understanding will be ours forever.

REUNION

Reunion

Chapter One

My hometown was noticeably unchanged since the last time I had been there ten years ago. Even the hotel I was staying in was the same – the decor and paint never altered only the staff was new and thank goodness for that. As I unpacked my toiletries, I still wondered whether coming back for the class reunion had been a good idea. It unnerved me to think about the questions I was going to have to answer, that is, of course, should anyone recognize me. Above all, I hoped that Dario, Tate, and Edie (oh sweet little Edie – not!) would not attend. Three people that had had such a huge effect on me, three people I had hoped never to see again in my life. Again I considered packing up and returning to my home and the safety of the miles between me and this place of painful memories. I hovered between the bathroom and my suitcase on the bed – do I pack or unpack? What did I have to fear? Nothing! I was single, and a successful businesswoman and I owned my car and house. The woman they had all known at school no longer existed and in fact, I should be proud to show them all the new and improved me. I knew and believed this; only I feared my reaction when or if I came face to face with the three people I less than desired (hated at times) the most in this world.

From the balcony, where I reclined with a bottle of water, I watched the sunset and calmed my overactive mind and its fears. It was still two days till the reunion, and the event would probably take care of itself without any help from me. I had a lot of reminiscing to do the following day when I planned to take a drive down memory lane to the places where I used to live and the spots I used to frequent.

After a satisfying meal in the hotel restaurant and a relaxing hour or two on the balcony, I went to bed and settled for a restless night's sleep. Events of years gone by plagued me, washing up old history and familiar faces that revisited me, unraveling along with them the torments and frustrations that had led me onto the path of destruction that had nearly destroyed me.

The weather was cool for May in Worcester. I recalled the stifling dry heat that used to irritate most of us as we sat in our classrooms sweltering away while trying to concentrate at the same time. I dressed casually and had a cup of coffee on the balcony. The view was magnificent; the mountains were so close I was able to distinguish between shrubbery and trees and was even able to see water flowing from the mountain streams. During the "eat as much as you can" buffet breakfast I ate as much as I could from the usual hotel breakfast selection. The restaurant filled with the aromas of bacon, eggs, and coffee, inviting our empty stomachs to feast there. I sat alone at a table by the window, the view of the swimming pool and the neatly trimmed garden was peaceful even with the hum of the general restaurant noises. The water in the pool slightly rippled from the breeze coming around the corners of the building, and I stared at it blankly, my mind wandering again.

After breakfast, I got into my rental car and started on my day of revisiting the places that had been such a big part of my life so many years ago. I drove passed my old school, noticing the huge banner promoting the reunion – I shivered. I went passed the house I had grown up in; the garden was now immaculate, definitely in better condition now than when I had lived there, but still, the house wore the same color of paint and had no additions or renovations. I slowly wandered through the center of town noticing that the shops were mostly abandoned when they had all relocated to the mall. Buildings were in dire need of attention – the town hall, the library, the police station - Oh dear, the police station - My bones quivered at the memories that washed over me, and suddenly I was right back in the past.

***

I puked all over Constable Pienaar's boots in the front garden of the police station. The evening long ago spent and the early morning hours resulted in those who were stupid enough to be seen, staggering through the streets in a drunken stupor getting afforded a ride in the back of a police van and escorted to the joys of a holding cell. For whatever reason, the constable that found me felt a heap of sympathy for me. I was so grateful it was not the same constable from my previous escapade.

'I'm slo shorry,' I spluttered through the vomit still hanging in my throat, spitting the last bits of slime out of my mouth. I tried to straighten myself up and stand like a normal person but my head was in another dimension unbalancing the rest of my body, and I was unable to plant my two feet together on the ground at the same time. I did try ever so hard, but it hurt my head too much.

'Whoa, there young lady. Just get it out of your system before I take you inside, don't want that stuff all over the charge office floor now do we?'

'Uhm...Yeesh oflicer.'

He left me alone there in the corner of the garden and allowed me to finish my retching and to empty the contents of my insides. It seemed to take forever. Once we were inside, I was led to the holding cell, and I was not alone in that horrid hellhole that reeked of urine. There were five other ladies – prostitutes and thieves –, and I was no better than they were. My head was still spinning, and the stench gripped my senses to the point of throwing up the little bile I had left in me. I staggered to the toilet in the cell and bent my head over it, oh the horror – one of the ladies must have been menstruating as the bowl was full of blood and on top of it floated a used tampon. I had never smelt such a disgusting odor shoved so close up my nose in my entire life, and my gut retched to vomit, my mouth opened, but there was nothing left to emit, and instead, I sucked the dirty smell of used blood into my mouth. I tripped backward and fell to the floor, it was wet but not with water; it was wet with urine, strong yellow pungent urine. I lost consciousness right there lying in the putrid, stale urine of another dirty human being.

Keys rattled, and screams from a woman awoke me along with the sun shining through the small window of the cell. The smells of the lowest level of society grabbed me immediately, and I recalled some of the events of the previous evening. Partying, drinking, popping pills of various kinds and then ending up here. What a nightmare! The remaining woman in the cell watched as I scrambled to the bench, then laughed at me, calling me obscene names and throwing threats of the worst kind at me. Was I already in hell?

'Miss!' an officer shouted from the door of the cell, and we both looked at him.

'You there with the red hair!'

He was shouting over the yelling of the other woman who was begging and demanding that he release her too. I walked like a person walking the plank – slowly, hesitantly, with the urine infested puke smell hovering over me and clinging to me. The officer took a few steps ahead of me to avoid the smell and every person I passed held their hand over their nose in objection to the scent I was carrying. I was given the only possession I had – my wallet, and all it contained was my driver's license and a fat help that was when I did not even own a car.

'Constable Pienaar told me to give you this card,' the officer said as he handed me a white business card with the address of a shelter nearby.

I nodded, took my wallet and the card and left the station. The sun was extremely bright, and I squinted, and the wind was fierce, mixing my matted hair into bigger knots. I had no idea where to go; I had no home thanks to the landlord that had kicked me out of my apartment the day before. I had no friends anymore; all had deserted me – who wanted to be friends with a drunk that enjoyed a few pills every so often? I studied the card, what did I have to lose? And in my heart, I knew I needed help so very desperately.

Chapter Two

I had not realized I'd driven over 200 kilometers to Vredenburg. Well, what was I supposed to do here? I drove to the harbor and went to a restaurant overlooking the entrance to the small fishing harbor. The seagulls squawked non-stop hovering over the spoils from the fishing trawlers and tourists. I ordered a meal of fish and chips and settled by the window with a glass of mango juice. I tried to remember if I had ever been to this place before but if I had the memory was escaping me. The waitress almost dropped my plate of food without so much of an apology, and instead, I got a click of her tongue. Well, this place would certainly not go on my "to visit again" list, that was for sure. The fish I was served was so oily, the oil was visible on my plate as a sauce, and the chips had been fried in old oil. At the first bite, I felt nauseated and called the waitress. When I complained, she simply shrugged her shoulders and when I asked to speak to the manager, I was told he was not available as he had gone to the bank. I got up and left with the waitress running after me to pay. I gave her my phone number and told her to tell the manager to phone me as I was not going to pay for a plate of oil. She clicked her tongue at me again, rolled her eyes and flew off back to the kitchen. This day was not boding well at all with the flooded visits of my past and now this place. I headed back to the hotel hastily.

By the time, I had showered and changed I was starving and made a beeline for the hotel restaurant as fast as possible.

'Yvaine, Yvaine Wolton, is that you?' a voice called from a few meters in front of me.

Oh no! Who had recognized me and who was also staying at this hotel? I had so hoped this was not going to happen. I looked up and saw a face with a wide smile moving steadily towards me. I had no idea who she was, I had to think quickly, but I couldn't think quickly enough.

'Yvaine, it's me Julia, Julia Feguria.'

I smiled back. I still had no idea who Julia Feguria was, and I racked my brain for the connection.

'Hi,' I said finally, but the blank expression on my face gave me away.

'You don't remember me do you?' Julia laughed still standing in front of me.

'Sorry, I don't,' I cringed as I admitted defeat.

'It's okay; I was a year below you. I married Jonathan Breed. He is going to the reunion, so I get to tag along,' she giggled like an excited little school girl.

'Oh okay. I remember Jonathan. How is he, how are you both?' I was not inviting conversation but merely being polite, but Julia seemed to think otherwise as she sat herself down at my table.

'May I?' she asked already sitting.

What could I do but nod?

'Jonathan will be here any minute; he forgot his phone in the room.'

She still wore a wide smile as she spoke and she giggled after every sentence. I did not remember anyone so friendly from school.

'Well, I never. Yvaine Wolton, you are looking good girl!' Jonathan stood next to his wife, who was still giggling and if at all possible even more so now that her husband had arrived.

'Jonathan. Hello, how are you?'

He was as happy as she was and sat himself down too. We went through almost the entire matric class trying to match the faces we remembered to names. I quickly skipped over the names of Dario, Tate, and Edie.

When the feared question was inevitably asked, "What happened to you, you just disappeared?" I felt the blood drain from my veins.

There was no running away from it; this would be the first of many times I was going to get asked. I was not ready to explain myself to Jonathan Breed just yet.

'Exactly that. I disappeared!' I took a sip of my coffee.

'So no babies yet?' I changed the subject.

Julia's face practically exploded, and immediately her hands affectionately held her stomach. 'First one on the way, due in seven months.'

Maybe that explained their happiness. I feigned fatigued to get out of a long evening of interrogations and returned to the balcony of my room. The balcony of my room faced on the mountainside so that the flow of the water sliding down the mountain slopes were loudly audible and so soothing. I sank back into the comfy recliner, closed my eyes and was asleep in a few seconds. Then I was suddenly back at the shelter...

***

I knocked on the door of the shelter, looking down at the card Constable Pienaar had left for me. My mouth felt like a crocodile had died in it and I could smell my body odor, which was anything but pleasant. I stank like a sewage farm. Somewhere between the last pub I had been at, and getting thrown into the police van I had also lost my shoes so there I stood knocking, as a beggar, a homeless vagabond, a drunk, a junkie and completely lost in my hometown. The door swung open to reveal a big bold woman standing in the door frame. When she spoke her voice sounded like an echo from someone else, it was soft and kind, unlike her frame and features.
'Yes dear, can I help you?'
I had no idea what to say or of the protocol at these places, so I handed her the business card.
'I got it from Constable Pienaar.'
My head hung in shame.
'Well that man is your guardian angel dear, do you have any belongings with you?'
'No, I have a few clothes at the apartment I used to live in.'
The words came out so sheepishly, and there was this lump sitting in my throat. As a breeze wafted down the passage, I smelled bacon, and my stomach growled. It had been days since I'd had a good meal so much so that I was dizzy at the thought of it.
'Come on in dear, before you faint on my doorstep.'
'I...Uhm...I don't have any money...' I said before taking a step toward the door hoping beyond hope that this was not to be a problem.
I was so hungry!

'Yes dear, I gathered that. Come in now; I won't hurt you.'
She indicated the way with her hand.
'If I must say you smell worse for wear, so what do say to a shower first before you sit at the breakfast table? We don't want to be upsetting the other guests now do we?'
I stood in the middle of a large hallway; doorways and passageways led off from it, and the walls decorated with paintings of flowers, very bright red, orange and yellow flowers.
'I will have to get my clothes first.'
I felt like Alice in Wonderland as the walls surrounding me grew larger, or I grew shorter and shorter.
'Oh no, no, you're not going to faint on me deary, come and eat first then. You can eat on the back porch; then when you've finished, and your blood sugar levels are up, you can have a shower.'
She held me up by my arm, and with quick steps walked me to the back porch and sat me down in a chair at a table with a plastic pink checkered cover. A young girl brought a glass of orange juice and put it on the table in front of me. She scrunched her nose and left, and not long afterward the kind lady returned with a bowl of warm oats.
'No bacon or the like for you at the moment, it will come straight back out. A few days of good old-fashioned Jungle Oats and you will be ready for the lekker stuff.' Her smile was so sweet.
'Thank you so much. What is your name?'
'Gretha.'
'Thank you Gretha.'
She left, I lifted the glass of juice to my lips and savored it as my taste buds delighted in it. My throat was so parched the juice burnt as it slid down. Slowly I took a mouthful of the porridge, and as the substance hit my stomach a savage hunger overcame me, and I almost inhaled the bowl of food. I shoveled spoonful after spoonful into my mouth before I had even swallowed the previous mouthful. The bowl of porridge was consumed in seconds, and so was the juice that washed down the last scoop of much-needed nourishment. I sat back in

the chair and waited until Gretha came back for me; a shower would be more than wonderful right now.

Gretha accompanied me to the showers and handed me soap, shampoo and a towel with the assurance of fresh clothes kindly borrowed from another resident. The hot water washed over my filthy skin, and as I lathered soap all over my body, a frantic sensation engulfed me. I started to wipe and wipe, which led to fierce scrubbing but the dirt did not seem to want to come off my body, and mentally I was unable to wash off the urine and vomit that stuck to my skin. The harder I scrubbed the harder I began to cry till eventually, I broke down releasing the anguish of my destitution. I dug my nails into my scalp as I tried to scrape off the filth; I scratched and scraped my hair, and then my body, then my hair again, in desperation I cried and wailed and sobbed until my cries were so loud Gretha was summoned to help me. She climbed into the shower and held me, sinking with me to the floor. She wrapped her large arms around me, easing my pain, and at the same time allowing me to release my anguish until I could cry no more.

***

I woke up with the sunrise when I realized I was still in the recliner on the balcony. I had slept through the night there consumed by more of my painful past that I had buried for so long. Why was I going to this reunion? So far nothing good had come from being back in Worcester. The past was just too painful. I kept asking myself why was I here? Why did I have this compelling need to be at this reunion when all it was doing was bringing memories to the surface that I did not want to be exposed? And I most certainly did not want to meet Dario, Tate, and Edie ever again, so why, why, why did I have this nagging urge to stay?

Chapter Three

I had one last stop before the reunion and before I left the next morning. I had to visit Gretha. I knocked on the front door of the shelter house, at least, this time, I smelt like Chanel No. 5 and not like a urinal. The door opened, and a young lady answered wrapped in an oversized apron and adorning a hair net.

'Hi, can I help you?'

'Is Gretha here?'

'Who are you?' she asked very bluntly.

'My name is Yvaine; I was a resident here just over ten years ago.'

'Yvaine, we have all heard about you!'

She stepped aside and gave me just enough space to get passed her and into the large familiar hallway before she shut the door and locked it. I looked around at the same pictures hanging on the walls; nothing had changed at all. The lady moved ahead of me.

'Come with me,' she instructed.

We went through the main house and the kitchen, and as we reached the door to the back room, she stopped and turned abruptly to face me.

'I am only permitting you to see Gretha because she spoke so fondly of you.'

I was bewildered.

'Is there something I should know before I see her?'

'You don't know?'

My heart started pounding, and I shook my head.

'I have been out of the country for over a year now, and all the emails I sent her were returned.'

She frowned and mumbled something that sounded like "stupid lawyer." I stared at her with wide eyes waiting for an explanation. She took my hand and hurriedly led me back to the kitchen and pulled out a chair indicating for me to sit down. I sat, she put the kettle on and prepared two cups for coffee.

'My name is Luanne,' she started, 'Gretha is dying; she has possibly a week maybe two left.'

She let her tears roll freely, and although her words were blunt, they were meant with love that was as clear as daylight. I gulped in horror. I could tell my throat had swollen double its size with instant distress.

'What? How?'

'It started as cervical cancer and before you could say "bless my soul" it spread to all her organs. Not a day goes by without her asking for you. We all just put it down to her lapses in memory, but clearly, she has been hanging on in the hope of seeing you.'

'In the hope of seeing me?' I said, so astonished as I was having a difficult time absorbing all of this news.

'The doctor told us two months ago she only had two weeks and every two weeks it has been two weeks since. They have been amazed that she is still here with us.'

Then I cried. The bubbles of tears ran down my face while my body jerked from the convulsions. What a shock to receive such sad news so unexpectedly.

'I never knew, all, this time, I thought she probably outgrew our friendship with me traveling so much. If I had known, I would've been here sooner.'

I wiped my eyes and blew my nose on the numerous tissues Luanne offered me.

'Then she would have died sooner.'

Again so blunt but so full of compassion. I shuddered at the door to Gretha's room; Luanne had warned me about her minuscule form (I had a hard time trying to visualize her with a small body frame). Softly Luanne turned the door handle and went to stand at Gretha's bedside.

'Gretha, you awake? You have a visitor. Gretha, wake up dear.'

She gently nudged her, continuously prompting her to wake up. I stood in the doorway shaking with fear that I was too late. Was I too late?

Oh Lord please, please don't let me be too late. Let me say goodbye. Please, please, I begged silently still frozen in the doorway.

Luanne tried without hesitation for a good few minutes without any response, and I felt my knees weaken – I was surely too late. She turned to me pulling me toward her with the motion of her waving hand. I had to fight my legs to make them walk, and when I managed to move, I moved ever so slowly, my heart beating aggressively against my ribcage, my body shaking with apprehension expecting to be confronted with the dead face of my dearest friend. I looked at Gretha; she was almost grey in complexion and nothing but a skeleton lying in the middle of the bed. Her eyes moved toward me, and I fell to my knees grabbing her frail cold hand and bursting into heartbroken sobs. I was not too late. Her hand moved in mine comforting me until I had myself under control and was able to give her a big but ever so gentle hug. Her smile was woeful but full of delight to see me. I begged for forgiveness that my emails had not reached her, and I had not been there for her when she had needed me the most. All she did was move her head slightly sideways assuring me it was all okay, and I was there now, and that was all that mattered. It was difficult to hear what she was saying, so I lay down next to her with my head right next to hers. She insisted on hearing all about my travels, especially when I had gone to Venice – it had always been her wish to go there one day.

'I will stay here tonight rather,' I said once the subject of the reunion was raised.

'Oh no, you need to forgive,' she rasped.

She insisted I attend, even on her deathbed she was telling me what to do, and I teased her about it. I was rewarded with a half chuckle and at this stage that was worth a million loud, boisterous laughs. Luanne made me a cheese and tomato sandwich for lunch with a glass of orange juice that I had sitting on the bed with Gretha. She had her dose of whatever it was that she was being fed via the intravenous tube along with the morphine. Luanne sat in the chair on the opposite side of the bed, and I listened to her story of how she had landed up at the shelter house. She was young at only twenty-five and dressed in a gothic fashion although she insisted she was not into that at all. I had to love Gretha for the way she goaded Luanne.

'Goth child this one,' she whispered and lifted her finger ever so slowly towards Luanne.

Her story was like so many others that were abused by their husbands and their fathers. Managing to escape a prison of a home she had found Gretha in the front garden of the house watering the few plants and instantly knew this was where she was running to for safety.

'Still goi…Church?' Gretha whispered slowly; her dull eyes moving to my side of the bed searching for mine.

I leaned down near her face, so she was able to hear me clearly, 'Yes my dear, I always find one to attend no matter where I am.'

She nodded her head once and closed her eyes again. I hoped I sounded convincing enough; the truth was I hardly ever went to church anymore. My life was so wrapped up in my antique import-export business that I used Sundays to catch up on the sleep I missed during the week. It suddenly dawned on me that I had not noticed any other residents in the house since I had arrived earlier.

'Are there any other residents in the house? I haven't seen any.'

'When Gretha got the news of how her cancer had spread, and she became so weak; she found new shelter homes for the five residents and shut down the place.'

'But you stayed?'

Luanne swallowed and with her lips trembling, her head facing down to her hands as they rested on top of her knees she told me, 'I couldn't leave her, I wouldn't leave her. She tried to force me to leave, but for once she was not going to get her way.'

She wiped the tears trickling down her face.

'It's the least I can do for everything she has done for me. She sorted my divorce not only from my husband but my family too. She led me to Jesus, and now I have a reason to live because of her.'

She stopped unable to say anymore. I got up and went to her and reached forward to hug her, to cry with her and to share a similar pain of losing the most caring person we both had ever known. We consoled each other and wiped our tears. Gretha was in a deep sleep, and so we went back to the kitchen and sat at the table once more.

'What are you going to do when Gretha passes on?'

Luanne shrugged her shoulders.

'I have not thought that far yet. I have been so concerned with caring for Gretha, and I suppose I've been in a state of denial. I don't have anyone to talk to about that, yes the minister at church would listen, but I am still very embarrassed about my past so that would be very difficult for me.'

As the conversation flowed, I discovered that Luanne got married three months after she had left school and had not studied or gained any form of experience since. What was this beautiful, gentle woman going to do with her life when Gretha was gone? It worried me immensely that she might get so lost she'd land up in another shelter house one day.

Reluctantly I left around five o'clock. Luanne had to attend to Gretha, and I had to get ready for the reunion. It was ridiculous that I had to attend this event when the only person that ever really cared for me was dying and refused to have me for company, insisting I enjoy myself at the reunion. How on earth did Gretha expect me to enjoy myself while she lay there slowly ebbing away from this life? And what was her comment about "I must forgive"? What was that about? I was just so consumed with questions and concerns as I trudged to my car and drove back to the hotel.

Once back in my room, I found my flight tickets and phoned to extend my return flight for two weeks, and if need be, I will change it again. I was not going anywhere again as long as Gretha was alive. The closer the clock ticked toward seven o'clock, the tighter my stomach knotted. I put on a black cocktail dress and my high black Jimmy Choos and left my red hair natural and loose. I applied a little makeup, only enough to hide the fear and anticipation written all over my face, to accentuate my grey eyes and to hide the freckles that came with the red hair. I also hoped it hid the puffiness around my eyes from a day spent in tears and high emotions. Picking up my red leather jacket and my red clutch bag I made for the door. It was now or never, and I made sure for the hundredth time that I had my cell phone, and it was fully charged in case Luanne phoned with the worst news. As I stepped out of the elevator and into the foyer of the hotel, I groaned when Julia and Jonathan stepped out of the other elevator, with Julia about to detonate with enthusiasm.

'Do you want to drive with us?'

'No thank you. If I want to leave, I don't want to have to put anyone out.'

'Okay well we'll drive behind you, safety in numbers,' Jonathan offered, and I offered a pathetic excuse for a smile in exchange.

Chapter Four

Judging from the full parking lot and the crowds at the entrance to the school hall it was clear that a lot of people had already arrived. Julia and Jonathan were stopped en route by classmates, but I was able to escape. In the foyer of the hall, some people were looking at the old photos on the walls and trophies in the cabinets. I made my way passed them and to the registration table. From the corner of my eye, I could tell some were staring at me, probably trying to figure out who I was.

On the table were labels and a pen and I wrote my name on the label, and the lady sitting at the table exclaimed, 'Yvaine, gosh is it you? I did not recognize you at all.'

With her little outburst, several others took notice, their memories finally jogged.

'Yep that's me,' I smiled and walked through the huge entrance doors and into the hall.

It had been set up with the same decor we'd had at our matric farewell.

'Nice touch,' I muttered.

They had gone to a lot of effort. The lady that had been sitting behind the desk ran up to me and handed me a card with a gift bag. She smiled and told me to enjoy the evening. At the door stood two schoolboys, wearing their uniforms that adorned their achievements. One asked for my card, which I presented to him, and then he ushered me to a table. I had hoped we would be able to sit anywhere as I would've chosen the one table right in the back corner. My appointed table was in the middle on the right side of the hall against the wall – slightly hidden from the spotlight. I thanked the young chap and immediately looked to see who I was sitting with and breathed a huge sigh of relief that none of the names on the place cards were Dario, Tate or Edie. A Sharene was on my left and a Jordan on my right, along with their partners. Why was it so hard for me to remember my old classmates? The minute I sat down I checked my phone – no messages. I sent Luanne a quick text to enquire of any change in Gretha; her reply was almost immediate and stated that there was no change. I sighed and closed my phone. While I stared around at the decor and the people milling about my mind wandered back to the night of my matric dance...

***

Tate arrived on time, dashingly dressed. I was so in love with him, and I knew in my heart that we were going to be together forever. My parents said goodbye without any happy send-off; they weren't the kind of parents that took much notice of their teenage daughter's life, as long as she was passing that was all that mattered to them. They were very unaffectionate, and this was most probably the reason I thrived on the attention and love I received from Tate.

We walked in through the arched entrance and had our photo taken together underneath it. The dance was just so perfect as we laughed and had fun all night with our friends. We danced till our feet ached so much we had to kick our shoes off. It was natural that Tate and Edie danced together, we were all very close. Not too long before the event was going to draw to a close Tate and Edie danced together again. I went to the bathroom and chatted to some other girls for a few minutes longer than expected. When I got back to our table, the song had changed, and I presumed since Tate and Edie were not there they were still dancing. I looked for them on the dancefloor, but they were not there. I wondered if they had gone to the courtyard for fresh air, so I went there to look. When I could not find them, I asked one of the guys if they had seen Tate and Edie.

'They left,' he said.

I thought he was playing the fool being in the drunken state that he was. But I went to the car park to the spot where Tate's car had parked, and it was empty. I started to panic, and confusion muddled my mind. What on earth was going on? I went back to the hall and asked a few other people if they knew what had happened to Tate and Edie, but they all said the same thing.

'They left.'

Everyone presumed I had gone with them, and so they looked as confused as I felt although I detected pity in many of their faces too. Well, now how was I to get home? My heart ached at the thought of betrayal by my boyfriend and my best friend. I collected my shoes from under the table and saw that Edie's were gone, and then I went outside and sat on the steps of the main school entrance. I had no idea what to do. If I phoned my parents, they would just tell me to get a lift with someone and to think for myself. My heart was beating like crazy. What had happened? Tate loved me; he had told me so earlier while we were dancing, so what was going on? We had been dating for sixteen months now and had never even had a serious argument. We declared our love for each other every day, several times a day. Edie always tagged along, but that was because she was my friend. There I sat, in a beautiful evening gown of rich purple satin feeling so befuddled I wanted to cry.

'Hey Yvaine, I heard Tate left with Edie; bummer.'

Dario appeared next to me. He was the rebel of the school. He was only at school because the law insisted he attend. His life out of school was wild and involved things us normal school children had never even dreamed existed.

'What do you mean?'

'Your boyfriend, your best friend; bummer.'

'It's not like that. There is probably a good explanation.'

'Nope, it is like that.'

He was very direct, a trait that infuriated the teachers immensely.

'Shut up, go away.'

'Tell you what. I will take you home, and we can take a drive past his house and her house and around the neighborhood. I bet you we will find them.'

'What do you care? Do you get some kind of a kick out of other people's misery?'

'Just an offer, best you see it now with your own eyes than believe what isn't true.'

I wanted to lash out at him, but he did have a point, and I was desperate to believe it was all just a misunderstanding. I also needed a lift home. I got into his car, and first, we drove to

Tate's house – nothing, and then to Edie's house, and still no sign of Tate's car. I breathed a sigh of relief.

While we were driving around looking for his car I asked Dario, 'Why do you think they have run off together?'

'I am very observant, and when they were dancing, they were much closer than friends ought to be. They were under the impression no one could see them in the dark corner of the dancefloor, but they were wrong. I also saw how they scurried out of there, hoping to disappear before you returned.'

I sank into the seat wishing it would swallow me. Everyone knew Dario was a "head case" at school but if he were one thing it was truthful. It did not matter to him who would get hurt in the process because he wasn't friends with anyone, so he didn't care who he hurt with the truth. As Dario drove around the neighborhood, my heart would race as we turned a corner and then slow down again when we didn't spot Tate's car. I kept hoping we wouldn't find it.

We landed up at Nekkies Dam. One of the after parties were held there and so Dario pulled into the campsite area. He got out of the car and told me to wait, and I obeyed, too frightened to face the possible reality I feared. He returned not much later, opened my door without a word, and I got out and followed him. My heart sank at the site of Tate's car. In front of his car was a tent.

'I dare you to go into that tent,' he said with a smile.

I did not know what to do; I was too naïve in these matters to truly think the worst.

'Why would you want me to do that?'

'If you don't you will never believe it,' he said very matter-of-factly.

Hesitantly I walked towards the tent. I was shaking and breathing so heavily the cool fresh autumn air cut my throat with every intake. I reached for the opening; it wasn't closed all the way, so maybe that was a good sign.

'Go on,' Dario egged me on.

I quickly unzipped the rest of the flap and peered inside. In the background, the sound of music and laughter and loud conversations obliterated the scream that escaped my lips and the horror of what my eyes beheld. Oh, the betrayal! Oh, the deceit! Oh, the pain that my heart was consuming! Tate and Edie lying naked together wrapped in each other's arms; I was so overwrought that I wanted to die, and while Dario was laughing himself something stupid, Tate and Edie were scrambling for their clothes. I ran, I ran and ran out of the campsite and down the road. I ran into the frosty night, tears stinging my cold skin as they ran down my cheeks, my throat struggling to pass enough air to my lungs along with the choking sobs. I just ran.

Chapter Five

'Hi Yvaine, gosh don't you look lovely!'
Sharene arrived at the table. I remembered her now. Jordan also arrived, and I was relieved that I remembered him too. They all said the same thing when first laying eyes on me, and I wondered why it was that the lasting memories we have of our classmates are those from the last few months of school, particularly from the matric dance onwards. Jordan offered to get drinks for all of us at the table and left with Sharene's husband. I had to admit I was beginning to relax and enjoy the memory lane we were all traveling down together. I had forgotten a lot of the good memories.
'You keep checking your phone, is everything okay?' Sharene asked, the others waiting in anticipation for my reply.
I sighed. I suppose it was that obvious and also it did not help to hide the truth, they all knew what had happened to me.
'It's Gretha, the lady that saved my life. She is dying. I only found out when I arrived here.'
I stopped speaking; my throat was too clogged up to carry on.
'Oh Yvaine, that's terrible. Why are you here and not with her?'
'She told me to come. I wanted to stay with her, but she wouldn't have it. Kept going on about forgiveness.'
'Tate. Edie. Dario.' Sharene hesitated between their names.
'I guess so. But I'd rather not see them at all. I nearly didn't come tonight because of them.'
'Well you did, and you are stunning Yvaine.'
I was flattered. I honestly had not seen myself as such, but then they had last seen me when I was in the depths of despair, so it was no wonder they thought now I looked better. Jordan returned with our drinks and as he sat he kindly informed me that Tate and Edie had arrived.
Immediately I started to rev up into panic mode but then Sharene said, 'Think of Gretha,' and patted my hand.
Yes! That's what I had to do. I had nothing to fear from them, and as I had been told a million times, "That was the past, they did not destroy you."

Minister Caldew came to mind when I thought of that, along with a great deal of gratitude.

Remember what he said to you all those times, "With the grace of God you can overcome anything," I told myself once more.

Being the only person at the table without a partner left me alone when they all got up to dance when a favorite song came on, but I sat quietly and continued my trip down memory lane...

***

I was still running, my feet were cut and bruised from the stones on the road, but I still ran. I was not much of an athlete, but the adrenaline drove me further and further. Dario pulled up in his car and ordered me to get in, but I refused. I kept running until he eventually pulled the car over, got out and caught up to me, grabbing me by my arm and forcing me into the car. I huddled in the seat and leaned against the door, shivering, unaware of where Dario was taking me until we stopped at a house.

'Where are we?' I managed to squeak.

'A party, you need a distraction.'

'Just take me home.'

'No,' he said emphatically.

I looked a mess; my hair was wet and frizzed, and my makeup was smudged all over my face. I looked like a Halloween freak.

'I can't go in like this,' I pleaded as we reached the door.

'You can clean up in there,' he said and pushed the door open.

I walked into the house trying to hide behind Dario. People were sprawled about everywhere, over couches, on chairs, on the floor. They were just chilling and listened to music that I did not recognize. He led me to the bathroom where I loosened my hair and washed my face, crying all the time. The image of those two in the tent fixated in my mind. Dario tapped on the door and enquired as to whether I was going to come out at some stage. It had crossed my mind to remain in there. When I finally did, he ushered me into the living room and gave me a glass of wine that I refused at first. Everyone got on my case encouraging me to drink it.

"It will make you feel better," and, "It will help you forget," were some of the things I was told. Feeling cornered I swallowed the wine in one gulp and almost immediately my glass got refilled. And this happened several times. They were right, though, I did feel better, I had no idea what I was feeling, but it wasn't anguish or pain. I took whatever it was that they gave me to eat or drink after a while. My head was spinning, and I felt out of control, but I was also exhilaratingly happy. I just wanted to feel like this forever.

When Dario took me home at some unearthly hour of the morning, I threw up in his car, on the pavement and again in the house. I woke up later in the day to a massive headache, a reminder of what had gone down the previous night. My parents were somewhere in the house, and I remained in my room thinking it best to avoid them. I began to feel the heartache all over again as I lay on my bed, trying with all my might to understand why Tate and Edie had done what they did and how I was going to face them at school on Monday. How was I going to face anyone when they all knew about my humiliation?

I snuck silently to the kitchen hoping there was some leftover food lying around. After a small meal of chicken and pasta, I opened the cupboard where the alcohol was kept. I stood there deliberating, and while I stood there I smelt myself – gosh I stank, I needed a shower. Perhaps the alcohol should wait. Hygiene first.

I was barely out of the shower when my mother yelled at me from the living room; I had a phone call.

'Hello?' I said when I was sure my mother had put down the extension, trembling with the fear that it could be Tate or Edie.

'How you feeling?'

'Dario, um…Hello. I'm not sure yet.'

'Fetch you in half an hour.'

'No, wait...'

But he had hung up. Why on earth was he so interested in my life suddenly? Since he'd arrived at our school three years ago, he had never paid any attention to me. I got ready nevertheless.

We went back to the house from the previous evening. Everyone was still, or again, sprawled out wherever there was a spot. The wine was already flowing, and I drank it eagerly. Later other alcohol appeared and I smoked something, but I didn't know what and ate cookies that were delicious. I was so incredibly high, and everything seemed blissful again. How I got back into my house without my parents suspecting a thing I had no idea.

I felt so lost at school the next day. Usually, Tate, Edie and I met at our spot in the courtyard, but because I had no other close friends what was I supposed to do and where was I supposed to go until school started? I had no idea how I would or should react when I came face to face with the both of them. I heard people snickering as I walked passed and saw the way they looked at me – everyone was on a gossiping hype over the whole affair. I slumped along to my registration class in the hope that it'd be open, and I might escape the masses. En route Dario caught up with me, another person I would have preferred to avoid.

'How you feeling?' he asked with a sarcastic smirk on his face.

'Oh just peachy.'

'Here,' he said offering me a small cloth bag.

To everyone else, it looked like a small material handbag and probably would be admired by most women, but I knew what was in it. A small bottle of vodka.

'No one will smell it on your breath.'

'Why?'

'Dutch courage,' he said and continued to walk with me in silence until we reached my classroom.

I had just enough time to put my bags down on my desk before the bell rang. I took off my jersey, leaving my blazer on, and wrapped the bottle in it, placing it in my school bag before closing it securely. But not before taking a huge gulp.

'Dutch courage,' I said offering the bottle to Dario.

We both chewed vigorously on gum on our way to the hall. The school, still very strict on tradition, had the boys sit on the left and the girls on the right. I always sat next to Edie. I shuffled through the side door and found the first chair closest to the door – all eyes fixated on me; I could feel it. I thought how good another swig of that vodka would be right now. I never looked anywhere but directly in front of me or at my hands resting on my legs. It was impossible to clear my mind and think rationally. The dagger that jabbed in my heart was so fierce along with the humiliation I felt, and the tears flowed silently. The only way I was going to get through the day was with the help of that bottle of vodka.

When it was over, I vanished from the assembly hall like lightning and rushed to my classroom. Edie would have to find another seat; she was most definitely not going to sit next to me. I waited nervously, my stomach in knots for her arrival. Then I changed my mind and moved to the back of the class, to the corner desk, hidden from all the eyes. I wished I was permitted to wear sunglasses not only to avoid everyone's stares but also to hide the red, puffy bags around my eyes. Edie walked in, and I gasped and looked down at my shoes, resting my head on the desk. The class was deathly silent. An explosion was imminent, and everyone held their breaths in anticipation. Our register teacher was giving a lecture of some sort about the upcoming final exams, and I wanted to choke on my panic. How was I expected to write exams in this state? The buzz of the intercom interrupted my inner hysteria.

'Edie Ashdown and Tate Kestell report to Mr. Joubert's office immediately.'

The hush in the classroom erupted into a hoard of "yeahs" and "ooohs" and surprisingly to me; there were a lot of comments about expulsion, not directed at me. It then dawned on me that perhaps I was the victim here and that people were, in fact, sympathetic to my pain. Alas, it did not appease my desire to slither away and never be seen again. During the day, I heard many rumors about what had happened in the principal's office, but they meant nothing to me, and I only wanted to drown my sorrows and fill the void in my heart. The first opportunity I had, I dashed for the bathroom and downed a large amount of vodka, waited for a few seconds and then sent another swig down my throat.

'Dutch courage,' I told myself again.

The inevitable confrontation was around the corner at first break when I wandered sluggishly toward a bench and sat down before I fell from my spinning head. A shadow appeared in front of me and when I looked up there stood Tate and Edie, holding hands. Rage replaced the alcohol and overcame the anguish. Tate opened his mouth to say something but I replaced it with my fist, and before Edie could retaliate she found the other side of my hand flat on her cheek. I was fuming, no, that is too calm an expression, I was in a furious frenzy, screaming and shouting filthy obscenities, crying and trying to assault them physically in any way possible. I didn't hear a word they were trying to say; they didn't have much chance of saying anything. All I knew was that killing them at this point would be greatly satisfying. Hysteria, wild fanatical hysteria burst from the hole in my heart, and I flung anything and everything I could lay my hands on at them, including a rock lying next to the bench that just skimmed Tate's head. Before I was able to do any serious damage, unfortunately, two prefects restrained me, forcing me to sit back on the bench once more. My chest was heaving, and I was completely out of breath, and then I fainted, waking up a half an hour later in the sick room.

***

My table guests arrived back at the table panting from dancing to the very fast songs. They guzzled their drinks and Jordan, and Sharene's husband made their way back to the bar for another round.
'Sure you only want orange juice?' Sharene's husband asked me.
'Definitely,' I replied, and Sharene gave him a stern look as he left.

<u>Chapter Six</u>

I needed the bathroom, so many glasses of orange juice had to come out at some point, and there was no way I could hold it in any longer, so I had to make the trip reluctantly. I had wished to spend the entire night glued to my chair. As most women do, for whatever reason, we go to the bathroom in numbers. Sharene and Jordan's wife Elisbe thankfully joined me. We made it to the toilets without too many hellos along the way. Relieved and a few pounds lighter we exited the bathrooms and walked smack-bang into Tate and Edie. Time froze for a second as we stared at one another in anticipated surprise. Sharene and Elisbe were soldiers at my side instantly. Edie paled dramatically and reached for my arm, but I pulled away immediately. Her eyes welled up with tears, but Tate remained frozen. It felt like school all over again as everyone went deadly silent, waiting for my reaction.

'Yvaine, can we talk?' Edie stuttered through her tears.

I expected a different reaction from myself. All the years of pent-up anger, ideas of revenge and imagined scenarios of this exact moment dissipated, and I was calm and in control of my emotions and the situation.

'No. We have nothing to talk about,' I replied assertively.

'Come on Yvaine, don't be childish, we're all grown up now,' Tate threw his words at me.

By now a large audience had gathered.

'Tate, excuse you for pointing out the obvious! I have the right to speak or not to speak to either of you, and I choose not to. What happened in the past is what you have to live with, I am done with the past. You and Edie, however, do not have to be a part of my future.'

Edie reached for my arm again, and I refused her advance once more.

'Please Yvaine, please forgive me, forgive us.'

Tate was about to say something and Edie shushed him. Tears were ruining her make-up – she had a lot of it on.

'If you truly need to hear the words to move on then yes, I do forgive you. Goodbye now.'

I turned my back on a sobbing Edie standing alone as Tate left her to get a drink from the bar. The world had lifted from my shoulders. I felt strong and refreshed. I had never guessed I would've triumphed, but I realized if I had God with me then who could be against me? A round of applause went out from the onlookers, but I shook my head and walked back to my seat. Sitting down Sharene and Elisbe were babbling like school girls re-enacting the scene for their husbands.

'I cannot believe it went that way. I dreamed of the worst possible outcomes; blood and bruises included and yet I was so calm it was incredible. It's such a fantastic feeling to have that behind me now.'

'It's just like your Gretha said; you are here to forgive,' Sharene said.

I nodded. When I felt I'd had enough, as much as I had unexpectedly enjoyed myself, I said goodbye to everyone at the table with affectionate hugs and promises to keep in touch. I took in a deep breath of the frosty air and smiled at myself as I stood on the steps of the entrance hall. I was very proud of who I had become right then and there.

'Hello,' a voice said, and Dario was suddenly standing next to me.

I'd forgotten about him; I had in fact forgotten about him. It was a case of déjà vu meeting him for the first time again at the same spot.

'Dario!' I exclaimed.

'Can I get forgiveness too?'

'You heard all that? I haven't seen you all evening.'

'Hiding in the shadows too afraid to speak to you.'

I squinted at him in the dim light. He looked different, cleaner or more decent, perhaps gentler, or perhaps it was just the light.

'Since when are you afraid of anyone?'

'Since I grew up. Can we talk somewhere, or have you nothing to say to me as well?'

'I'm tired, maybe another time. What is your number? I will be here for another week or two, perhaps then.'

Why I did not treat him the same as Tate and Edie, I was too tired to try and figure out. I punched his number into my phone, checking for any messages from Luanne at the same time, then left. In bed, I mulled over the evening and felt extremely pleased that I had ended up going to the reunion. The hole in my heart had finally been stitched up. The horrid feelings I'd not been able to get rid of had finally been buried beneath the stitches of the hole. The rest of my past, the part with Dario, I knew I was now capable of discussing as a mature adult without any reservations or bitterness. I also realized I needed to tell him I forgave him too.

***

By the time the school nurse let me leave the sick room, the school was over. Exhausted, I walked home, but before I got even halfway down the road, Dario pulled up alongside me in his car and indicated for me to get in. I did, but he didn't drop me at home. Instead, he stopped at a liquor store, and from there we went to his apartment. From then on, I was incapable of functioning or controlling my emotions without the use of vodka and whatever alcohol I was able to get my hands on. At nightclubs I gladly helped myself to pills of all sorts, encouraged to fix my loneliness and sadness by Dario.

I somehow made it through the exams, but the discussion with my parents over my future was disastrous. I was not prepared to study anywhere or anything, and they insisted I go to college. The result was that I was told to leave the house, and I landed on Dario's doorstep, where I was free to feed my addiction as I pleased. I spent my days high and drunk, selling anything I could get my hands on since I was unable to keep a job for longer than a month or two. I sank so low I even broke into my parents' house on a few occasions to steal things and sell them for pennies so that I could appease my addictions.

Dario came home one evening and informed me that he was leaving Worcester, but that I could stay in his apartment for as long as I paid the rent. I was mortified. Again I was being dumped by the person closest to me, at least, this time, it wasn't my boyfriend, but, this time, it was my addiction support. He had introduced me to this life of degradation, and now I was supposed to carry on by myself. He was the only person I was able to call a friend if you could call someone like that a friend. 'How do you think I am supposed to pay this rent?'

'Well that is not my problem now, is it? You will have to keep a job for longer than a month I guess.'

And I tried to do exactly that, several times, and the same situation repeated itself – arrive late and hungover, and after the third warning, I was fired. I only had money for my desired needs, which were alcohol and the weekend pill popping and, needless to say, my hygiene and personal health went for a loop to nowhere. Without Dario I went further downhill so fast, it was frightening. Even my parents had by this time publicly disowned me, and I had not a friend in the world. The last straw was when I was kicked out of the apartment and ended up at the shelter house. But this is where Gretha came into my life saving me from death.

**

At first light, I was at the shelter house having a cup of tea with Luanne telling her how the evening had gone. She was so delighted for me and was eager for Gretha to wake up so I could retell the story. Once Gretha had woken up, I repeated my story, and she smiled and squeezed my hand timidly with the little strength she had left.

'God good,' she said in her weak, wispy voice.

I laid my head on the pillow next to her and cried. Why had I not tried harder to keep in touch? I could've spent so much more time with this wonderful woman. She went back to sleep again, exhausted from simply listening to my news and I felt sorrow and happiness all at the same time. I was happy that I had forgiven, and I had released that bitterness, but she was leaving us soon. I knew it was going to be very soon too.

'I think she feels she can go now. Now that your life is in order,' Luanne said sadly.

'Don't say that; my life is not that important.'

'You have no idea how she felt about you. You were the daughter she never had. She loved you so much, yes she loves me too, but not like she loved you.'

I burst into a mass of choking sobs.

'Then I was a terrible daughter for not trying harder to contact her this past year. I should not just have assumed things.'

'You're wrong. She knew you'd show up one day. She knew you loved her like a mother.'

I had no words and simply cried my shame away, or tried to.

Chapter Seven

Gretha was holding on by a thin thread, and I had with Luanne's permission moved out of the hotel and into the shelter house. The only time I went out was when we needed groceries. Luanne and I were always at Gretha's side unless she was sleeping and even then we were just down the hall and checked on her every fifteen minutes or so. We grew very close, sharing a common bond in Gretha and having similar personal histories.

Early one morning the doorbell rang, and we presumed it was either the doctor, the minister or the lawyer. When I opened the door, I was extremely surprised to find Dario standing in front of me.

'Dario! What are you doing here?'

'You haven't called me yet.'

'I didn't say I would call you…'

'Yes that is what I was afraid of,' he said half smiling.

'How did you know I was here?'

'A very long process of elimination.'

This time, his reply came with flushed cheeks and a proper smile.

'I guess you had better come in then.'

I opened the door, so he was entitled to gain entrance, and he followed me to the kitchen. I told him to sit down and went first to check on Gretha and then to inform Luanne of my guest. Luanne flew off her chair.

'Oh I have to meet the infamous Dario!' she said teasingly.

A soft voice caught our attention.

'Dar…here?'

I went over to Gretha and leaned in next to her ear, 'Yes. Surprise visit.'

Gretha nodded and smiled ever so slightly then went back to sleep. I introduced Luanne and Dario, and we made idle chit-chat while we drank coffee. I had to admit it was strangely comfortable having them both with me in the same room.

Luanne excused herself to attend to Gretha; it was time for her regular bed bath.

'Want to go out for a bit?' Dario asked, or rather suggested.

'I don't know. I do not like leaving Gretha even for a minute.'

'Then we will only go out for a minute.'

'Still have an answer to everything I see.'

I knew it would be pointless to resist, so I let Luanne know, found my jacket and left with Dario. We decided to stroll around town a bit instead of driving to a coffee shop or a restaurant. There was a chill in the air, but after a while after walking around, it was not so inhibiting.

'You are different,' I decided to be the first one to delve into the conversation that I knew was looming.

'Yes, when I left here and you, I went to Mossel Bay to work for a drug dealer. I can't tell you the hellhole I was in – or maybe you will be able to relate from what I have heard – but one day I landed up at the wrong house. I was supposed to deliver some drugs to a new guy in town, and instead, I knocked on the door of a preacher. Man did he chew me up but in a nice way. I know God led me there, I know that now, but on the day I was so confused that this man even invited me into his house let alone talked to me. It was very rough, but he got me clean, and eventually, I was baptized, and now I am a minister in a small church in Ceres.'

Well, you could have blown me over! I knew he had changed but not even for a moment had I imagined to such an extent.

'Wow Dario, that is some story. I bet your congregation loves your sermons; you have so much to offer them in the way of repentance.'

He simply laughed at my assumption.

'And you? You have cleaned up well.'

'Gretha,' I said and told him my story of regret and woe.

'Oh shame man, so you're staying until she passes? Would you mind if I pray for her, with her?'

'Of course, you can. She will love that; I know she will. I did not want to go to the reunion, but she insisted, forever telling me to forgive. I guess I did not realize what she meant until I was there and came face to face with Tate and Edie.'

He laughed.

'Now that was a scene any movie director would relish!'

I punched him lightly on the arm, laughing with him.

'You know we have never had a friendship per se. I like this moment; I hope we can be friends as proper friends should be.'

He stopped abruptly and for a moment was very still, his head bent and his eyes on the pavement. Then he looked up, and I hardly believed my eyes when I saw his face streaked with tears.

His lips quivered as he uttered, 'I have been praying for all of these years to be forgiven by you, and for this exact friendship.'

He stopped trying to get the words out; it became too difficult to speak as he sobbed in front of me, on a pavement in front of the central park in Worcester. Instinctively I wrapped my arms around him and held him, the bonding of our friendship sealed in forgiveness. My tears were not held at bay, and we shared a pivotal moment in our lives.

'Thank you,' he said as we released each other, wiping our wet cheeks.

'And thank you,' I said back with a kiss on his cheek.

We got back to the house, and I went immediately to Gretha leaning into her ear as always and asked her if Dario could pray for her. Her face lit up; I knew I did not imagine it, as she nodded. With Dario, Luanne, Gretha and I all holding hands Dario prayed for Gretha. The kind of heartfelt prayer I had not heard in a very long time, and we were all brought to tears. I knew this was the moment Gretha had been holding on for; she was now at peace with her world, and she was ready to meet Jesus and live forever. At the end of his prayer, we remained as we were, each saying our own prayers. A few moments later I opened my eyes as Gretha's hand moved in mine. I looked at her; her eyes were searching for mine. I leaned in close to her face, and she gave a limp smile then closed her eyes as she exhaled her last breath.

What was there for us to do other than to feel despair and sorrow? Silently I thanked God that Gretha had been spared until this perfect moment before He took her away. While Dario consoled Luanne, I made the phone calls to the doctor, minister, and lawyer. In a matter of half an hour, they were all at the house. Dario and the minister chatted easily while

Luanne and I were summoned to discuss Gretha's will in the study. The lawyer slowly and with much deliberation put his briefcase on the desk, opened it, pulled out a file filled with a few papers, set it down on the desk and put his briefcase on the floor. Then he took off his jacket, hung it over the chair, pulled out the chair, sat down, pulled the chair towards the desk, opened the file and silently read from the first page in the file. I was exasperated watching this process. He silently read every single page before opening his mouth to speak. It took forever. Finally, he cleared his throat a few times.

'Right.'

He cleared his throat again and fidgeted in his seat. I wanted to rip the papers from his hands and read them myself; it would certainly be less frustrating and far quicker. He then read the legal terms and conditions and obvious facts that Gretha was dead. Luanne and I sat in our chairs numb and heartbroken, tears spilling down our cheeks as we listened. Gretha did not have much in the form of an estate and not having had any children of her own; her small estate was awarded jointly to Luanne and me. The estate consisted of a provident fund that had a value of approximately five hundred thousand Rand, as well as the house and all its contents. I felt relief that Luanne had a chance at a new life, and she would not be stranded as I had first feared.

'If I want to waive my share of the inheritance, how would I go about it?' I asked to the surprise of the lawyer and Luanne.

'We would need to draw up some legal documents, and that would be it.'

'Okay. I need to do that as soon as possible.'

'Yvaine, what are you doing? This is what Gretha wanted!' Luanne was stunned.

'Yes that is true, but it is mine now, and that entitles me to do what I want with it. In any case, I know Gretha would approve of my actions.'

The lawyer and Luanne both looked surprised and confused at the same time.

We waited a week to have the memorial service for Gretha at her church. I was pleasantly surprised to see Constable Pienaar at the service, and he felt very much the same when I told him who I was. The wheels had gone full circle.

Chapter Eight

For the next week, Dario remained with Luanne and me at the house to tie up all the loose ends. I had given my inheritance to Luanne much to her objection, but it fell on my deaf ears. One evening we sat around the kitchen table, our favorite place, I asked Luanne what she was going to do with her life now.

'Get a degree in counseling. I want to help people like Gretha helped me.'

I was overcome with admiration for this wonderful woman, with such an innocent and pure heart.

Dario looked up and smiled, 'So...We have a rehab center similar to Gretha's shelter, and if you like, you can work there and study at the same time.'

Luanne's eyes grew wide.

'Truly, you mean that?'

There was a special glint in Dario's eyes as he reassured her of his offer.

***

I turned around one last time before disappearing through the boarding gates, waving goodbye to Luanne and Dario. After returning to my hometown, never would I have imagined that I would be leaving with a free heart, an open spirit, a love for humanity and grateful compassion that made me want to burst. Never had I imagined I would leave with friends like Dario, Luanne, Sharene, and Elisbe for a lifetime ahead. Never had I imagined God would lead me to forgiveness.

God had led me back to my hometown where forgiveness lay when I had not fully understood or trusted in His plan for me. For so many years I had led my life, pretending to have forgiven and forgotten but God knew better. Until I had truly forgiven and released the resentment that limited my faith and belief in God, I would not have the relationship with Him that I was meant to have, nor be able to do His Will.

For we do not know the Will of God. If we die to ourselves and allow Christ to live in us, we will know an abundance of love and peace as never before.

"If anyone is in Christ, he is a new creation; the old has gone, and the new has come."
2 Corinthians 5:17

THE
BOOKSTORE

The Bookstore

Chapter One

My feet were killing me. Served me right for wearing new shoes – high heels too – on a day that I had to investigate five MaxiS Superstores. Why you might ask, do I need to visit and investigate so many stores? Well, it is my job. My job requires me to go into the chain of MaxiS Superstores as an ordinary customer and pretend to be shopping. In fact, I am scrutinizing the operation of the store, its contents and the employees. I am the KGB, super spy of MaxiS Superstores. How did I land up in a job like this? I know you're curious to find out.

I worked in the buyers' department at the head office of MaxiS Superstores, and after being treated appallingly by our local store during a lunch break one day, I stormed into our large office and threw a hissy fit of note. Boy, did I throw a tantrum! Unbeknown to me at the time, one of the directors was in the building and within earshot of my performance. A few days later I was called to a meeting on the top floor. Usually, when an employee was summoned to the top floor something seriously bad had occurred, and you undoubtedly got fired.

As I rode in the elevator, I sweated and tried my hardest to figure out what I had done wrong. By the time I was ushered into the director's office, I was shaking like an earthquake. Mr. Bartlett indicated with a friendly smile and hand gesture that I could sit on the chair in front of his desk. I sat and held onto my legs trying to assess the situation. He was not angry, so perhaps I was not in trouble. I had never had anything to do with the big bosses before, so why now? He picked up the phone and told whoever was on the other end to join us. My nerves were in shreds, how many more people did I have to face and why? A few seconds had passed before three more gentlemen joined. Fainting was a distinct possibility for me.

'Miss Asbury, thank you for joining us.'

He thanked me. Why would he thank me? I remained silent, too afraid to speak and so he continued.

'A few days ago I happened to hear your rant about the service at one of our stores.'

He stopped and probably took a few moments to gauge the horror-stricken expression on my face. I had no thoughts; I only knew that I was waiting in anticipation to get.

'Well, it got me thinking as to how we can circumvent this sort of service in our stores.'

He motioned with his hand to all the men in the room.

'We put our ideas together and have come up with a possible solution.'

I was not sure if he expected a response from me when he paused, but he didn't get one and so carried on.

'We have created a position in the company called "Investigator." This person will be employed as an investigator and will go to all the branches under the assumption of being a normal customer.'

I listened, fascinated, as he explained that the person fulfilling this position would be given a credit card to enable any purchases, a company car, a clothing allowance, and an expense account. A report, which was still to be designed, on every store visit was to be completed and emailed to him every day.

'This position is subject to absolute secrecy. We do not want anyone to know about it, in case it leaks out to the stores. They are not to know that they are being scrutinized. The only people that will know about this will be the five of us here in this room.'

I had to blink, my eyes were bulging from their sockets in surprise, and my mouth hung open.

I took a short intake of air, refocusing on the man in front of me and hesitantly asked, 'So, you want me to take this position?'

He smiled and said, 'Absolutely. We think that since you are so passionate about the quality of service, we will get honest feedback from you.'

'Of course, you will have time to think about it,' one of the other men added.

I shook my head. 'No need to think about it, this is a fantastic offer, I don't know what else to say but thank you.'

Everyone breathed a sigh of relief, and for the first time, I relaxed, still overwhelmed by the prospect of this interesting offer. I resigned and entered into an agreement with the directors as a freelance agent. My colleagues in the buyers' office were horrified when I told them I had resigned. The directors and I had made up a story that I had been told off for my tantrum which led me to resign. Shoo! My colleges were upset with management and begged me to sue, complain, strike and who knows what else. I wanted to laugh and fill them in with the truth so badly.

And so I spent my days shopping – literally. The feedback I provided helped immensely, and in some stores, I was able to see the improvements. But others, well, they were difficult, firstly to accept the criticism and secondly to implement the changes I recommended. Naturally, I loved going to the upmarket stores in the more affluent areas, and when I had to go to the stores in the dodgy downtown parts of town, I dressed accordingly and held my breath almost the entire time.

***

On that point, it would be unfair to assess a store like the one I was entering now in the Doonside Mall as I would, in let's say Umkomaas where there were different logistics, different criteria; and, in the end, it all made my job so much more interesting. The only downside – that I was forbidden to let anyone know what I did for a living. Doonside was my last store for the day. It was only three in the afternoon, and usually, I'd investigate the store and go directly home, to begin with the reports, but today I felt like browsing through the other little shops in the mall. It was not a very big mall in comparison to the major city malls, but it had a quaint family feeling about it. The first store I went into was a shoe store, and I purchased a pair of flat sandals and left them on my feet immediately after trying on them. Aaaah, that certainly felt so much better!

From there I stumbled into a bookstore. I loved to read but never seemed to have much time for it these days. I looked along the shelves at the vast number of books that all required the time to read them, and my heart yearned to have the time to do just that. I pulled out a book, read the blurb and the bio of the author and replaced it, repeating the sequence as I slowly passed along the shelves. I sighed as a particular book appealed to me, reaching out for me to read it and possess it. I kept it in my hands and continued with my inspection of the varied genres. The store was so welcoming, peaceful and relaxing; it had two leather chairs in a corner where I chose to sit for a few minutes and flip through the magazines on the table in front of me. There was a coffee machine against the wall next to the chairs with paper cups, and I helped myself to a cup of delectable smelling coffee and sat in the chair again.

'If you need any assistance, please let me know,' a young very pretty lady said to me.

I smiled and nodded, sipping the hot beverage at the same time. She went back to her counter and her computer. These were such an odd few minutes for me; chilling in a bookstore in the middle of the afternoon. I was not familiar with the slow pace. The door suddenly swung open and a man probably also in his thirties, like me, burst in. My heart stopped – I was sure it was out of fright – and he greeted me and walked behind the counter until he stood next to the young lady. By young, I mean probably mid-twenties. They conversed softly for a few minutes then he disappeared to the back of the store, and I presumed his office. Perhaps they were dating; neither wore any rings; not married I thought to myself. After some contemplation, I decided to buy the book. I went to the counter, handed it to the lady and got out my purse.

'This is a good choice; you will not be sorry, it's a wonderful story,' she said with a bright smile.

'Oh, that is good to hear, this is such a lovely store, I regularly shop at the MaxiS but have never been in here. What is your store called?'

I realized this probably sounded stupid and quickly added, 'I just walked in without looking at the shop name.'

She giggled, 'Readers Rest.'

'Well that is a perfect name,' I smiled, and she giggled again as I took my book and my receipt from her.

'I'm sure I will be back for more.'

I walked to my car not bothering to visit any other shops in the mall. I was eager to get home, finish the reports and start reading my new book. While driving home, I tried to remember when last I had read a book, and I came to the conclusion that it was three years ago – just before I started my job with MaxiS. The reports took me a little longer than usual as I'd had a problematic time in the first store of the day and this, therefore, involved more descriptive information. The email to Mr. Bartlett finally flew through cyberspace three hours after I arrived home.

I had a shower, a leftover pasta salad to eat and then snuggled on the sofa with my newly purchased book. I became completely engrossed in the story I was reading. It was about a young lady who had lost her father and fiancé in a car accident, her struggle to overcome her heartbreak and how she found a support system in her family and mostly God. I hadn't realized that Christian Romance could be so enthralling and captivating, and I battled to put the book down to get some much-needed sleep. Tomorrow was only a few hours away, and I required sleep. Reluctantly I switched off the lights of my townhouse and fell asleep.

Chapter Two

I awoke to a bright sunrise, and my first thought was what a lovely day it was, and then immediately I thought back to the story of my book. I had a hard time throughout the day focusing on my job as I kept thinking about the protagonist, Tali, and her story of woe. I wondered if I could ever overcome a tragedy like hers.

At one o'clock in the morning I was sobbing my eyes out, so deeply touched by this beautiful story with such a fabulous ending. I put the book down on the bedside table, switched off the lights and cried myself to sleep. When was the last time I had even cried let alone sobbed until my tears dripped onto the pages of the book until my heart ached so much it wanted to break not only from the sadness of Tali's loss but also from her happiness? The story also made me realize I had not been to church for a very long time, or even visited my parents for some time. I felt awfully guilty and ashamed.

I had made it a personal rule to stay away from shops in any form, shape or size over the weekends – that would be like working overtime – but I was eager to get back to Readers Rest to buy more books by this author. Somehow I resisted and instead packed a bag and went to visit my parents for the weekend. They were delighted to have their only daughter home for a few days, while my much, very much, younger brother at only eighteen (now there was a big accident!) was unperturbed by my presence. He was such a surfing fanatic, that if he was not surfing – for instance, if he was at school – he was dreaming about it. I was pleasantly delighted to discover he had got involved in the Christian surfing school at the local beach.

'So how come the sudden visit?' my mom asked me in the kitchen as she put the kettle on to make us coffee.

'I read this book, yep, don't look at me so strangely, I did buy a book, and I did read it. Its story was so beautiful, and it just made me think a little about my crazy busy life, so here I am, sorry that I have been so scarce...' I had a pathetic sorrowful expression on my face.

'And I also realized I need to go back to church.'

I felt a burst of happiness at seeing delight across my mother's face on hearing that little bit of news.

'Oh Salma, I am so thrilled. Now we need to get you a nice Christian boyfriend!'

She loved teasing me about my single status. I raised my eyebrows and shook my head. It was great to feel the love and harmony of my family home again.

On Sunday, I went to church with my family and listened to a riveting sermon and was made to feel so minuscule in my devotion to God that the guilt overwhelmed me. That, coupled with the stirred feelings that had surfaced from my book, caused me to cry as I sat there in God's house. I had fallen so far away; I needed Jesus to take my hand and direct me back to where I belonged. My mother, hearing my tiny sobs, took my hand and squeezed it gently, giving me a look of love and acceptance. We visited with the members over tea and coffee at the building after the worship service. A few people I recognized made an effort to say hello and to find out how I was and also to encourage me not to stay away for so long again. I honestly did appreciate that. While I walked to where my car parked, I noticed a man getting into his car and knew that I knew him from somewhere but could just not place where. He had a nice face, sharp features, and black hair – not too thick, but with a definite kink in it. He was neatly dressed and relatively tall. I smiled to myself.

After a scrumptious meal delivered as only my mother could deliver, I had a nap for an hour or so. This weekend seemed so surreal to me; I felt as if I had ascended to another plane and become someone completely different. On my way home I stopped off at the beach and soaked up the last few rays of sunshine. I watched the surfers catching a few final waves for the day, and one of them happened to be my brother Brice. He put his board on the ground and before drying off wrapped his big arms around me in an affectionate, marvelous, tight wet goodbye hug. That hug that was given so freely by Brice was the first of its kind between us siblings ever.

'Don't be such a stranger sis, we all miss you.'

His show of affection deeply moved me, and it confounded me after my already emotional last few days, and I had to swallow the lump sitting in my throat before I replied, 'Nope, will make sure of that, you're even going to get sick of me.'

He laughed, and I got awarded another relished hug.

***

It was a long three weeks later before I made a stop at the mall again and popped in at Readers Rest. I went directly to the shelf with my new favorite author's books and purchased two more. The young lady was almost laughing when I presented the books to her to cash up.

'I told you that you would enjoy the book.'

'Oh my gosh! I couldn't put it down, and I have never cried so much in my life. I just haven't been able to get here sooner to get these.'

She presented her hand to me and introduced herself, 'My name is Jayce.'

I introduced myself to her, and we chatted briefly about what I might expect in the next two books, without Jayce giving too much away. Another customer required her attention, and I made a cup of coffee and sat down in the comfortable leather chair. Slowly I opened the pages of one of the books, glancing through it but not reading the ending. The door to the store opened and the man coming in stood aside to allow an elderly lady out of the store before he entered. I remembered him from previously, and it was almost like watching a replay of that day as he retraced his footsteps in the same manner, first to Jayce then to his office. He greeted me as he passed me too. I stood up to leave and said goodbye to Jayce, who quickly came around from behind the counter and handed me a pamphlet.

'It's our programme for the month, we have lots of things going on here all to do with books,' she offered as I read the information.

'Wonderful, thank you!' I replied, having noticed that most of these events happened over weekends.

I knew I would not attend them but did not tell Jayce that.

It was good to be out with my friends for a change. We sat in the non-smokers section of our favorite club and watched people dance and be merry. When we did go out in the evenings, we came here unless we took the trip to Durban, which did not happen very often. Women traveling on the roads at night these days was just too much of a risk for such a long distance. I recognized Jayce and waved and smiled at her when she also recognized me. I also noticed that she was very comfortable with a man more her age and so my theory that she was dating her boss flew out of my thoughts.

I had enjoyed a few dances with the men that had come up to ask me, but never more than two dances in case they got the wrong impression and tried to take it a step further. I had learned this from experience. As I was moving from the dance floor to my seat, I fixed my eyes on the owner of the bookstore. I followed him with my eyes as he walked past several people and into the men's toilets. My eyes remained focused on the toilet door waiting for him to exit it and to follow him again. I was curious as to whether he was going to join Jayce or not. The door opened, and out he walked and headed straight for the bar buying only one drink, then he weaved in between people until he had indeed reached Jayce.

'Uh-huh,' I said to myself, but then I had to mentally slap myself when it was obvious that there was nothing between them as Jayce's complete focus was on her male partner.

A few minutes later after he'd finished his drink, he made for the exit and left. He did look familiar other than from the bookstore, though, but I couldn't think why. My friends and I decided to leave at about one o'clock in the morning. If I'd had my way, I would've been at home reading my book, which I reluctantly had to put down to go out. People were milling about the tables set up just outside of the club and also in the parking lot. Sometimes one had to be very accurate to dodge a drunken person falling over. As I passed a bunch of people, a set of eyes caught mine, and my heart went fluttering out of its shell.

Wow, that has never happened before, I told myself silently.

He smiled, and I blushed as I smiled back.

'Hi,' he said still smiling.

'Hi,' I replied still walking towards my car.

He didn't follow me or try to have a conversation with me, and so I finally got home with that man's eyes drilled into my mind. I wondered, or rather I hoped I would see him again. But when that would be, I didn't know. It was time for my MaxiS country visit, and that meant I was going to be away from home for a few weeks. I sighed and fell asleep.

Chapter Three

The next morning I got to church, missing the announcements and welcoming but just as the first song was being gloriously sung. I slid into the pew and inched my way next to my mother. She smiled as she sang and handed me a songbook, and my dad nodded and smiled continuing to sing as well. I looked around for Brice and eventually saw him sitting with the rest of the young boys and girls to the right of the auditorium. He smiled and offered the tiniest wave of his hand. I giggled at his attempt to stay cool among his peers. As my eyes made their way back to my songbook, they rested upon the man I had seen last night.

It can't be; I thought as my heart thudded in my chest and I kept glancing in the direction of the man I found so intriguing. He, fortunately, was unaware of my constant stares. All day I wondered who he was since as soon as service was over he disappeared and I was too embarrassed to ask Brice or anyone else who he was.

After an uneventful day of doing nothing but relaxing and spending quality time with my parents, I was on my way home again. My mother begged and pleaded with me to be safe during my country visit over the next few weeks. I stopped to say goodbye to Brice at the beach. He was still in the water, so I waited, sitting on a bench and absorbing the wonders of the ocean. When he got out, Brice awarded me with a sublime hug as he had done previously.

I relished every touch, and before getting in my car, he said, 'You must join me at Bible study one evening. It's a fantastic group, some about as old as you,' he snorted, 'and mostly us surfers.'

After a punch on the arm for his sarcastic wit, I replied that I would do so on condition that I had my reports done on time.

'Reports won't get you into Heaven,' he smiled knowing he was right.

As I drove away, I passed a van and, noticing a man packing his board into the back, I gasped, 'No it's him again!'

My heart fluttered mildly, fortunately for me, as I easily could have driven my car into a lamp post with my eyes glued on him instead of the road. All the way home I wondered if Brice perhaps knew him and if he attended the Bible study since he went to church.

***

Well, my curiosity had to wait until I returned from my country trip. Between the towns of Durban and Ladysmith, I only visited two stores a day as they were miles and miles apart hence I was more exhausted from driving rather than shopping. With a tired and sore body, I checked in at a country-style guesthouse in Estcourt and nestled into bed delving immediately into my book; another from the wonderful shelves of Readers Rest. Country trips were not my favorite. As much as the people were friendly, there was something unnerving about them – the trips, not the people. I was completely out of my comfort zone, which was so ridiculous since I was probably safer here than in the city.

There was a nip in the air when I left the guesthouse the next morning and trotted to my car, hurriedly turning on the heater. The first store was fifty kilometers away, and I had another to visit after that. On entering the first store, there was a stifled atmosphere, as though if someone spoke a little higher than a whisper the whole place would explode. I stood in front of the shelf of various detergents when a choir of screams erupted nearby. At first, I thought it was a group of local ladies having an excited conversation, but then I realized the screams were from fear. Another customer who had passed me not too long ago came rushing back to my aisle, which was farthest from the check-out counters and hovered around me. Her eyes were huge, and she was panting, wheezing in fact, and trembling with fear.

'What is going on?' I questioned her.

She shook her head unable to speak. There was a deadly silence in the store; I only heard my whispers to the terror-stricken woman.

A security guard came hastily walking by and said, 'It's okay now. They have gone.'

'Who has gone? What happened?' I questioned again.

The woman burst into a hysterical release of anguish.

'Ma'am, we have just been robbed. The men, there were three of them, went up to the front check-out and held knives to the lady.'

'Did they catch them or are they still near the store?'

The idea of bumping into them made me shudder.

'No, they were caught as they got to their car.'

My hands and knees became very unstable as it dawned on me what had gone down in the store. I had always wondered if this day might ever happen. I had read of similar cases so many times in the papers and heard it on the radio often enough, but somehow I had been confident it would never happen to me. Well now it had, but I was not affected except of course that I had been in the store during the robbery. That was enough to unnerve me and make me cancel my visit to the other store for the day. Exiting the store, people clustered around to watch the paramedics attend to the traumatized cashier. I said a prayer for her once I had locked myself in my car and thanked the Lord no one was physically hurt.

As soon as I reached the guesthouse, I phoned Mr. Bartlett, who was already notified by the store manager of the incident. He, of course, did not know that I had been in the store at the time, and he was horrified when I informed him. And since I was "not employed" by him, it was a risk even answering his phone, but he did so without hesitation. After a lot of convincing, I managed to assure him that I was okay to complete my country trip. For today though I stayed at the guesthouse, calming my festered nerves. I sent my report to Mr. Bartlett who was no different to what I had already told him. Then I phoned my father – telling my mother over the phone was just not a good idea. Fifteen minutes later I had a hysterical, sobbing mother's love pouring down my ear through the phone. She hated my country trips and now even more so. I was reminded by her to thank our Lord for His mercies in sparing everyone's lives. And as soon as I hit the end button on my phone, I did exactly that.

I'd never done it before, but when I reached my hometown after three weeks in the country, thankfully without further incidents, I went straight to my parents' home. The first to greet me was my mother who held me so tightly and did not let me go until my father practically pried her off me. Then he did the same anyhow, and then Brice pulled my father off me so he could have his turn. I had never felt so much love as I did at that very moment. As it was the weekend, I remained at their home, snug as a bug around two doting parents. Mr. Bartlett phoned as soon as he heard I was home safe and sound. I did appreciate his call since my job was so secretive that we never communicated over the phone, and we had spoken twice since the time of the incident. Brice coaxed me out of the house on Saturday afternoon to go with him to the beach, and I teased him that he only wanted a lift from me. It was good to relax and empty my mind at the edge of the ocean.

'Hi,' a voice said behind me, startling me.

I looked around, thrilled to see a dark-haired man with a lovely smile looking at me.

'Hi,' I replied and waited for him to make the next move.

He sat down on the sand next to me.

'I think I saw you at the club a few nights ago.'

It was him!!

I blushed and smiled, 'Yes I think that was me...I saw you at church a few Sundays ago too.'

He looked at me quizzically, 'Uhm, maybe...'

He was friendly and easy to talk to, but I must say my heart did not flutter all over the show as I had expected it would. Perhaps curiosity had killed the cat – satisfaction brought it back, and now the nerves were settled.

'Sorry, I am very rude, my name is Salma Asbury.'

I extended my hand toward him, a little snubbed that he had not introduced himself first. He shook his head.

'Oh my bad, I am so sorry, Lex Conley.'

He offered his hand, and I shook it.

'Wait,' he paused and looked toward the surfers in the ocean, 'Asbury? Are you Brice's sister?'

'Yes. He is a lot younger than me, a "laat lammetjie."'

Lex laughed a little. 'He is a good kid, good surfer, too.'

'Yes, Surfing is his passion.'

The words were hardly out of my mouth when Brice joined us.

'Hey, Lex, what's up?'

He nodded at Lex. I got up and dusted the sand off my bum and legs, Brice waited still holding his board.

'Hope to see you at the club again,' Lex said winking at me as he spoke.

I smile and nodded.

'Sure,' I replied at the same as I listened to Brice's explanation of the waves.

After dropping Brice at home, I closed the car door and let my window down to say another goodbye. He bent down so that he was at my eye level and reminded me that study was on Wednesday night, and I'd "better be there."

Chapter Four

I parked outside Zeke's house and messaged Brice to meet me at the door. I did not particularly enjoy the feeling of walking into homes of people I did not know, especially when it was full of people I did not know. Brice introduced me to the few people that were there. Most of the regulars were unable to make it that night. But of all the people that did attend, one was Lex, and when I smiled at him, he looked sheepishly at me and sent me a gentle smile back. Okay! So that was not the reaction I had expected, perhaps it was because he was deep in conversation with someone. When the study started, he sat for a few minutes behind everyone else and then left. Everyone simply said cheers as he left. I was confused and thought of asking Brice more about him but then reconsidered, Brice was after all only eighteen. Besides that, I thoroughly enjoyed the study and knew I would attend whenever it was possible.

That weekend it was my friend Britley's birthday which called for celebrations at the club we frequented. We sat in our usual corner filling our souls with such laughter that we cried. On my way to the bathroom, Lex obstructed my pathway with a huge smile on his face.

'Hi.'

My heart added a few extra beats to its rhythm.

'Oh, hi.'

'Want to dance?'

He pointed at the dance floor, but I was already doing a little dance of my own – I needed the toilet in a hurry.

'When I come back from the bathroom,' I said hoping he hadn't noticed my urgent need.

'I shall be waiting right here.'

And there he stood as if to attention. He was still waiting there when I finally returned from the bathroom. He sure did deserve a dance for his patience. One dance led to three or four, and after a while, I lost count. We tried to have a conversation above the noise on the dancefloor, but that did not work out too well, so we finally decided to take a seat together. He was introduced to all my friends and made to wish Britley a happy birthday and to buy her a drink – it was done all in good cheer. I found out that he was an architect, had an apartment in town, had two brothers, no sisters and that his parents were still alive. He enjoyed surfing occasionally but mostly loved to have fun; loved extreme, adrenaline pumping sports with his mates. A real man's man I figured. But he seemed to be a nice person, and he made me laugh even if the adrenaline stuff frightened the daylights out of me. By the end of the evening, we had exchanged phone numbers, and I went home looking forward to having Lex as a new friend. Strangely enough, the idea of anything more than that did not excite me as much as I had originally thought it would. I felt confused.

I looked around at church for him the next day, but he was nowhere. I remembered mentioning to him last night that I had seen him the previous Sunday, and he had just shrugged his shoulders. When I'd asked him why he'd left the study so soon, again, he had only shrugged his shoulders. After that, I'd laid off the subject as he clearly did not want to talk about it. Unfortunately, it only peaked my curiosity.

From church, I went to the mall. Now I know I have a hard and fast rule never to go to the malls or shops on weekends, but I had to get my hands on some more books. The leather armchair was waiting for me to sit in it and page through a few books as I made my mind up on which ones to buy. Readers Rest had become my favorite shop. I looked up from my comfy position on the leather chair as the shop door opened and the door chimes jingled. I yelped as I saw double – literally. Lex walked into the shop twice. Lex seemed to have been shocked himself at the look of shock on my face. I opened my mouth to say something but to no avail as it was already open and no words wanted to slide from my lips. Now I knew where I had seen Lex before! Or was it him I saw? Or was it the double?

'Hi, um hi, what you doing here?'

He stumbled over his words still greatly surprised.

'Buying books, having coffee…'

And then I gasped, 'Aaah, you!'

I pointed to the two men standing in front of me, both identical, my heart freaking out, its pounding stabbing a bruise into my ribs. The one that looked like the other one stood with the biggest grin on his face and quickly stretched out his hand.

'Hi, I'm Dax, Lex's twin brother. I'm the one you have seen here.'

I offered my hand.

'That explains a lot. I thought I was hallucinating for a second.'

I looked at Lex, 'You said "brothers" – you never mentioned a twin! Wait, is the other brother also a clone?'

They both laughed, the same laugh with the same movements, it was so weird to watch.

'No. He is older than us,' Lex answered.

In the meantime, Jayce was crying with laughter from behind the counter. Dax retreated to his office while Lex got some coffee and sat in the other armchair. I closed the book on my lap and swallowed my coffee, drowning the flutter of upturned nerves.

'So you're a bookworm?' Lex asked with a smirk.

'Yes. Love books, and you? Do you read?'

'Of course, I read. Everyone has to read; I just don't read books. They're boring.'

'You would prefer to jump off a cliff or something to that fashion I guess?'

'Totally. So what are you doing next weekend?'

'Not planned anything yet. Why?'

'You're coming rock climbing with me. Before you say no – I can see the horror on your face already,' he chuckled, 'you don't have to climb, just come along.'

'Hmm. Okay, but I promise you now I will not climb anything,' I said in a very stern voice, stamping my resolve.

'Okay. Point taken. I will call you in the week then.'

He got up and went to Dax's office.

'Sorry, I laughed so much. Your face was too classic,' Jayce piped up.

'I believe you. That was a scary moment there.'

I had to laugh with her.

'They might look the same, but in personality, they are complete opposites. Dax is the quiet bookworm, and Lex is the extroverted adrenaline junkie.'

'Have you known them long?'

'They're my cousins,' she giggled as she watched all the pennies drop into place in my brain.

I left with my head still reeling from the surprise. When I got to my parents' home, I relayed the episode to them and Brice, much to their amusement. Brice informed me that it was Dax I had seen at church and Bible study. He knew Dax better than he knew Lex although he did not know either of them that well.

Chapter Five

I had to wait until Thursday for Lex to phone me to confirm the date for Saturday but in the interim, I had delved into the world among the pages of my newly purchased books. How much I had missed this passion – and I only realized so now. On Saturday morning, I packed my book in my bag as I left my house to meet Lex and his climbing friends. They can climb; I can read.

I sat on a huge rock observing Lex and his four friends excitedly gear up for what they anticipated being an awesome climb. When Lex had fetched me earlier, and I was introduced to everyone, I thought the only other woman, Shantel, would join me watching them. However, she was the most eager of them all. They all coaxed, begged, pleaded with and bribed me to give it a try. I stood my ground and rejected them all. The rock I was sitting on, me and my book were very content together. They had been gone for hours, and it was baking hot, so I moved from my rock to another one that was shaded at least. When they eventually returned they babbled on and on about the massive rock face they had conquered, mostly to themselves and now and then to me. As if I was in the least bit interested.

Lex dropped me back at my house, and I truly believed that would be our one and only date, but he surprised me by asking me out again – Saturday night at the club. While I soothed my sunburnt skin in a fragrance bubble bath, I wondered why that initial excitement at the thought of him had dissipated. Perhaps it was because we were so different, but maybe once we kissed that feeling would return. I imagined our first kiss – still nothing. It was so strange not to feel anything more than just friendship for Lex after my heart had fluttered so when I'd first seen him. He was handsome, tall, well built and had a lovely manly voice. His eyes were gentle but not as gentle as Dax's eyes. Dax! I wondered what he was like? What kind of date would he offer? Definitely not climbing rocks in the middle of nowhere. They were so identical it was scary, the only way to tell them apart – besides from their interests – was that Dax's lips were slightly fuller. I wondered if he kissed better than Lex. I jumped up from my lazy position in the bath.

What are you thinking? I scolded myself, got out of the bath, made some hot chocolate and settled myself on the couch, forgetting my ridiculous thoughts as I got lost in the world of my book.

I had not heard from Lex by the time Bible study came around again, and I wondered whether our date for Saturday night was still on. Lex was not in the study, but Dax was, and he greeted me with a lovely smile and a "hello" this time. He also did not leave so early. During the evening, we veered off course a little and were discussing how easy it is to step away from the path we walk along with God when we get faced with disappointments. There were a lot of people at the study and the young ones especially – not having experienced much in life yet – listened keenly. Some of the older attendees spoke of tragedies that cast a sad shadow over the room as they struggled to relive their traumatic experiences without completely breaking down. I opened my stupid mouth and told the group about the incident at the store a few weeks ago and how it was possible that the lady who was attacked or that even those around her might easily let go of God's guiding hand because of such an experience.

There was a moment's silence when I had finished speaking before Dax exclaimed, 'What store was this at?'

I suddenly realized this was the first time I had ever spoken about my job in any way to anyone other than my family or Mr. Bartlett and even my family only got tidbits from me. I kicked myself for being so dense.

'It was at a MaxiS Superstore,' I replied hoping the conversation was over with now, and they'd move on to the next person's story, but no, Dax seemed overly curious.

'Where? Where was the store? I have not heard of any robberies in the area.'

Argh! I was so annoyed with myself now.

'In Estcourt.'

'Estcourt!' Dax exclaimed, 'What work do you do that takes you all the way there?'

Now I was very angry at myself.

What do I say to them that isn't a lie? I began to fidget.

'Uhm…I am a rep.'

Dax considered this for a moment, and I was sure he wanted to ask more about my job but Zeke, bless him, moved on to someone else. After we had closed the study with prayer and were enjoying a coffee and I was getting to know a few people, Dax stood himself next to me, and by the look on his face, I feared more questioning concerning my job.

So before he made any attempt, I asked, 'Do you own the bookstore?'

'Yep, I do.'

'It's lovely; I stopped reading for a while and for whatever reason I strolled into yours that day. Well done with it.'

'Why thank you, ma'am,' he proudly replied.

'How long have you had it now?'

'Just over a year. I can't rely solely on the shop for income, so I lecture at the college, which is my proper vocation.'

I was impressed, and it showed when I asked, 'What do you lecture in?'

'English lit.'

If he were a peacock his feathers would be sprayed out in full flare; he was quite proud of himself or of the fact that he had impressed me. I did not mind which.

'Wow, really well done.'

'So, you and my brother?'

He raised his eyebrows in question.

'Me and your brother – nothing. I went with him to the rock climbing thing, and that has been all.'

He smirked and took a sip of his coffee. On my way home I contemplated phoning Lex to confirm Saturday night but stopped myself not wanting to sound desperate. But Lex did phone on Friday night. Wherever he phoned from was a public place, there was so much loud background noise from both people and music. We yelled at each other over the phone having to repeat what we said several times. Trying to get an answer as to where he was would have been too much PT, so I did not bother.

Saturday night arrived and my thick black hair, which matched Lex and Dax's hair almost identically, I tied up loosely leaving a few strands randomly hanging out. I applied a little makeup, just enough to make me look like I had made an effort, put on an emerald green sleeveless lace top – the color of the shirt enhanced my green eyes, and then pulled on my pair of faded jeans. I finished off with my favorite pair of genuine cowboy boots. Boots were perhaps not the best choice in humid Natal, but I loved them and wore them any chance I got.

Lex was already inside when Britley and I arrived. I was nervous but not excited to see him and slightly miffed that I had to look for him, but when he saw me, he did seem pleased that I was there. All his climbing buddies were there too, and they were talking about some new adventure for Sunday involving mountain bikes. No way was I getting roped into this one as there was a wonderful book waiting to get finished – which I could easily be reading right now! And besides, a bike and I had never got on well together. I introduced Britley to everyone amid their conversation then we excused ourselves and went to greet our friends on the opposite end of the club in our usual seats. I sat with them for a while before returning to Lex and his friends. They were still talking about these mountain bikes; it was ridiculous. So I stood next to Lex, silent, not being able to contribute to their enthusiasm in any way. It was, at least, an hour or so later when Lex finally asked me to dance, but by this time I was so bored I had already contemplated leaving a few times. A slow song began. It was our first slow dance, and we link into each other's arms may be both a little shy at first. As the song progressed, we edged closer to each other until our chests were pressed tightly together. He lifted his head and automatically I did the same.

His eyes hooked into mine while his lips without moving, asked the question, 'May I kiss you?'

I tilted my head toward him, and his lips met mine. Our first kiss tenderly happened as we swayed to the music. But it was indifferent. I was indifferent. It was just a kiss; the expected thrill and relish of a first kiss were unfounded. It disappointed me so, but obviously, I did not let it show and finished the dance in his arms. It was a long, tedious night either spent in the company of Lex's friends or on the dancefloor with him, but all the time I preferred to either be with my friends or even better – at home with my book. I kissed Lex goodbye when the evening finally ended and left without the promise of another date; I was so relieved.

Chapter Six

The following Wednesday Lex called and asked me out again. He had to leave me a message as I was unable to answer the phone in time. I thought about it for the rest of the afternoon and, in the end, decided to give it another go. Perhaps if we were alone, without the company of his friends, it might be better I reasoned with myself. So Friday night we would be going to Rafiki's for dinner.

The next day it was time to investigate the store at our mall. I was so happy I could get to Readers Rest again and buy some more books. By the time I got there, it was four in the afternoon because my day got delayed by a major accident on the N2. I got out of my car, grabbed my bag and hurriedly walked to the store. Since the bookstore closed earlier than the MaxiS, I quickly dashed in there first. Jayce was as always like a breath of fresh air, and happy to see me. We chatted briefly about new books that were delivered that week and then I went to my favorite shelf to browse. I was turning a book over and over, reading the description and looking at the cover when a tap on my shoulder interrupted my thoughts.

'Not read that so I cannot recommend it, but buy it, in any case, I need the sales.'

'Haha, Dax, funny!'

I laughed and put the book back on the shelf. Dax pulled a sad face, and I chuckled then took the book back off the shelf and got rewarded with a happy face. I could not resist the temptation to put the book back on the shelf to see if he would put the sad face on again. He did, and so I took the book off the shelf again, and his happy face returned. We went on and on until I was unable to lift the book from laughing so much. Jayce was lying with her head on the counter crying with laughter. I paid for my book amid fits of giggles and snorts from the three of us. I should have received a discount purely for the entertainment.

Trotting to the MaxiS store much, much later than I had planned and occupied by our amusing little episode in the bookstore, a smile stuck to my face; I was oblivious to everyone around me. I entered the store and wandered down the first aisle that my feet took me to. Suddenly there was a huge commotion. I heard lots of screaming coming from deep male voices and in return many high-pitched female shrieks. The men's voices were barking out orders, and I spun around on my heels to see what horror was before me. The men were running around herding people to the ground, jabbing them with their guns. Men, women, and children sank to the supermarket floor. I froze in fear and terror just long enough for one of the gunmen to run up to me and knock me down to the ground. It hurt so badly I started to cry which seemed to infuriate the already enraged man. He yelled at me, hurling all sorts of abuse – about me being a woman and what he would do with me if I did not listen to him. I shook in horror and tried to stifle my crying in case it set him off again. A woman close to me was hysterical, and the man turned on her kicking her with his foot. Some of the gunmen went to the cashiers, yanking them up out of their chairs at their stations and forcing them to open their tills as they filled bags with money. I tried to count how many men there were and I got as far as fifteen before I had to stop for my head was lifting too high off the ground.

A few of the men were forcing the manager to the office, and when he didn't walk quickly enough they hit him over the head with a gun, and he fell to the ground bleeding. They forced him up again, holding a gun to his head. I looked at the store entrance and saw that more armed men were guarding the entrance. The alarms were shrieking out adding to the deafening chaos, and before long the sirens of the entire police force were heard tearing their way to the mall.

When the men finished with the tills, they made their way to all the people lying on the ground and demanded their personal belongings – cell phones, wallets, jewelry and anything else they deemed theirs to take. The same man that had hit me earlier bent over me and grabbed my bag, ripping at my arm at the same time. I felt excruciating pain as a bone clicked in my shoulder, and I cried out in agony, unable to stop myself. The man yanked at my bag until it was free and I screamed in utter pain and terror as he hit me hard on my back with his gun. It was all that I could bear, and I begged him to stop, which only seemed to encourage him more. He was about to take another swipe at my back when there was another big commotion, this time at the entrance to the store. I lay there crying and praying that God would end this and that He would spare the lives of the innocent people.

I prayed despite the pain searing through my body, *Oh please, Lord help us, please.*

I begged God to stand between these men and the innocent people. Suddenly the loudest and most horrifying sound I had ever heard echoed through the store. It was a terrifying sound, and as soon as one gun went off, it seemed as though an explosion of ammunition had gone off when the gunmen fired at the police. More cries for help and screams of fear were let loose from us terrified people at the mercy of these madmen. Mayhem ensued; gunfire, shouting, screaming, yelling, more gunfire, glass shattering, things breaking, feet running – all at the same time. Suddenly there was what seemed to be a scramble for cover and a whooshing noise, and then there was smoke everywhere, and my eyes burned insanely. A scurry of footsteps, more shouting and then all at once there was a lot of quiet. I lay dead still firstly because I was so terrified and yet calm and secondly because it hurt too much to move. I waited for the next sound or for the crazed man to come and attack me again. I lay on the cold floor and prayed to God. I groaned as my shoulder throbbed against the floor; the sudden silence was deafening. I tried to lift my head enough to see what was happening but even if I had been able to, my eyes were stinging and watering so intensely I had no vision.

I remained on the cold floor praying, praying that God would protect me and the others that had unwittingly got included in this anarchy. Different voices were drifting between us now. They were gentle and compassionate, and a hand touched me, and I groaned, and immediately the voice yelled for a medic. He was here to help; help had come, help had won over the bad guys. I was so overwhelmed I burst into a spurt of hysterical sobs. The kind voice left me and another voice, a woman's voice, this time, assured me it was all over and that she was going to help me. There was someone with her, a man, and together they turned me over. A burst of pain shot through my body, and I shouted out loud pleading with them to stop. The lady injected me with something to help with the pain, and at the same time, they started to secure my neck in a brace. I could only weep. I was lifted onto a gurney; the painkillers had begun to do their work, and as I was being wheeled out of the mall among hordes of bystanders I heard my name getting called out repeatedly. There was a bit of a scuffle when the person calling my name was prohibited from reaching me, but he got his way and before I was pushed into the ambulance his hand gripped mine.

'Salma, Salma it's me, Dax. You're going to be okay. You have to be okay; you hear me? You have to give me a chance to steal you from my brother! Salma…Salma…'

I floundered in darkness hoping that I had heard him correctly.

Chapter Seven

The doctor stood beside me and informed of my broken shoulder blade, fractured collarbone, a few cracked ribs and just for good measure, some internal bruising. But more than the injuries everyone was concerned about shock. I had been through a horrific ordeal and would need help getting over it. I tried to listen but I was drowsy, and my head was pounding so instead I started to cry, which was not what I wanted to do, I wanted to sleep. He left me alone with strict instructions to the nursing staff to carefully screen any visitors. The last thing I needed was a headline-seeking journalist at my bedside.

I had slept for two days. Naturally, it must have been a drugged induced sleep but who cared, I had managed to sleep without much pain. The first person to visit me according to a nurse was a gentleman named Dax. She went on to tell me that he had followed the ambulance and had remained at the hospital until I was back from the operating theatre and he knew I was going to be okay. Dax was also the one who had phoned Brice to inform my parents of what had happened. I knew my mother would have become hysterical and probably collapsed, which later on I found out was what had occurred. Dax had visited twice every day since the incident. The next person to visit other than my parents and Brice had been Mr. Bartlett. Those were the only people who were allowed to see me. Britley and my other friends had been to the hospital but were not permitted into my room. The nurse explained very sweetly to me that they could not take the risk that one of them would run to the media. I appreciated their efforts.

I tried to move but gave up almost straight away sensing the pain. I thought of Dax and how diligently he had been at my side, and a warm fuzzy feeling floated over me. I wondered if it had perhaps been Lex that was here, and since they were so identical, the nurse had only presumed it was Dax.

I smiled at the funny memory of the bookstore moment, just before I had entered the war zone. I shuddered at the realization of what could have happened, and once I could talk without crying, I enquired as to whether any other people in the store were injured. There had been several casualties, and sadly one had been fatal. My face was instantly wet with tears, and I prayed to God for comfort for the victim's family. While praying, I tried to keep the visuals of the attack out of my head, but it was difficult. How was I going to keep them at bay and not allow them to turn me into a nervous wreck?

I slept on and off for most of the day until Mr. Bartlett arrived at 3 o'clock for visiting hours. I detected that his eyes were watery, and he had to swallow hard before he was able to say anything to me. He had me holding the sheet over my face to try and combat the overflow of emotion and hysteria that had been building up inside of me.

He cleared his throat once more then said, 'Salma, I am so sorry, I would never be able to live with myself if anything fatal had happened to you.'

'It's not your fault and how were you to know this would happen?' I croaked.

'After the last incident, I should have pulled the plug.'

'Pulled what plug?' I was confused.

'This position of investigator. I have retracted the position, and I have something safer and more stable for you if you're still willing to stay with the company.'

'Why did you do that?'

'Why?' he exclaimed. 'Who is to say this is the last time this kind of thing is going to happen? I am not taking the risk, not for any of my staff. Life is not worth it.'

As much as I tried to convince myself he was speaking the truth, I wanted so badly not to be so weak as I lay there sobbing helplessly. Mr. Bartlett sat in the chair next to my bed and held my hand allowing me to release the waterworks freely.

When I had calmed down, he said, 'I have a new position for you, working with me in an advisory capacity.'

Okay, so this was strange. How could I advise him, he was a director?

'I have created the position very much like we did with your investigator position and it will be the same except you will be working from the office, and it will not be such a secret.'

I found myself breathing a sigh of relief as now I did not have to lie to Dax about my job. I also found it strange that I was only concerned about lying to Dax. When my parents arrived, Mr. Bartlett left and promised to discuss things further with me once I was discharged from the hospital. I knew immediately I would take the job with him, there was no one I would rather work with than him especially now after he had made such a concerted effort to create the new position for me.

The doctor popped by when my parents were there, and we were all told that should I not have any complications I would be able to go home on Friday. My mother insisted I move back home where she could faff over me until I was ready to go home and fend for myself once more. With the doctor egging her on I had no hope of getting myself out of it, and actually, I was quite looking forward to her pampering. The doctor also started talking about the importance of therapy after such an episode. I knew I would have my parents backing him up on this so I promptly cut him off by thanking him for his suggestions of several therapists and said I would rather seek therapy from my God and my fellow Christians. As soon as Brice arrived that evening, I asked him to speak to Zeke for me – to have therapy sessions with someone that loved the Lord as much as he did was the perfect solution.

Later when my family had left, and I was almost asleep, a light tapping on the door made my eyelids lift. Dax – or Lex? – was standing in the doorway.

'Hey Salma, how you?'

It was Lex. My heart sank.

'Hi,' I replied softly, 'come in, please. Sit down.'

The nurse walked past my room and doubled back sticking her head into the doorway.

'Only a few minutes, sir. Salma needs her rest okay.'

Lex nodded and returned his attention to me. He shook his head unsure of what to say next.

'You doing okay? You need anything?'

'I'm okay thanks. How're you?'

He shook his head again. Something was bothering him I was sure of it. Perhaps he was not a hospital kind of person.

'Better than you that's for sure,' he half smiled at me.

'Well, thanks!'

I tried to laugh, but it hurt too much.

'How was the mountain bike ride?'

He nodded. 'It was great. When can you get out of here?'

'Hopefully on Friday.'

'You okay?' I asked as he seemed out of sorts. 'If you don't like hospitals I understand, you don't have to be here.'

He looked at me oddly, 'Why would you say that?'

'Most men don't like hospitals and situations like this. I just thought maybe you were uncomfortable here.'

As I spoke I closed my eyes; I was getting really tired.

'Well, that is true. But I wanted to see for myself that you were doing okay and not only take Dax's word for it.'

My eyes found a surge of energy to open. 'Dax's word?'

'Well, you know he has been here since you arrived and well, you know, he has a thing for you.'

I didn't reply and only stared at him.

'Yeah, I can see it from a mile away and let's face it, the two of you are far more suited to each other and from what Jayce has told me you have a thing for him too.'

'What?' I asked shocked.

Lex laughed.

'That Jayce might be young and beautiful, but she is very sharp and observant.'

By now I must have been beetroot from embarrassment.

'Listen Salma, we're good right, we're friends and as much as I do like you, I know we would date a few times, and that will be it. So I'm asking you to give my poor brother a chance. He has never dated much, but I must say I have never seen his face light up like it does when he talks about you.'

I had no idea what to say between a headache that was forming, and the tiredness that was taking over, and absorbing this load of information was too much even if it was what I precisely wanted to hear. All I did, instead of replying to Lex, was burst into tears. The nurse was in the room in a flash and shooed Lex out sternly. She gave me a few tablets and comforted me until I dozed off but not before I set the record straight that I wasn't getting dumped, but that Lex was the bearer of good news.

<u>Chapter Eight</u>

The morning rounds were finally over, and I was packed and ready to go home. My parents arrived promptly, and once home I was tucked into bed and banned from leaving it until much later in the afternoon. Zeke came to visit, and we spoke about doing therapy sessions that he was willing to do, but only after he had given it to God in prayer and asked for guidance. Instantly I knew I had made the right decision with Zeke. Just before dinner, Dax arrived to check up on me. My parents asked him to stay, and he gladly accepted. During dinner, he explained that he had been away for a few days at a conference for the college, which was why he had not visited the hospital lately. My father was interested in all this and threw Dax question after question. My mother and I sat quietly and listened as if we weren't even there.

After dinner Dax and I sat on the back stoep of the house. I was wrapped up in a warm blanket, and the wicker chair stuffed with extra cushions and pillows for my comfort. It was a perfect, still and warm evening, only the crickets dared to break the tranquillity. We sat in silence for a while then we discussed my upcoming therapy, and I knew that the biggest therapy I needed was to tell Dax what my job had really been. The secrecy of my job had never bothered me until now until I knew that I never wanted to lie to Dax.

'I have something I need to tell you,' I started, and Dax looked at me curiously as I began my confession.

Well, it felt like a confession. He listened quietly, and when I finished, I sighed.

'I know God guided me to Readers Rest that afternoon. I know that now,' I smiled at him.

'How do you know that?'

I knew what I wanted to say was, "Because He led me to you," but I was too shy to be so bold, so I just shrugged my shoulders that then hurt, and I winced from the pain.

'Hey are you okay, is sitting out here too much for you?'

I smiled again, 'No that was my stupidity, trying to use my shoulders too much; I'm fine, I like it out here it's so peaceful.'

'Just kick me out if I overstay my welcome.'

'Don't worry; my mother will do that when she deems it necessary.'

We both laughed, or rather I smiled as it still hurt too much to laugh.

'But before I do get kicked out, I must tell you something,' he paused contemplating or choosing his next words carefully and I, if I could have seen properly in the dim light, am sure he was blushing.

'Lex told me about your little conversation the other day.'

'Oh! Uhm, okay…' I did not know where to take the rest of the conversation, so I left it hanging - Dax continued.

He looked at the ground as he spoke, 'Well it is all true.'

Then he looked at me. I'm sure he did not know what to expect, but he did get the hugest smile that wrapped around my face.

'I am very pleased to hear that. I was praying it was true.'

He giggled a little and picked up my hand, taking it in his. A perfect fit. His eyes sank deep into mine as he leaned forward and placed his strong lips on mine, sending my body into a tingling fit from pure delight. He placed his free hand gently on my cheek, securing my face in his grasp. His lips parted mine, and I wanted to disappear into his kiss forever. A passionate and loving kiss that was to be repeated for many, many years to come. Even when we had become old, and grey and my joints felt as sore as they did on that day – not from injury but old age – our kiss would still tickle my senses and send me into a frenzy of wanting more from him.

***

How does God protect you each day? He sends us on paths that will help us when the time comes, and He puts people in our lives that will be there for us when we need them most. When the time comes for us to have to deal with ordinary traumas like death and illness, or when we get forced into dangerous situations, God is always there for us. Call out His name, and He will hold your hand. The outcome might not always be what you desire, but if you leave it in God's hands, it will be God's outcome, and somewhere in the future, you will discover that. When trying to deal with trauma in your life, why not go to the Creator of all things, the One who loves you more than any human ever could? Why not let God be your therapist? He is the best therapist of them all.

WHERE

WE

MEET

Where we Meet

Chapter One

I dashed into the convenience store for water while the attendant filled my car with the necessary fuel. My thirst was at its limit, and I still had, at least, half an hour's drive to the airport. I stood impatiently in the queue to pay for my one bottle of water. The lady in front of me insisted on giving the exact amount required and fiddled with all her coins until she had finally paid. Then she took her merry time putting the leftover coins back into her purse one by one, battling to pick them up with her long nails. The line behind me was getting longer, and as I presumed most of the people had come in while their cars were being filled up, the service station was now congested with unattended vehicles.

Behind me, a young man had his arms filled with goodies and a young boy. The boy was restless and fidgeted with everything on display at the check-out point that was within his reach, and when he was bored with that, he attacked the sunglasses perched on my head. I felt them move and automatically grabbed for them with my free hand and turned around. The child could not have been more than a few years old, not that I was an expert, and the young man must have been in his mid-twenties. He blushed with embarrassment and offered some apologies, at the same time moving the child from within grabbing distance of anything else. I merely smiled, accepted his apology and made idle chatter with the little boy. He had such a mischievous face and the cutest but naughtiest smile – it was easy to tell he was a handful on a good day. Finally, I was able to pay for my water, and in doing so, I bade the man and the boy goodbye and dashed back to my car. By the time, I had reached the exit of the service station I had finished the water.

Thanks to a major accident on the highway, which caused a huge traffic jam and thus a very long delay in my travel time, I barely made it to the check-in counter at the airport in time. The result of this inconvenience meant that I got whatever seat was left on the flight and who knows next to who I would land up sitting. I was the last passenger on the flight but in front of me was the man from the convenience store, with the little boy. I realized they would also have been caught up in the traffic jam, but somehow they had managed to get ahead of me. The boy recognized me and smiled as I walked behind them into the plane and walked down the aisle between the rows of seats right to the back. They were seated in the back too as they also kept on walking. My heart sank as I realized they were my companions for the next two hours. That's what you get when you arrive at the last minute and cannot choose the seat you want! The man smiled at me, probably thinking the same thing. He settled the boy in the middle seat, and he took the window seat. I had hoped he would put the child at the window. I had the aisle seat, and we were in the very last row of the plane.

'Hi. So we meet again,' he said when we were finally all strapped in and ready for take-off.

'Yes, we do. I suppose you also got caught in the traffic on the highway?'

'That's why we're in these seats,' he smiled as he spoke, 'my name is Callum, and this little fellow is Logan.'

'Hello Logan,' I smiled at him, and his eyes glinted back mischievously.

I turned to Callum, 'Hi Callum, I'm Skye.'

'Bet you get teased a lot,' Callum grinned.

'You have no idea how much, so please don't add to it.'

'Sorry, I can't promise that.'

I was grateful the flight was only two hours if it meant I would be teased for a name my parents thought I would enjoy having my entire life. I ordered a very expensive bottle of water from the stewardess and Callum placed his order while I was already opening the bottle. Logan reached over me to grab his packet of chips and kindly knocked over the bottle. The water rushed out onto my lap, drenching my jeans and my top. Logan, unperturbed at his clumsiness, ripped open the packet with such force that the chips landed all over the floor. All this happened in a matter of seconds. Callum took the chips away from the screaming child and tried to salvage what he could to appease him and to get him to stop screaming. In the meantime, I tried to dry my clothes with a tissue. I had a very important audition to attend in Durban and what impression would these wet clothes make? I had no others to change into either. I was very annoyed, and it showed all over my face.

'Logan just stop it and eat your chips,' Callum pleaded until eventually, he bought another packet which shut Logan up.

The stewardess gave me another bottle of water for free and offered me a towel to dry off as much water as possible.

'I am so sorry,' Callum apologized to me a good few times, clearly very embarrassed.

'Logan, tell Skye you are sorry for bumping over her water.'

'No,' Logan defiantly replied every time.

'Please just leave it,' I said wanting to tell him his child had no manners at all, but I managed to swallow the words.

Callum stared out of the window, and I was grateful for the last thing I wanted to do now was have a conversation with him. Logan kicked his legs non-stop while eating his chips and our chairs were jolted with every kick. It was just not possible for him to sit still. I did not mind an active child, but a child that was cheeky and insolent was not something I easily tolerated. I bit my tongue to prevent myself from reprimanding him.

'Logan, stop kicking,' Callum said and put his hand on Logan's legs to still them.

'No!' he screamed and threw his chip packet on the floor, spilling the last few chips that brought on a forced cry and an even louder scream.

Callum picked up the chips and the packet once more while Logan's screaming continued. I sensed the rest of the passengers were annoyed by now, probably all wondering why this father was unable to control his unruly child. Logan stood up on the seat and began to stomp his feet, jumping up and down in between the stomping. I couldn't take it anymore.

'Stop it now!' I yelled at him with a "do not cross me" expression on my face.

Logan hesitated for a second contemplating how far he thought he might be able to push me and as he lifted his leg to initiate another round of stomping I said very sternly, 'Sit down now.'

My finger pointed at him almost touching his nose, and my eyes shot spears at him.

'Callum, naughty aunty,' he reached over to Callum with his arms and sat in his lap cowering away from me.

'Sorry about this. I don't know what to do with kids. He's my nephew and as you can see he is very spoilt. He was visiting my parents in Cape Town, and I am chaperoning him back to my sister in Westville. As much as I love him, I have never been in his company for longer than a few hours, so I have no idea what to do with him.'

I felt sorry for Callum when I realized he wasn't the father. He was embarrassed at Logan's behavior, but at the same time I was annoyed and frustrated, so I accepted his apology and remained silent for the rest of the flight. Logan sat on Callum's lap, and if he so much as moved a muscle, he got a glare from me. When the seatbelt sign came on Callum, put him in the seat by the window rather than next to me. He was very intrigued by the sights outside the plane and kept quiet during the landing.

On the way out of the airport, Callum walked passed me and said goodbye, apologizing again for Logan's behavior. I smiled and greeted him back, grateful I would never see either of them again. I had a headache and hoped that the hot Durban weather would dry off my clothes by the time I reached the studio for my audition.

Chapter Two

I stood in the center of the white studio grateful my clothes had dried out almost completely and that the people in charge of the auditions were understanding, if not rather amused as to why I looked as if I had peed my pants. My head still ached making it difficult to concentrate on giving the audition my best shot. I had studied the lines I'd been given to read, but every time I looked up, a sharp pain stabbed through my eye causing me to squint and grimace. The piece I was reading was a happy section and a frown on my face would certainly throw out my chance of getting the part. After a few trial runs by myself in the waiting room, I figured if I moved my head slightly to the left instead of up there was no pain. I mentally smacked Logan for putting me under such unnecessary stress.

'Go ahead,' the lady said from the back of the studio.

I cleared my throat and went ahead with the reading, with the pain a constant reminder not to look upward. I pulled off what I felt was a good audition, full of expression and with pauses at just the right moments. I felt confident when I finished even if my head was still throbbing.

'Thank you,' the same lady said, and I thanked them back and left.

As I exited the waiting room and was walking towards the elevator, I heard a scream coming from the adjoining studio. My head wanted to burst from the high-pitched sound waves pulsating through it. I shuddered and pressed the button for the elevator hoping it would not take ages to fetch me. While I waited, the studio door opened, and Logan came running down the narrow corridor at top speed.

'Good grief, no, this is not possible...' I muttered aghast.

'Wow. Hi Skye, third time we meet in one day,' Callum said with a huge grin while rushing passed me to catch Logan before he wreaked havoc in the building.

'Well, I think you are following me around. I thought you were taking him to your sister's?'

'After I'm finished here, which was probably a bad idea in the first place, this child is so busy and loud.'

'And naughty!' I added.

'Yes, that too. So what are you doing here?' he asked while struggling to keep Logan in his arms.

I gave Logan one of my stares. It was easy to look very stern as the pain from my headache enhanced the seriousness on my face. He took one look at me and calmed down, probably remembering what had happened on the airplane.

'I need to learn how to make those evil eyes. Maybe then I would hang around with him a bit more.'

'He's the reason I have a pounding headache, so he deserves the evil eyes,' I said as I rubbed my forehead trying to erase the pain stretched across my brows.

'So you still haven't answered my question?'

'I had an audition in Studio Five. What are you doing here?'

'I had a meeting with the sound engineers for the same project that you auditioned. I work freelance for them.'

'You're going to be working on the movie?'

The surprise showed on my face.

'Yes, why does that sound so surprising?'

'I don't know. It's a Christian production. I didn't think you were a Christian…' I trailed off.

'Well that is not very good now, is it? I guess I'd better work on my people skills.'

'No, sorry I'm rude. Please don't listen to anything I say. I'm probably the worst example right now. Sorry.'

I felt so rude and so bad for judging him. I was not in a good mood, and, therefore, reviewed everyone in a negative light. I did not know him from a bar of soap so who was I to judge him?

'I have another hour or so before I leave so how about I buy you an apology coffee?'

He had that same mischievous grin Logan had, clearly a genetic trait.

'As long as I can get painkillers to go with it,' I said stepping into the elevator and turning to face the doors, watching Logan try to press every button before Callum moved to the back eliminating anything from his reach.

'I hope the painkillers are for your head and not Logan.'

'Don't make me laugh, it hurts,' I laughed rubbing my eyes.

Before I ordered anything, I begged the waitress to bring me a glass of water so that I could swallow the pills I had bought at the store next door, and I prayed that the pain would ease quickly.

If job titles had looks, then Callum looked more like a painter than a sound engineer. He seemed to be a gentle person with a good sense of humor. His smile enhanced his deep-set green eyes. His mop of pitch black hair sloppily shaped around his oval face, and his fashion sense matched his sloppy hair.

The waitress brought some paper and crayons to keep Logan occupied, along with his milkshake. It was not even a minute, and the milkshake was spilled all over the paper and Logan himself, which sent him into a very loud tantrum. I held my head in my hands in case it exploded. Callum took him to the bathroom while the waitress cleaned the table and removed the paper and crayons. I apologized on behalf of Logan and explained that he did not belong to either of us. Then I ordered another milkshake. When they returned, I could see that Callum was highly annoyed and frustrated. He was not used to having a child around him, let alone a spoilt one like Logan.

'So how come you got the task of being chaperon?'

'He was supposed to stay with my parents for another week, but they could not handle him anymore. He has been with them for a month, and they are exhausted. My parents are in their late seventies so having a busy young boy that does not know how to listen was too much for them. When they heard I was flying up today, they grabbed the opportunity to send him home earlier. Can't say I blame them, I've had him for less than a day, and I've had enough already.'

Logan sat still and drank his milkshake and for that very brief time if anyone had seen him they might have thought him to be a perfectly well-behaved little boy – but only for that very short time.

'Are there any brothers or sisters?'

'No just him. My sister struggled to have children so when he came along, well, it was truly a blessing that turned into a nightmare. She cannot have anymore so this little fellow is all they have. I don't know how they will deal with him when he's older, he's three now and is already impossible.'

I had an image of Logan in his late teens sitting in the headmaster's office for the umpteenth time, on the verge of expulsion for his behavior. I smiled ruefully. Our time was up quicker than expected and we both had to be on our way. We exchanged contact numbers and left the coffee shop.

My head still pounding, I rested it gently against the headrest of the plane's seat and prayed that I had done enough to get a callback. I thought about seeing Callum again and how nice it would be to work with him on set. Very nice indeed!

Chapter Three

My voice was exhausted from repeating itself over and over again in the voice over studio. It was not where I wanted to be, but since the role I'd auditioned for in Durban had not come my way, I had to be grateful for whatever work did. Still, I sullenly wondered if that big break would ever come my way.

I collapsed onto my couch not bothering to put even the TV on. My head found a comfortable spot on the cushion, and I closed my eyes searching for sleep. Much to my annoyance, a "doof doof doof" sound bounced off the walls, and I knew that the sleep I so desired was not going to happen anytime soon. My neighbors were a bunch of students that love to party almost every night. However, there were never any complaints as the all the residents of the apartment building joined in and had the best student years of their lives. I was the odd one out in the building, simply because I was the only one that was not a student and worked for a living. Sometimes I went to the parties, and for an hour or two I had a bit of fun, but it always ended up the same – the smoke-choked my throat and trying to keep up a conversation with a drunken twenty-something was impossible.

Tonight I chose to stay home and nurse my sullen mood. There was another reason for my downcast mood, and perhaps it was more this than work – I had not heard from Callum since we'd said goodbye to each other in Durban. It bothered me why he had taken my number if he had no intention of using it. And what irritated me more was that I liked him, even if I had only known him for a few hours.

My mother had made it her mission to find her twenty-five-year-old daughter a husband. She had set me up with more dates than I could remember but they'd all failed after the first attempt. Even the young men at church failed to make an impression on me. It was not that I had exceptionally high standards or a peculiar taste or that there was anything wrong with the males in my world, there was simply no enthusiasm from me. With Callum, I thought that might all change, but I guess I thought wrong.

One morning on my way to the studio where I would repeat myself over and over again, my phone rang, and since there was a cop car behind me, I thought it best to let the call go to voicemail. Sitting in the parking lot before getting out of my little old Ford I listened to the voice message.

'Skye, this is Jeska, please phone me as soon as you get this message. I have a terrific audition lined up for you.'

I returned her call immediately, 'Hi Jeska.'

'Oh Skye, I have a fantastic audition for you. There is a huge international production happening here in Cape Town at the new studios and lucky for you I know most of the local directors and producers on a personal level. I've sent them your résumé, and you have an audition next week Wednesday.'

'Oh really, really? Oh Jeska, how perfect that will be for me, maybe this will be my big break at last. But it's unfair to all the other women auditioning for the part if you've arranged it already.'

'Oh no my dear, I've only put in a good word for you and they might take special notice of you, but nothing is a given. You'll have to fight for the part as much as any other woman. I've sent you an email with the part you will have to read as well as all the audition details. Good luck Skye, I know this part will be perfect for you.'

When I got the email from Jeska during my lunch break I read through it and immediately knew that she was right, this role was perfect for me. I just had to get it. I had such a difficult afternoon trying to concentrate on what I was supposed to be saying when all I wanted to do was learn the lines for the audition.

At home, I studied and studied the part and did the same whenever I had even a moment free. I threw myself into the character of the woman I hoped to play. Even the parties at my neighbors' apartments did not deter me from perfecting the part.

When the day of the audition finally arrived I woke up nervous, but a good nervous, a positive nervous. I walked between the huge ominous buildings of Faure Studios, feeling minute and insignificant. My long mauve skirt fluttered with the breeze that blew through the alley as I pushed passed people. People carrying props, people carrying papers and files, people hurrying, running, walking slowly, some driving in carts or riding bicycles or even mopeds, and, all in all, it was a truly fascinating hive of activity.

I reached Studio Two and opened the small door cut out of the huge sliding door almost the size of the studio's front wall. When I arrived in the audition room, I sat next to an old lady and wondered why she would be auditioning for the role of a twenty-two-year-old. I greeted her with a pleasant smile and looked at the other ladies also waiting. They were all elderly. Was I in the right studio? Quickly I reached for the confirmation email in my bag and checked the details. I had it wrong! This audition was for the role of the mother, and my audition was for the next day – it was only Tuesday! Blushing like an idiot and knowing now why I'd been given such strange looks when I'd walked in, I laughed and hurriedly disappeared from the room feeling stupidly foolish.

It was a long evening trying to pass the time, so much so that I eventually went to visit my noisy neighbor for a few hours. The usual bunch of young men and women occupied the small apartment, talking more and more rubbish the more alcohol they consumed. By ten o'clock I'd had enough and left. I watched a movie on TV to pass the time and finally fell asleep in the wee hours of the morning.

Chapter Four

With a feeling of déjà vu, I made my way from my car to the audition studio dodging people, objects and things that moved with little motors. Cautiously I opened the door to the studio, praying I did not have the wrong day again. It was the right day thank goodness, as I looked at the young women anxiously waiting to impress the producers. While I was mentally running through the lines for the umpteenth time, the lady I'd reported to on arrival called my name and told me to proceed to the audition room. I introduced myself to the two women sitting on large comfortable chairs behind a desk.

'Hello Ms. Porter, my name is Paula, please proceed,' the woman with huge purple hair said with a smile.

I adopted the expression I'd been working on and got my mind into the role I was meant to play. When I finished, I took a deep breath, blew it out slowly, lifted my head and smiled at the two women across from me. They were both still watching me which I hoped was a good sign. I waited on the spot marked with an X as they simultaneously looked down at their papers and wrote notes. The lady with the purple hair got up and took a few short steps to the urn with her glass, filled it up with water and returned to her seat.

'Thank you, Ms. Porter, that was well done.'

'Thank you for this opportunity,' I said earnestly and left the room.

When I was outside the huge studio and in the alley, I did a little jig, squealing ever so loudly. I was so happy it had gone so well I just had to get the excitement out of me.

'You get the part?' I was interrupted by a male voice, bringing my exuberance to an abrupt halt.

I turned bright red as I recognized the man's face.

'Callum, what are you doing here?'

It was his turn to blush as he looked at his feet and then into my eyes almost as if pleading. I was so extremely happy to see him I forgot how disappointed I was not having heard from him.

'I'm so sorry I haven't been in touch. When I got to my sister's house with Logan, he got hold of my phone and flushed it down the toilet! I managed to recover most of my contacts but a few, yours included, were lost. I thought of finding you on Facebook but realized I didn't even know your surname.'

He stood still, fiddling with his hands as he continued his confession sheepishly, 'Then I heard about this audition, and I knew it would be a role you'd love, so I found out when it was and have been skulking around here hoping to bump into you. And here we are.'

He laughed a little apprehensively and motioned with his hands confirming that I was, in fact, standing in front of him. I stared at him for a few moments not quite believing my good fortune.

My face colored, and I laughed before replying, 'Uhm, so I wonder if I should be happy that you stalked me or if I should make a run for it now? I hear a lot of crazy stories about stalkers.'

I couldn't help laughing, taking the seriousness of stalking completely out of the threat.

'You doing anything now, or can we go for coffee?'

'Coffee will be super.'

'But before we go anywhere please give me your number again…'

He stopped and got his phone out of his pocket ready to tap in the numbers.

As I repeated my number and my surname he asked, 'Why did you not contact me?'

'Let's get coffee, and we can put all our cards on the table.'

There was a quaint restaurant on the studio premises, and we made ourselves comfortable at a table near the entrance. It was almost full as lunch hour was upon us.

'Honestly, I did not think you were serious about staying in touch with me and that you only took my number to be kind.'

When I looked at him, he had a look on his face that immediately made me regret my actions.

'I wish you'd contacted me; you'd have saved me many, many sleepless nights. I gather men "play the field" as they say, but I'm not one of those men. Maybe I'm old-fashioned or boring, but when it comes to dating, I take it seriously. I've been hurt too many times to be cruel to a woman.'

I wanted to hug him so badly. Was this the man of my dreams or what?

Before we left the restaurant, we had accepted each other as friends on Facebook, had taken a selfie and uploaded it to an album on our profiles and had even given the albums the same name. Since he would be working on the production I had auditioned for, I prayed and prayed my audition was successful; if not for the lead role then for any role just so that we could be together as much as possible.

The following two weeks I checked my emails almost every half an hour and pounced on my phoned when it rang in the hope that it was Jeska with good news. Callum visited every evening, and on weekends when he was not working, we spent time exploring the beautiful Cape. He was adventurous and excited about discovering new places and enjoyed visiting old historic sites. There was never a dull moment when he was around unless he was sleeping. It was not long before we declared our love for each other.

I still worked in the voice over studio and one Friday at lunch I switched my phone on to check for messages. There was one from Jeska – I had to call her back immediately.

'Hello Jeska,' I nervously said when she answered.

'Did I or did I not tell you-you were perfect for the part?'

'Jeska don't tease me, please, tell me!' I pleaded.

'Oh yes my dear, yes you did it. You got the lead role! I am so happy for you!' she almost shouted over the phone, thrilled on my behalf.

I did my happy jiggle dance and shrieked with joy before I calmed down enough to thank her properly.

'Oh Jeska, thank you so much. I promise I will be forever grateful to you.'

'Just remember to thank me at the Oscars,' she laughed before we ended the conversation.

The first thing I did was thank God for answering my prayers, and then I phoned Callum to tell him the happy news, and then my parents. I was so happy I wanted to burst. My big break had finally come. I resigned from the voice over position at the end of the work day and met Callum in the restaurant at the studios. When he saw me, he ran and flung his arms around me, hugged me tightly and then gently kissed me. He drew his face away from mine by just a few inches and looked directly into my eyes and my heart.

'Well done Skye, I'm so happy for you,' he kissed me again before drawing away, still holding my face cupped in his hands, 'and I am even happier because we will be working together, sort of.'

He hugged me again, and I wanted to remain there in his arms forever. When he held me, even if he so much as just held my hand, I felt at peace and secure in the world; as though I was in the right place at the right time, in God's universal plan. I was sure I had found my soulmate. I was completely and utterly in love with him.

Chapter Five

We met at the studio every day and spent every evening together. By the time the Christmas holidays arrived, we were joined at the hip. I fell in love with him more and more every minute of every day.

Rehearsals were exhausting as the director was an absolute perfectionist and wanted things to be perfect by the time filming began, but I loved the character I was playing. She was a vibrant woman who did not let her disability from polio deter her from her commitment to God and to serve Him in all things. Through playing this role, I found my faith getting strengthened and my commitment growing stronger, and in turn, I influenced Callum positively as well.

For the two week break, I went with Callum and his parents to visit his sister Cora, her husband, Bernard and Logan in Westville, Durban. We spent the days and nights in the swimming pool as the heat and humidity were unbearable, especially for me as I had never experienced this kind of weather before. Logan was an absolute water baby and since I was in the pool almost all the time he was allowed to swim too. I think Cora was only too happy to have him occupied by someone else for a while. Logan was his usual spoilt self and even more so on Christmas Day when we opened gifts. He was like a kid in a candy store carrying on as though he had never seen a Christmas present in his life. If he'd exploded from sheer excitement, it would not have surprised me at all. He opened every present, even those that weren't his. Everyone simply let him get his way rather than face a scene of tantrums and have him ruin the occasion.

Callum was delighted with his gift from me – a new device that had just come on the market that had something to do with sound engineering. It made no sense to me at all but he was overjoyed with it, and that was all that mattered to me. It felt so wonderful to be able to spoil him as I had never bought gifts for anyone other than my parents before. His appreciation openly expressed in his kiss was all the gratitude I needed.

'I should buy him a gift like this every day,' I thought to myself after getting my breath back.

His gift to me was a necklace with a heart-shaped locket that already had a photo of us in it. The photo was the selfie we'd taken at the restaurant at the studios on the day of my audition. On the other side of the heart, he'd had engraved: *"Forever yours, Callum."* The tears of joy flowed freely as my heart overflowed with happiness. There was not a perfect gift better fitted for me in the world, or so I thought!

Two days after Christmas, Callum and I were relaxing on the sunbeds beside the pool, but there was a lack of sun since it was almost ten in the evening. Callum sat up suddenly swinging his legs over the side of the chair so that he was facing me. I glanced at him through the corner of my eye, wondering why he was staring at me.

'And now?' I asked sitting up and turning sideways over the chair too, my sarong slipping off as I turned so before I focused my attention completely on Callum I reattached the sarong to my waist.

'What do you think of marriage?'

'Pardon me?' I asked in a very surprised tone wondering where this conversation was going.

'Well, um, do you want to get married one day and have children and the house with the white picket fence, you know, the whole fantasy dream thing?'

'Yes I do, but I do have one criterion that must get fulfilled before even considering it.'

'And what is that?' Callum asked a bit cautiously, fearing perhaps it was not what he wanted to hear.

'He must be a Christian too.'

Callum wrapped the biggest smile on his face and took my hands in his, playing with my fingers, and looking intently at them for a while. Then he looked at me; he really looked at me, he looked deeply into me.

'Marry me,' he said.

Stunned I found no words but instead just stared into his sincere and honest eyes, brushing aside the sloppy hair with my fingers that had fallen over his eyes.

'You see, I don't want to wait until we have money in the bank, all the furniture, the house, the long-term plans or even until we have a dog, to get married. I want to do all those things and so much more with you, together, married. I know we have only been together for four months but why wait? I love you; I have since the day I met you at the petrol station. Please, marry me.'

With his thumb he dried the tears on my cheeks, his face only millimeters away from mine. I swallowed the rest of the tears somehow finding words through my elated brain.

'Oh yes, oh yes!' I squealed and threw my arms around him holding him as close to me as humanly possible.

There was sudden cheering from inside the house that drew our attention away from each other. Everyone was standing on the porch with their eyes fixed on us. Callum and I looked at each other again and burst out laughing. He helped me to my feet, wrapped his arm securely around me and we walked to the others and into their outstretched arms. Veronica, Callum's mother, rushed to the kitchen and came back with a bottle of bubbly while Callum disappeared and returned to stand in front of me – all in a matter of seconds. He held out a little blue velvet box, his face lighting up like a thousand stars. When I opened the box, the sparkling white gold ring shone so brightly with the cluster of small diamonds; it reflected all the love we held for each other.

The cork popped and the bubbles overflowed from the bottle as Callum placed the ring on my finger. Now to tell my parents! It was probably wrong of me to lay this news on my mother over the phone, but I was so excited and happy I could not wait a moment longer.

Chapter Six

'Hello, Mommy. How are you and Dad?'

'Hello love. What's the matter? Why are you calling so late?'

'Sorry, I forgot it's so late, is Dad still awake?'

'Skye, what is it? Yes, he is.'

'Nothing is wrong. Well, the holiday has taken a bit of a different direction…' I paused to add a bit of drama.

'You getting married?' Mother blurted out so loudly Callum heard her through the receiver, causing him to giggle.

'How did you guess? And here I was worried you would not approve.'

'Oh my darling, the two of you are perfect for each other. So tell me, when, where? Come now, I want all the details.'

I relayed the event as it had happened and my mother listened with delight, squealing now and then with elation.

'Let me speak to Callum,' she interrupted, and I handed the phone to him watching the color drain from his face as I did.

He inhaled deeply before placing the receiver to his ear, 'Hello Mrs. Porter, how are you?'

'Callum darling, I am so happy, but first, you will have to ask Joel for permission, hold on.'

Before Callum had a chance to get a word in edgeways, she gave the phone to my father.

Callum went transparent he was so pale, his hands began to shake, and he rubbed his forehead nervously.

'Good evening Callum,' my father's gruff voice echoed through the phone.

Callum looked at me for help, but all he got in return were five pairs of eyes teasingly laughing back at him.

'Good evening sir, hope you are well.'

'Yes, very good, thank you. So son, what is this you need to ask me?'

Callum took the phone away from his ear and held it to his chest as he took a deep, deep breath, wiped his forehead once more, exhaled and then replaced the phone to his ear. He turned his back on all of us realizing he was not going to get any support from us.

'Sir, I asked Skye to marry me, and she said yes but I would very much like to have your blessing. Sir, I know this should not be over the phone, but Skye did not want to wait until we got home to tell you. Uhm, please sir. Please?'

A round of giggles erupted from behind him, and Callum waved his free hand at us, pleading for us to stop agitating him.

'Well Callum, if she has already agreed to marry you there is not much else I can do about it. But yes, you do have my blessing, I am very pleased she has agreed my boy. May I speak with her, please?'

Callum passed the phone back to me on his way outside to the pool area without saying a word.

'Hello Daddy,' I said a little on the weary side as I watched Callum bend over with his hands on his knees.

I wondered if my father had decided to be difficult.

'So what do you think?' I asked.

'Skye my dear, I would not wish a better man for you, I am very happy for you my darling.'

He went on about a few things, but I did not pay much attention, my eyes only focused on Callum. As soon as I put the receiver down I rushed outside to Callum, still bent over.

'Hey, what's wrong?' I asked, tenderly placing my arm on his back as I spoke.

He stood up and faced me and then I realized what a big step it had been for him. His face smeared with tears.

'I love you; I am so happy.'

He grabbed me and hugged me for the longest time. I was in awe that someone loved me so much.

'I love you. Did my father give you a hard time?'

'No, I think the moment just got the better of me and all the long nights wondering if you would say yes, the relief was probably a little overwhelming.'

'All the long nights? How long have you been preparing for this?' I teased watching the creases disappear from his face.

'Since the day, I found you at your audition.'

What was I to say in response to that? I kissed him instead, and the passion of his kiss in return made my toes curl.

'I love you,' I said again, just in time before we were interrupted by everyone else waiting to celebrate.

On our arrival back at my parents' house a few days later we walked into a celebratory party.

'Congratulations!' everyone shouted as we walked into the house.

Callum jumped from fright, and I squealed.

'Mom, what have you done?'

'I invited your cousins and a few family friends over to celebrate your engagement.'

She didn't wait for me to respond, instead threw her arms around Callum and then finding the ring on my finger proceeded to parade me, my hand and my ring around the room.

'Sorry son but it's going to be a tough affair reigning Faye in with the wedding plans if she's like this now already.'

Callum shook my father's hand.

'Thank you, sir, sorry I had to ask you over the phone.'

'None of this "sir" business, please call me Joel.'

'We want a small, simple wedding and would rather have a really good honeymoon.'

'Have fun telling Faye that,' my father laughed, and Callum chuckled along with him as the two of them watched me being shuffled alongside my mother like a ragdoll.

It was only two days later that we finally had the chance to sit down alone with my parents to discuss what we wanted for the wedding.

'A small affair will not do,' my mother exclaimed in a high-pitched voice, 'I only have one child which means this will be my only wedding! It has to be a grand occasion, not a small affair.'

'Mom, it is what we want it to be, we would rather use the money to go on a great honeymoon than spend it on other people's stomachs.'

Mother gasped, mortified, 'Rubbish; it's tradition and besides what will the family say?'

'What will they say, Mom? Half of them are not going to get invited.'

'Oh no, no, you have to invite them all!'

And so the argument went on and on between my mother and me until finally, my father put his foot down.

'Faye, it is their wedding, not yours. I am sure you will be the most glamorous mother of the bride that has ever existed, but if it's a small affair that they want, then that is what they will get.'

He turned to us, 'Skye, Callum, plan what you want but Skye, please appease your mother with an elaborate wedding dress. Callum come with me son.'

Callum obeyed and left the room as fast as lightning to escape the evil glares of my mother.

During filming, getting into the character of a woman with a disability was very difficult – even if she was so vibrant and we were filming the scenes when she was at the lowest point in her life – when I was so happy.

Filming was to be completed in about six months but rather to be safe than sorry we set the wedding date for July. Callum was able to get a week's leave for our honeymoon.

Chapter Seven

It was very difficult to rein my mother in with the wedding plans. Both families agreed to have the ceremony and reception in our garden, which was big enough and rather exquisite. My cousin Moira was to be my bridesmaid as she had always been closest to me and Callum's best man was his best friend, Millar.

While shopping for dresses, I found a beautiful soft mint green dress for Moira. It was not a color I would normally have gone for but the minute I laid eyes on it I was sold. Moira not too keen on the color but willingly went along with my choice. My dress was a different story; there was nothing in the bridal shops or the material shops that interested me in the least. Styles and designs had my mother and me at loggerheads constantly, so much so that at one stage I considered eloping as a better option. Veronica, Callum's mother, came to the rescue with a design and a dressmaker she knew who lived in Cape Town – much to my delight and relief. My mother, on the other hand, was not very impressed that her ideas had not made an impact. Her dress was going to be elaborate, stylish and celebrity-like and, as expected, she would most probably outshine me, the bride.

It was difficult enough trying to find the time to deal with all the arrangements, dress fittings and my mother when the filming schedule was taking up almost 24 hours a day. On most days I was too exhausted to care what happened. If the cake came out purple, well, that would be okay too.

With a week to go, all I wanted was for the wedding to be over so that I didn't have to endure an endless battle with my mother over my lack of grandeur and finally be Callum's wife. On a glorious day for winter, I relaxed outside in the sun while Callum and Millar behaved like little boys in the pool. The water was freezing, and yet they deterred not. Millar, being a great athlete, was doing backflips from the pool edge into the water, Callum clumsily trying to copy him.

Several times I heard Millar say, 'Wow bru that was close to the edge,' and Callum would laugh as they both climbed out of the pool to repeat their antics.

For a while all was quiet. Millar had to answer a call, and Callum wallowed in the pool like a seal. It was so peaceful that even the clinking of dishes from the kitchen was pleasant. Disturbing the peace was a crack, the oddest sound of something breaking.

I sat up and looked around, squinting from the sun's rays and then heard Millar shouting, 'Callum, Callum!' as he jumped into the water.

It was then that I noticed Callum floating face down in the pool. By the time I had stood up and rushed over, Millar was pulling him out of the water carefully holding his neck in one position as best he could.

'Callum, Callum!' I screamed, 'What happened Millar? Callum, Callum!'

I was almost hysterical as I continued to scream while trying to help Millar at the same time. My parents were by this time alerted to my screams and had rushed outside to find out what all the commotion was. Millar was checking Callum's breathing and calling out to him as I continued to scream his name desperately. My father, with one glance at the scene before him, yelled at my mother for her to call the paramedics, but she just stared at Callum, numb.

'Faye! Call them now!' he said firmly shaking her out of her frozen state, and she turned and ran.

I had never seen her run so fast in my life. My father took over from Millar, trying with all his might to resuscitate Callum. Millar breathed air into Callum's lungs on every count of five, and my father thrust pressure onto Callum's chest. They worked as a team, vigorously, pleading Callum to come back to us.

'Callum, Callum!' I continued to call him, begging him to make a movement, take a breath, to call out my name.

Nothing. Millar and my father kept their pace until the paramedics arrived. It must have been a very few short minutes, perhaps even seconds from when my mother ran off to phone them to when they arrived. My mother pulled me up from my frozen position on the ground as close to Callum as possible. I resisted with all my strength not wanting to be away from him.

'You must let the paramedics have the space to work with Callum,' she insisted as she wrapped her arms around me as we stood a foot away from my motionless husband-to-be.

They worked with speed, checking vital signs and taking over the CPR efficiently, all the while asking questions. Millar was quite breathless from pumping all his oxygen into Callum and slowly gave them the details of what had happened. I was cold as I stared at Callum lying like a washed-up jellyfish on the ground, and as much as I told myself it was not true, the blue shade to his lips could not go unnoticed. My father also exhausted from pushing Callum's chest for those few minutes stood aside aiding the paramedics whenever they requested him to do so. For a brief moment, he simply stood silently with his eyes closed. I could see he was praying. After what felt like hours, one of the paramedics stood up and looked at the four of us staring at him hopefully.

'I'm sorry,' he said with compassion etched into his face, and my heart shattered into a million pieces.

'What? NO NO NO!' I screamed until I had no more voice and flung myself onto Callum, hugging him, holding him, shaking him, begging him to come back to me.

'Oh no! Oh no!' I cried as I sobbed on top of the lifeless body of my only true love.

I faintly heard Millar sobbing behind me as he put his hand on my shoulder encouraging me to let go.

'NO!' I shrugged his hand away and held on tighter to Callum's body.

My father held my mother in his arms as they consoled each other. The paramedic somehow got me off Callum, kicking and screaming. How had this happened? In a week's time, I was to marry him, and we were going to spend the rest of our lives together in peaceful bliss.

'How? Oh, why has this happened?' I asked Millar whose only reply was to engulf me in a hug and sob as hard as I was sobbing.

Our chests beat thunderously. Who was going to phone his parents?

Chapter Eight

How was I going to get through this day? It was supposed to be my wedding day, but instead, the wedding guests would be saying farewell to the man I loved, in the garden where we were supposed wed. I was supposed to wear my beautiful wedding dress that still hung in its plastic bag on the back of my bedroom door, but instead, I was expected to wear black. Why? Why? Why? How would I do this? How could I say goodbye to him? I wasn't ready to say goodbye. Not now, not ever!

My mother peeped into my bedroom, 'Skye darling, I brought you some coffee.'

I rolled over pulling the blanket and pillows over my head. I felt the bed move as she sat down next to me and then I felt the blankets move and a pair of arms were lovingly wrapped around me as she wiggled her way until she was lying tightly next to me, her head snuggled into my neck.

'Oh Skye my darling, if I were able to take this burden and sorrow from you I would in a second.'

And then she cried. I turned around and held her, crying with her. My heart was so overcome with gratitude that when I needed a loving, unselfish and caring mother, it was what she had become. After a long while, my mother left me alone to get ready. I got up and dragged my body to the bathroom and noticed the wedding dress dancing against the door as I pulled it open. I took it off the hook and held it against my chest, longing for what this day was meant to be. I breathed in the smell of the dress as I held it to my face once I'd taken it out of the bag. I went back to my bed and lay down holding it. A deep sadness overwhelmed me, and soon the dress was wet with my tears. In a state of complete distress, I stood up and put the dress on without bothering to close up the buttons, and then I got back into bed with a shattered heart. I pulled up the big skirt into a ball and held it to my chest, my body convulsing with grief as I nursed my broken heart.

Hysteria overcame me, and I screamed into the dress, 'Callum! Callum! Why-why-why were you taken? It's not fair; it's not fair!'

With my screams increasing in volume, my words broke into colossal blubbering uncontrollable sobs, and even though muffled by the dress and blankets, my father heard me when passing my bedroom. He shot through the bedroom door, flung the bed covers off the bed and swooped me into his arms as he sat down on the bed. I lay limp as a ragdoll in his arms, clinging to the dress, still sobbing, still calling out for Callum. My father cradled me and rocked me as he'd done when I was but a baby, stroking my hair and softly, so very softly whispering sweet nothings to me. My mother, hearing the commotion, rushed to my room with Callum's parents, Cora and her family in tow. When they entered the room, our combined pain culminated in mass hysteria. Callum's mother, upon seeing me in the wedding dress collapsed into the chair next to the doorway, and Cora let out a squeal of anguish which set Logan off.

My mother sat with my father and me on the bed, and she gently rubbed my back although she was unable to speak as she was swept up in pain. When I – for the moment – was unable to cry anymore, my father helped me to drink the coffee that was by now cold. Everyone else had – for now – also calmed down after the initial shock of me in the wedding dress. It was a blatant reminder of the joyous wedding day we were meant to be celebrating, but instead, we were expected to celebrate the life of my true love, a loving son, and brother. My father, along with everyone else, only left when convinced I was able to function normally – as normal as was possible on this day. My mother helped me get out of the wedding dress and into the brown, long-sleeved dress for the memorial service. She even put my shoes and jacket on for me. Before leaving the house, I was given a mild tranquilizer to help me stay calm.

Outside people had started to arrive and were mingling in the garden, helping themselves to refreshments and softly talking to one another. We all braced ourselves and stepped out of the living room to encounter the swarm of sympathies and condolences faithfully given by those who had loved Callum. I was a walking zombie. Without encountering too many people I made my way to my seat and sat down just in time before my legs gave way. Moira was by my side all the time thankfully. When she felt that a person lingered around me too long, and I began to get agitated, she would shoo them off. I was so grateful to her. It seemed to take forever for everyone to get to their seats so the service could begin, and hopefully end soon. I was shaking as the minister stood behind the podium and cleared his throat. I was panicking and the urge to run away, far away and never return swirled within me like a whirlpool.

'I can't, I can't,' I stuttered shaking, but before I could move my mother and father, sitting on either side of me, both wrapped their arms around my shoulders.

'Shh, shh. Take a deep breath my sweet. Take a deep breath and hold onto us.'

My mother held my one hand with her free hand, and my father did likewise with my other hand. I felt my shoulders shake, and before I knew it, I was choking on the loud tortured grief-stricken pangs that flew out from deep within me. My parents through their anxiety tried with all their might to comfort me. I vaguely heard Veronica and Cora battling just as much as I was.

Finally, the drugs took over, and for the rest of the service, I sat numb and rigid in my seat, exempt from all the looks of compassion given by all those who offered their eulogies – until Millar stood in front of me with his hands requesting mine. I gave my hands to him; he held them with one hand and with his other shaking hand he held the microphone. He looked at each family member as he spoke but then stopped to force down the lump in his throat and to wipe the tears cascading down his face.

'I am so sorry we acted like foolish kids that day. I'm so sorry I was unable to save Callum…'

His shoulders slumped as he tried to console himself enough to continue, 'I loved Callum as my brother…'

He was unable to carry on, and I stood up and folded my arms around him slowly bringing him with me to sit next to me – my father moved up, so he was able to sit between the two of us. There was not a single dry eye in the garden. Millar leaned forward and rested his head in his hands, uncontrollably distraught. My heart cried out for this man who had loved my Callum so much. The minister ended the service realizing to continue would be far too painful and cruel for everyone.

While the guests and family had snacks and refreshments, I took Millar to the pool. I had not been there since that fateful day. We stood there and faced our pain and sorrow as the vivid images of Callum's limp, lifeless body brought to an end our lives as we knew them. We sat on the edge and dangled our feet in the freezing water and began to reminisce about Callum's life. It was good medicine for our souls as we found laughter amid all the sadness, remembering the fun times and the wonderful person he had been and always would be. We agreed to erect a memorial stone together for Callum right there where we sat, in the next few days. I told Millar about the wedding dress episode that morning. He looked skyward, and while brushing dry his tear-stained face, he said he had practically done the same thing with his suit.

'Let's burn the dress and the suit and scatter them with his ashes tomorrow,' I suggested.

Millar looked at me contemplating what I'd said.

'If I keep that dress I will become a morbid lunatic. It just cuts me too deep when I see it...' I said to Millar beseechingly.

He smiled and nodded without saying a word. Words were not required.

In the morning, Millar and I burnt the dress and his suit quietly in the back garden without anyone aware of our decision. Later that day we went to a spot in the hills where Callum had loved to hike, only the family, and Millar and Moira. Fletcher, Callum's father, took the ashes and before he threw them across the lush green bushes, I asked if I could add ours. The family was stunned, to say the least, but consented realizing that now was no time to argue. Callum, my wedding dress, and Millar's suit flew into the air with the breeze and settled over the land finally at rest. However, for our soul's rest was not to come for a long while still.

Chapter Nine

I hauled my heavy heart around like a ball and chain as the weeks following Callum's death slowly plodded along. Filming had thankfully ended, and instead of looking for work I chose to give up my flat and move back in with my parents and back to the comfort of my old bedroom. Having my parents by my side most of the day helped me put one foot in front of the other until the day was over.

With help, every day from the minister and many of my Christians friends, the anger I had slowly dwindled, and I slowly allowed God to heal me rather than try and heal myself. I understood God had needed Callum, and I had to wait my turn until we could both be His angels together. It was still difficult to put into practice the idea of God's plan, but every day I grew stronger, and every day I gave a little more of my pain and anger to God handle.

Six months had dragged by when Jeska phoned me.

'Hello darling, how are you?'

'Trudging along,' I replied.

'You ready to work again? There is a small part in a Christian short film. You won't have to audition; the part is yours if you want it.'

I contemplated this for a few seconds before I answered, 'Yes. I think it's time. Send me the details. Thank you so much, Jeska.'

After numerous meetings with the producers over a two-week period, we finally began rehearsals. I was slightly excited to be working again, but there were just too many reminders at Faure Studios to be truly motivated. I tried to avoid walking passed that studio door where Callum had waited hoping I was at the audition. I never went to the restaurant either.

On a very hot day in February, I made my way to the studios – filming had commenced. At a four-way crossing, I stopped to allow the car on my right to proceed first as was the law. Once the car passed me, I accelerated to cross the intersection. I heard a loud crash, glass shattering and the sound of metal crunching together. I felt a warm liquid running down my face and tasted it in my mouth as it accumulated in my throat. My eyes wanted to open, but my eyelids refused. There was an intense pain coming from my abdomen, and yet it was not sore. I was aware that I was lying sideways on the seats but made no effort to pull myself upright. I heard the sound of voices and sirens but acknowledged none.

My eyes eventually obeyed and flickered open, but my vision was clouded in darkness. I felt my heartbeat slow down and then it shuddered to cause a sensation similar to a bursting bubble that floated inside my body moments before everything hushed. My soul knew in the next few seconds that it would meet Callum again, and my motionless heart rejoiced in the knowledge that we were to be together for eternity with Jesus.

THE SPARKLE IN HER EYES

The Sparkle in Her Eyes

Dedication

To my dearest mother.
Lucille Daphney Naudé
28.05.1934 - 22.05.2013
This story is written from my heart that still holds so
much love for you.

For everyone, that has a family member or friend
who suffers from Alzheimer's I pray
that this little story about my mother will mean
as much to you as it does to me.

&

To The Helderberg Society for the Aged
Helderberg Lodge,
Flamingo Section.

The beautiful and caring
moms to my mom.

You serve with the biggest hearts
and I will forever hold
you dear in my heart.
Thank you for your dedication
and devotion during the time
of my mother's stay with you.
God bless you all always

Chapter One

'Where are we going to now?'

'We are going to the lodge, Mommy. You are going to live there now,' I replied.

This conversation had been repeated at least fifty times in the last half an hour. My mother's confusion and agitation was getting on my nerves so intensely I had to grab at every bit of patience I had left not to explode. It was not her fault; she had no idea she was repeating herself and if I told her she was it would confuse her even more. Then her agitation would most likely increase, and so the snowball effect just kept rolling on.

The day the retirement home phoned to inform me that there was a room available for her I had burst into tears from sheer relief. Her refusal to move into a retirement home left me no choice but to lie to her. Fortunately, the name of her new home was "Helderberg Lodge" which lent itself out to a white lie. We were met by the resident manager who had the softest smile and most caring eyes. Then we were shown to my mom's room, unpacked her bags and were given a tour of the facilities.

'Why are we here again?'

'This is your new home, Mom. Isn't it a lovely place? Just look at the garden, I am sure they will let you help with the gardening. You love that.'

'Oh yes,' she said as she gazed at the flower beds, examining every leaf and bud.

It was time for lunch, so we made our way to a table in the dining room, and joined some other residents. My mother made idle chatter with the lady next to her, and I felt a wave of relief wash over me. She would be safe here, safe from getting out the gate and wandering off into the streets, safe from falling down the steps, safe from being bitten by the parrot (she would always forget she shouldn't go near him), safe from setting the house on fire. She would be in a controlled environment where she would be reminded gently to have a bath and to eat. And she would receive a three-course meal, three times a day. I was so grateful to God for answering my prayers.

When it was time for their nap after lunch, most of the residents automatically went to their rooms and got comfy on their beds. It took the nurse some coaxing and coercing before eventually getting my mom to her bed. I sat with her until her eyes closed and then I left. I knew the first few days and especially the nights would be difficult for her. Unfamiliar surroundings unsettled her tremendously, and she did not sleep very well in any case. I knew she was going to get out of bed and wander around the corridors, and in doing so, she would undoubtedly throw herself into a state of total disorientation. The nurse assured me they were trained to cope with this kind of behavior.

Chapter Two

After a week or so Mom had settled in wonderfully. I went to visit her every day during my lunch hour as the home was only a ten-minute drive from my office. We were sitting in the garden on a beautiful spring day having the same conversation we had every day, but I did not mind as she was relaxed and had already started putting on some weight. She seemed content, but suddenly she deviated from our usual conversation.

'There's that man,' she said as she pointed to a janitor walking through the garden.

'What about him?' I asked curiously.

'He tried to rape me last night. I gave him such a punch and fought him off. I'm full of bruises now, and my wrists are sore from when he held me.'

'What! Did you tell someone?'

'No, I can't tell anyone. If I do, they will make my life hell here. They will all gang up on me.'

'Who is "they"?'

She pointed to the nursing staff that were mingling about the garden having their lunch. 'Them, they're all in cahoots. They all want to get me.'

'Get you for what?' I was so flabbergasted and not exactly sure whether to believe her or not.

'Oh, they're just evil people. They go around hurting everyone.'

The hair on my arms stood up. I had seen documentaries and headlines in the news about how old people had got treated in some homes and how it had been caught on camera. I shivered at the thought that it might be happening here. The notion was too horrifying to grasp.

'Where are the bruises, Mom?' I asked gently, trying to stay calm.

I picked up her arms and turned them over looking for the bruises she supposedly had. As I held her wrists I tightened my grip on them; if she had been hurt as she claimed she had been, it would hurt her. Nothing! I wondered what I should do about it. What if something had happened and her mind was not playing tricks on her? I watched her face as she focused on the nursing staff, she had a distrustful glare in her eyes, and it made up my mind for me. I would speak to the manager before I left. After relaying the story to the manager, I was assured it was a common occurrence for an Alzheimer's patient to conjure up stories such as this. They could have seen a movie way back in their past that had similar events in it and to them, now in the present time; it became a reality. Still, she was going to investigate to appease my concerns.

The following day we sat in the communal living room with the other residents, and when I asked Mom if her wrists were still sore and if she had found any more bruising, she became annoyed.

'What are you talking about? I haven't hurt myself. Who said I hurt myself?'

Well really now! I sighed.

I brought a photo of her wedding day and put it up on the wall above her bed. It stood alongside photos of her three children and a couple of her grandchildren and great-grandchildren. I also brought all Mom's photo albums too. They were full of fantastic black and white photos depicting a past full of memories and a time when her life was as clear as daylight.

We sat on her bed after lunch and looked through one of the albums. She named the faces in the photos and sometimes even told me the story behind the photo – who the person in it was, where they had lived and what they had done with their life. Sometimes she even told me tales of the lives behind the faces, like who was dating who or that the woman in the picture had been dating a fellow but had been in love with another man. She went on and on, reliving her life in all those photos as if her memory worked perfectly. We came across a photo lying loosely in the album of her latest great-grandchild, and she was unable to put a name to the face. She had seen him the past weekend, and yet it escaped her memory. She grew tired, and I left to go back to the office, wondering how the mind could remember so clearly a life so far back and yet yesterday's news was gone.

Chapter Three

I noticed a decline in Mom as the weeks slowly went by. One day I arrived and could not find her anywhere. I even had the staff running around looking for her. At least twenty minutes went by before a nurse found her in the adjoining section (how she got there no one will ever know) holding onto her framed wedding photo.

'Hi, Mom, where you been? We've all been looking for you!'
She clutched the photo to her chest.
'I found my photo in an apartment over there. That woman stole it.'

I guided her gently back to her room and placed the photo back above her bed. A nurse called me from just outside the door. I met her in the corridor while Mom looked through another photo album.

'Do you think you could take her photo home with you? Your mom keeps accusing the other residents of stealing it and then she wanders around as she did today. If it is not available to her, she will not know it is there at all. She won't miss it.'

I felt a pang of sadness tug at my heart. Just a few weeks ago she had told me all about her wedding day, naming all the people in the photo and I knew she had named them correctly. Now it had become an obstacle to her.

'Yes okay. When we leave the room, take it out and leave it at the reception. I will collect it on my way out.'

Her confusion and wild stories increased on a daily basis. I found that even going from the living room to the dining room confused her and she would ask if this was a new restaurant as she could not remember being there before. Her wandering at night had become so bad that I was called in for a meeting to discuss the situation. They wanted to move her to the upstairs section where there were a tighter control and a safer environment specifically designed for those who are not yet in the most advanced stage of Alzheimer's but are also not able to live comfortably without aid. It was next door to the dreaded section I feared, the last step before the end. It was too close for comfort and yet what could I do but agree, for the safety and health of my mother.

When I arrived to visit her the following day, Mom was having lunch in the dining room, and she looked awfully tired. I asked the nurse how the move upstairs had gone.

She replied, 'She was very confused. She was up and down the whole night, and they eventually had to give her a sleeping pill.'

I looked at Mom nibbling at her food, exhausted. My heart cried out for her. I wanted to shake her brain alive so that she could live a normal life again. I had seen this happen to my grandmother, and I anxiously feared what was still to come.

'Hi Mom, how you?' I asked as I sat down next to her.

She looked at me, and it took her a few seconds to register who I was before she replied, 'Hello.'

And then the smile and the sparkle in her eyes sent my heart whirling. I was not yet lost to her!

'I'm tired today. I don't know why because I just had a good sleep.'

I felt my eyes well up with tears, and I just hugged her. We went into the garden after lunch but it was too cold outside, so we went back upstairs to the TV room.

Although the TV was on, the sound wasn't, and not long after we sat down, she said, 'I can't sit for long, they will be wondering where I am.'

'Who will?'

'All the staff, if I am not there, they start to panic, and then they do everything wrong.'

I found it best to go along with her stories and imagination rather than point out the obvious.

'Where are you working now?'

'I'm still at the Hyperama; you know that!'

She gave me a "don't ask stupid questions" look.

'Oh yes, but I thought you were moving to a new job.'

'No, I changed my mind. They need me too much.'

From this time on we would have this same conversation about her work. On certain days, I was highly entertained by the goings-on at her imaginary workplace. Sometimes I wondered if those things had happened when she'd worked there. The names always eluded her, though, but maybe that was just as well.

Often I would take her out to lunch, mostly to a little restaurant up the road called Chatters. They got to know us very well and knew to get the apple pie warmed up when we entered the door. As lovely as it was to have her out and in different surroundings it eventually became too much for her to cope. After half an hour she would start getting frantic over her luggage that was probably misplaced. I would then assure her that it had been taken directly to the lodge. Five minutes later we would have the same conversation. If it wasn't the luggage, it was once more the staff that supposedly needed her. So instead of taking Mom out, it became better for me to take cake and coffee to her. So after lunch at the home, we would find a quiet place, and I would let her believe we were at a restaurant for tea. Was I a liar? Was I adding to the further deterioration of her already confused mind? These questions would haunt me later.

Chapter Four

Before Mom went to the upstairs section, it was easy for my daughters to visit with her. She could still have a relatively logical conversation with them, but once she moved upstairs, the pain and hurt were written all over their faces. At least once a month I would take her great-grandchildren to visit her, but it caused havoc with the other residents. They would zone in on the kids – who were only a few months old at the time too – and it would unsettle them terribly. The over-excited grannies wanted to touch the babies' toes and faces and squish them; bent right over the kids, their faces would almost touch the babies'. I felt sorry for both parties involved, the babies and the grannies.

As I walked through the entrance and before I got to the elevator one day a nurse stopped me and told me the residents were all in the common living room downstairs. I made a right turn and went to see what was going on there. A church group had come to sing to the residents, encouraging them to sing along. I placed myself against the wall behind everyone and watched and listened. The sweetest sound I had heard was echoing off the walls. The old people sang so loudly and every word that escaped their lips they sang with joy in their hearts. They praised God through their singing. Afterward, my mom was beaming.

'What a lovely time that was. We sang so much and all the old favorites too. I can't remember when last I sang so much.'

I just hugged her. For this brief moment, her mind was home and in the present. The happy moment did not last very long, though.

After a few weeks, I arrived to visit her at the normal lunch hour and found Mom lying in bed very drowsy. I sat on the bed once I had woken her up. She mumbled about how tired she was and just wanted to go back to sleep. A nurse entered the room and had to explain to me how the previous evening. Mom had been very disorientated and had woken up most of the residents looking for clothing they had supposedly stolen.

243

When they tried to get Mom back into bed, she had become violent and screamed and shouted and had thrown things at everyone and all over the place. I couldn't believe it. What had triggered her brain to make her go so crazy? I remained with her on the bed and listened to her constant mumbling; she was exhausted. The nurse was concerned that if this behavior carried on, they would have to move her to the next section. That was what I feared most.

After another week of very much the same behavior, she was moved to the Flamingo section. I was distraught. I had known one day she would land up there, but I didn't think it would happen so soon. It hadn't even been a year since she had first moved to the home and in such a short period she had already deteriorated so badly. Through no fault of anyone or anything of course, other than the awful, dreaded disease called Alzheimer's.

If you have seen the movie "One Flew Over the Cuckoo's Nest" you will have an understanding of what it was like in Flamingo. Some residents had resided there for a very long time, years in fact. They got to a point in their lives where they lived in a limbo state. They had no idea of where they were or what they were doing really but simply existed on a day-to-day basis. But let me also add that they were not all this way. There were many residents with whom I loved to converse. They told me wonderful stories (I could not tell how true they were), but they were certainly entertaining, and I wondered why they were there in that final section of the home. It was for the same reason Mom was there. They caused chaos in the evenings, and the wandering aspect of Alzheimer's meant they could be a danger to themselves or the other residents.

In case you are not familiar with this term "The wandering" – it is a term I use for the way Alzheimer's patients wander around aimlessly. You will often find after a meal they will walk around not knowing what they are doing or where or why they are doing it. As the disease progresses, it becomes a natural thing for them to do all day long. It becomes tiring watching them walk endlessly.

Mom was given a room with three other residents in the same state that she was in, but boy, did she complain about the snoring that went on in that room! She could even tell you how each one snored, who snored the loudest and the time that they woke her up (well according to her imaginary clock at any rate).

Somewhere in the midst of all her tangled memories, she knew she was in that section and that she was not going to move again. She was very unhappy the first few weeks, and I tried again to take her out to Chatters as often as I could. Again after a few attempts, I stopped.

Mom's walking gradually got slower and slower, and her sense of balance was failing her too. She would trip or fall over the slightest bump. I would still take her down to the garden on days when the weather was pleasant. She seemed to cope with this, but even then she would wonder where we were and would begin to get agitated after a while thinking that she had to get back to the office.

***

I would like to take the time here to mention the staff at Flamingo. If ever you have met the kindest, most caring, warm-hearted, helpful and loving people then you have met the staff at Flamingo. It goes without saying that their job is daunting and very emotionally and mentally exhausting, and yet they have a sense of humor and an ever-ready smile waiting to make your day a little more pleasant. They treated the residents with tender-hearted kindness and were always very informative whenever I enquired about any situation. They carried the minds of the residents that could no longer carry them alone and did so with the utmost love. I am and always will be forever grateful to them for being "moms" to my mom.

Chapter Five

Some days were intensely depressing but some days were highly entertaining. I know most people would frown upon making fun of the elderly and especially those with Alzheimer's or Dementia but without mocking them, I have to share a few incidents that occurred during the lunch times that I spent at the home.

***

Not long after Mom moved to the Flamingo section, I went to visit her as usual during my lunch break. She was sitting next to a gentleman, and they were chatting away, eating and laughing. It was a wonderful moment and not wanting to ruin it. I simply sat opposite them and let them continue their conversation until she noticed me. As usual, her eyes lit up when she saw me, and I was rewarded with a beautiful smile. I joined the conversation, and suddenly out of the blue, Mom went into a panic mode. I enquired as to what was upsetting her as she began to look for something in her pockets.
'I can't find my purse. I must have left it at home, sherbet, what now?'
The gentleman also began to search.
'Mine is also gone; someone must have stolen them!'
'What's wrong Mommy?' I reached over and held her hand to make her look at me.
'We haven't got any money with us, and we have already started eating this food. How are we going to pay for it?'
'Don't worry Mom; I already paid for it when I came in.'
'And what about my friend, can you lend him some money to pay for his?'
'I paid for his too, Mom.'
'Oh good, thanks! Shoo, I can't believe we left our money behind. My daughter has paid for our meals,' she said as she turned to the gentleman next to her and pointed to me at the same time.

'Thank you, dear,' he said to me.

Then he called out to the nurse, 'Waiter! Where is our dessert? I want it now.'

He turned to Mom and called her all sorts of sweet names. There they were, in the midst of a normal lunch at the home, and yet in their minds, they were in love and being served at a restaurant. I sat and watched them, smiling with the nurse.

***

One day Mom was merrily eating away at her chicken and vegetables when a gentleman a few tables away from ours started calling out a name rather loudly. I could not make out the name, but he tried to whistle each time afterward. I presumed he was calling his dog. He fussed and looked around for a few minutes before calming down and talking to the floor on the right side of his chair. He picked a chicken bone off his plate and threw it across the room and watched where it landed all the while talking to the dog. When he surmised that the dog had returned to him, he took his plate of food and emptied the contents onto the floor next to him. The nurse rushed to him and reprimanded him, bending down to pick up the food at the same time. While she was bent over next to him, he patted her head and told her to eat the food and enjoy it. She was not impressed at being mistaken for his dog, and when she stood up and straightened her hair, he yelled at her to finish eating the food. She walked away and left the food there to be cleaned up after lunch. The gentleman spoke to his dog all the while through lunch, not having taken a bite himself but instead making sure his dog had eaten. I am convinced he had a dog that he truly loved at some point in his life.

***

A lady that used to live with her husband at the retirement home was moved to the Flamingo section, and he would join her there for most of the day. Only on rare occasions was he unable to make it at lunchtime. On one such occasion, the lovely lady walked into the dining room and wandered around

247

a little before she was shown to her seat and persuaded to sit and wait for her food. She did so for a minute or two, and then she stood up again and wandered around a bit before being seated again in her chair.

It was a common occurrence with a lot of the residents, but what made this so entertaining was that the next time she stood up, and before a nurse, I, or anyone else could get to her, she had taken off her skirt and was halfway with removing her blouse. A nurse got to her in time, dressed her again and seated her at the table once more. Lunch was a little late that day, and after few minutes had passed, she managed to remove her blouse and her skirt before anyone noticed while still in her seat. She stood up and promptly started pushing down her panties. The nurses were onto her in a flash, and she tried to run away from them with her knickers around her knees! She told the nurses off with a few very eloquent choice words (not to be repeated) as they struggled to get her clothes back on.

By now the food had arrived, and the nurses were gathering to collect and deliver it to the residents. The lady was safely back in her seat – but not for long! While the nurses concentrated on serving the food, she disappeared out of the dining room and returned not a few moments later completely naked. Oh my goodness, those poor nurses moved with lightning speed to get her dressed again. Once she had her meal in front of her, she seemed to calm down. I was giggling so much, but by myself, as fortunately the rest of the residents had no idea what was going on otherwise it would have been a room of utter hysteria.

***

The last incident I want to share was maybe not so entertaining as it was interesting. I sat at the table with Mom and opposite me a lovely bright-eyed, beautiful old lady sat, holding a framed black and white photo. She seemed very coherent and made a lot of sense when she spoke. I asked her about the photo, at which she lit up like a thousand stars and eagerly showed it to me. It was a photo of her in her youth standing between two very smartly dressed men in uniform. She told me they were in the Navy at the time and that she had been a singer that traveled to all the army bases to sing for the troops.

That particular photo was taken at an admiral's dinner where she had sung as part of the entertainment for the event. She went on to tell me wonderful stories of her trips to the troops and the people she had met. Her stories intrigued me that I ignored poor Mom the entire visit. What a wonderfully exciting life she must have led. From that day on, we remained good friends, always sharing pleasantries every time I went to visit Mom.

***

I hope you don't think of me as being rude and sadistic. Sometimes you have to find humor in disheartening situations. I did this for some days with Mom left me exhausted and so depressed that when these moments occurred, I grabbed at them to make light of dark situations.

Chapter Six

Mom's ability to feed herself slowly declined, and it got to the stage where she had to be spoon-fed. Her appetite was not lost, though, and she still ate a healthy plate of food at each meal. By this stage, Mom was also wearing adult nappies. Although she would often say, she needed to go to the toilet she had no control over her bladder or bowel movements anymore. She was not even aware that she was wearing a nappy.

Every time I walked in and saw my mom, I would always face her directly and say hello, to which her eyes would sparkle and brighten, and I would get the loveliest smile. During lunch one day I noticed her words slur and the side of her mouth seemed to droop downward. Immediately the thought that she was possibly having a stroke entered my head, and I quickly went downstairs to the reception and asked if I could speak to the manager. At the time, I hadn't been able to locate the sister upstairs. As soon as I spoke to the receptionist, I burst into tears and was annoyed at myself for doing so as those tears would not help anyone. Nonetheless, there they were in full flow, and a doctor was arranged to see Mom later that day.

At four in the afternoon, the doctor arrived, and it could not be determined if she had suffered a stroke or not. The following day Mom was doing much better, but the doctor wanted a neurologist to have a look at her. The earliest appointment for her was the following Wednesday. Up until that day Mom had been fine, never showing any signs of slurring or that any form of imbalance or illness loomed.

On the Wednesday morning that she was due to see the specialist the sister phoned me to say that Mom was not waking up. She had fallen into a semi-coma state, and I should get to the home as soon as possible. I did. When I arrived in Mom's bedroom, she was lying in her bed sound asleep. Nothing would wake her. I still thought it was best to get her to the specialist. A nurse accompanied my daughter and me, to help with getting Mom in and out of the wheelchair. It was very difficult with her being in the state that she was.

The specialist took one look at her and immediately sent her to the ICU of the hospital. She was diagnosed with pneumonia. A horrible side effect to Mom's Alzheimer's was that whenever she got a simple cold or the like, her brain shut down. I had seen this on many occasions in other people. Now with pneumonia, it shut down almost completely.

My sister was fortunately down on business for the week in Cape Town and extended her stay until Mom was safe again. Mom spent, at least, three days in a comatose state and another week or so in the general ward before being discharged. Even when she was in the general ward, she slept a lot, far more than what was deemed normal. Her vitals were all good and normal, and yet all she wanted to do was sleep. To see Mom lying in bed unresponsive was just about all my nerves were able to handle. If ever I felt completely and utterly hopeless it was then.

When she returned to the home, she was moved to the frail care section of Flamingo. Here she remained in bed as an invalid for a few weeks. Slowly she became more alert and was once again speaking without a slur and able to eat solid foods. Only when the sister and doctors were a hundred percent happy with her recovery was Mom moved out of the frail care and back to her old bed. What a relief it was to visit that day and find her sitting in the dining room once more, and to see her eyes light up and melt my heart when she gave me the widest of smiles that I had not seen in almost a month.

Chapter Seven

Even though the residents were unaware of what day it was on any given day, on special days like Valentine's Day, Mother's and Father's Day and naturally Christmas Day and New Year's Day, the staff went to great lengths to dolly up the dining room. A special meal was prepared for the residents, and they were spoilt with cakes, sweets and little gifts. They would know something was different or special that day.

If I asked Mom how she liked the decorations, she would reply, 'Yes they're lovely. I told them not to spend too much money, but they just went ahead and broke my budget anyway.'

I would tell her what day it was, and she would say, 'I know that,' very indignantly.

Mom stayed alert and fit; her smile never failed to lift my spirits and the sparkle in her eyes when she saw me was worth more than gold. Even the staff members constantly commented on how Mom would light up when she saw me or even when she heard my voice nearby. It was those special moments that kept our bond as mother and daughter tightly knitted together. It kept the nagging thoughts at bay of how much longer I would be blessed to still enjoy the smile in her eyes.

Mom's appetite slowly decreased, and I found I had to spend my entire lunchtime visit feeding her, and at times that was not even long enough. Due to this, it was decided that Mom would go on a soft diet to help her chew and digest her food more easily. It was successful for a few days, and then it got difficult again. At times, I had to gently persuade her to open her mouth wide enough just to get the spoon into her mouth. One day Mom would co-operate well, and she would have a decent sized meal and the next day it was a fighting match to get her to eat a few spoonfuls.

I was later informed that Mom had developed a cold sore on her bottom lip, and that left me wondering if perhaps she was developing flu. The elderly easily develop bronchitis or pneumonia from a simple cold. The doctor checked Mom the next day, and she was diagnosed with mild flu and given medication. As I had mentioned before when Mom got ill, her brain tendered to shut down, and I was terribly concerned that this would happen again. The nurse kept a vigilant watch over Mom and her vitals. She seemed to be coping and on the mend quicker than expected and without the dreaded coma. That was short-lived, though.

When getting all the residents prepared for breakfast, the nurse found Mom in a worsened state and immediately notified the sister who in turn phoned me. Again the doctor was called in. I insisted that I speak to him once he had examined her. It was late in the afternoon, almost time to leave work for the day, when he called me. I immediately left and went to hear what he had to say. The diagnosis was not good. Mom's mild flu had worsened and become pneumonia again, and with the brain shutting down it was unable to inform the body to produce the antibodies to fight the infection. He was sure there was no way for Mom to turn back from here. I was shattered as I sat next to Mom on her bed watching her breath with difficulty.

She opened her eyes, and I leaned in with my face almost touching hers and whispered to her, 'Mommy, hello, can you hear me?'

She mumbled that she was able to hear me and then something else, but I could not make out what.

All the way home my mind was racing with the events over the past month. What could I have done differently to have prevented this outcome? How much longer would she still be with me? By the time I got home, I was exhausted and emotional.

I am truly blessed to have a family that is so loving, compassionate and supportive and who felt my pain and heartache as much as I did. I phoned my siblings, and as God's planning would have it, my sister would be in Cape Town on business for the next week. She would get given a chance to say goodbye to her beloved mother.

The next few days and nights, my sister, daughter and I spent as much time as possible at my mother's bedside, treated with love, compassion, and respect by the nursing staff. Several times when I wasn't at her bedside, the home would phone me and ask me to get to Mom immediately as her breathing was so erratic it seemed she would pass on at any second. I would arrive at her bedside and watch as her chest heaved up and down while her mouth gaped open as she battled to get air into her lungs. With each breath, it seemed as though it would be her last. I held her hand and spoke to her, gently stroking her hair and speaking calmly to her through the tears that trickled down my cheeks. I prayed and asked God to take Mom home. Was that wrong of me?

Wednesday morning the twenty-second of May 2013, Mom had to go to the hospital for X-rays. I met Mom and the nurse who accompanied her to the hospital, and it was not long when the X-rays were done, and we were with the doctor to discuss the results. The young intern doctor listened to Mom's heartbeat and chest for a long time. I knew she was prolonging the conversation she would have to have with me. The news she had to give me was written all over her face. I had to make it easier for her.

'I know what you are going to tell me. I know she only has moments left. Will you send Mom back to the home or are you going to keep her at the hospital?'

She looked at me still uneasy about telling me what I already knew. I felt sorry for her as perhaps this was the first time she had to tell a daughter her mother was leaving soon.

'I will order a bed, and as soon as one becomes available, they can move your mother to the ward.'

I thanked her and went back to the casualty section for the long wait for a bed. Mom's chest was heaving rapidly, and she made loud gasping sounds as she grappled for air. The nurse had been with Mom since very early in the morning, with nothing to drink or eat, and it was now past lunch. There was a little café at the end of the hospital, so I slipped out to get her a cup of tea. I returned holding her tea and a cup of coffee for myself. The first thing I noticed was that Mom's bed was missing. My heart fell to the floor – I knew, I just knew she had gone home, and I had not been there with her for her final breath.

The young doctor ushered me to where Mom lay privately in the corner of a little ward. There was no sound, no heaving of her chest, no gasping for air. There was no sound at all, just a peaceful silence with no suffering. Cyanosis had already kicked in, and I could see the blue was already beginning to color her lips, fingernails, and toenails. Her eyes were partially open, but there was no sparkle.

Oh, Mommy! What I wouldn't do to see that sparkle once more! To see your smile every time you looked up and saw me!
I bent down and kissed her goodbye. Her lifeless skin was cool, and I held her one last time. The urge to shake her, to reinvigorate the life back into her pulsed through me but just in time the doctor put her arm around me and gently persuaded me to withdraw from Mom and leave her in God's hands.

When I got back to the home, the staff, from the management to the nurses, overflowed with sincere sympathies. I stood by Mom's bed, her empty bed, and strangely thought of how lucky she was to know all the answers finally and to be living with Jesus for eternity. All I took was her Bible, thanked the staff once more for everything they had done, and then I left.

Chapter Eight

The slow decline of my mother's memory inflicted in her an aggressive personality and the sometimes vicious outbursts, both opposite to her nature. She had been an outgoing, lively, happy and lovely lady and yes, she was not perfect, but Mom had been respected and loved by everyone who knew her. To live with Mom in that state of mind was not only heart-breaking but very frustrating for all my family members. It was just easier to lose your temper with her at times rather than walk away and convince yourself that it was not just because she was old, but because her mind was a tangled mess and she was frightened and confused.

Having watched my grandmother (her mother) go through the same process, I should have seen the warning signs a lot earlier. My mother should have been more cautious and made an assertive attempt to ensure this dreaded awful disease did not attack her in the same manner. And yet Mom went down the same path, and before she realized it, it was too late. My and the family's attempts to confront her when I figured out what was happening got met with denial. There was no turning back from that point.

Alzheimer's is a nasty, dreadful disease and even with all the technology in the world, it remains a mystery vastly. Don't believe you will escape it once it begins and it can attack anyone. The best you can do is have a healthy diet, keep your brain as active as possible and surround yourself with people you love and who love you.

I don't know why such a disease exists – and it would be the same as asking why we have earthquakes. I only know that while we are here on this earth as human beings, we must trust in the God that created us. With faith, it will not matter what trials, illnesses or tragedies we are faced with because when it is our end, we will live a pain-free Spirit-filled life with Jesus.

Phil 4:13 I can do all things through Christ who strengthens me.

Psalms 9: 9-10

*"⁹ The LORD is a refuge for the oppressed,
a stronghold in times of trouble.
¹⁰ Those who know your name trust in you,
for you, LORD, have never forsaken those
who seek you."*

God Bless Always

Your Opinion

You've come to the end of this story; I truly hope you enjoyed it and it touched your heart.

Please be kind and leave your review for the benefit of the many to follow, I will be so appreciative.

https://www.amazon.com/Sparkle-Eyes-plus-Short-Stories-ebook/dp/B00SMW7KOM/

Thank you
God bless you

Aileen Friedman

More Books By The Author
Aileen Friedman

Changes From a Sunset
ISBN 978-0-620-52564-0

When is My Forever
ISBN 978-0-620-55793-1

Second is Best
ISBN 978-0-620-59758-6

The day God came to earth.
ISBN 978-0-620-68628-0

Radar Love
ISBN 978-1-543-29950-2

The Secret of Grace
ISBN 978-1-719-17242

Mr. Trolley Adventurer
ISBN 978-1-533-27328-4

Jamie's Discoveries
ISBN 978-1-533-27339-0

www.ingramcontent.com/pod-product-compliance
Lightning Source LLC
Chambersburg PA
CBHW060053150626
46556CB00017BA/112